From  The W
34 Great Sutton

Maud Farrell is currently working on a sequel to
Skid – The Big Overcoat. She divides her time between
Nantucket and New York where she is also a
photographer, a house-painter, and a chef. She has no
legitimate children, hobbies, or graduate degrees.

MAUD FARRELL

Skid

The Women's Press

First published in Great Britain by The Women's Press Limited 1990
A member of the Namara Group
34 Great Sutton Street, London EC1V 0DX

Copyright © Maud Farrell 1989

First published in the United States of America
by EP Dutton, New York, 1989.

All rights reserved. This is a work of fiction and any resemblance
to persons living or dead is purely coincidental.

Grateful acknowledgment is given for permission to quote excerpts from the
following works:

"Dirge Without Music" from *Collected Poems,* by Edna St. Vincent Millay,
published by Harper & Row. Copyright © 1928, 1955 by Edna St. Vincent
Millay and Norma Millay Ellis. Reprinted by permission.

"Brush Up Your Shakespeare" by Cole Porter.
Copyright © 1948 by Chappell & Co. (Renewed).
All rights reserved. Used by permission.

British Library Cataloguing in Publication Data
Farrell, Maud
  Skid.
  I. Title
  813'.54 [F]

ISBN 0-7043-4221-9

Reproduced, printed and bound in Great Britain by
Cox and Wyman, Reading, Berks

This book is dedicated to the memory of Leslie Anne Cook.

The author wishes to acknowledge the kind help and support of many friends and family members during the writing of *Skid,* including E. M. M., J. K. S., A. W. K., I. H., P. E. K., and to particularly thank the following: Malaga Baldi, Carole DeSanti, Pauline Margarone, SINN '88, The Nantucket Sapphic Consortium, and Mary Kathleen South.

Love is the only true adventure.

                Violet Childes

PROLOGUE

It was the edge of night. The cutting edge. The sky was taut, stretched thin as the skin of a drum, a pale membrane, an eyelid sinking shut. Its color was smudged-up yellow, congealed, smeared across the palm of a horizon. The light that remained, a veil of tinted smog, was receding all too quickly.

The man was running as fast as he could; his scarred shoes skimmed and cut through dusk. No graceful sprint, no evening jog, but a dance across the surface of a nightmare. The buildings seemed to split, veer backwards away from the street. The man—the tight sharkskin suit, the mottled hands, the crooked nose, the bloodshot eyes, the weak chin, the flying, spitting sweat—ran as one, slicing through air that was thickening with dark. The meaning of desperate was racing for that last chance, a sleight of hand, a miracle. His rasping breath sucked at the last of the day's light as if to draw his destination to him. No luck. The dark, chasing shapes sped closer, slick as submarines, determined. He was no match for them; it was astounded fear that lurched and sped the man along.

Finally the dark, sleek shapes caught up, and merged around him in a dizzying halt.

"Give it over, dead man. You know what I want," gasped one of the dark shapes. The hunt was over, the cornered man said nothing, knew it would do no good, could not talk anyway. The shape who spoke smashed his gold-toed boot into the man's groin, sending him swooping backwards on the pavement in a faint. The others slapped him awake.

"Speak up, Maxie, save yourself. Where is it, what have you got for that meddling bitch?" The cornered man was mute, a mass of jerking, live-wire dread.

The darkness was slipping around them like a shroud, encasing the scene in a plush black envelope. One of the shapes pulled out a long hunting knife. One of the other shapes nodded. With one hand he grabbed the prey by his hair, with the other he swiftly carved a deep, throat-wide grin into the man's neck. The sound was a hideous rip, blood sprayed out like an open hydrant, a splash of red on black air. The body shivered and bucked in its final protest, death arriving as a contortion; limbs flopped like a puppet freed of its strings.

The shapes jostled each other and laughed. They quickly searched through his clothing, ignoring the bubbling red. The shapes dragged the man who could no longer feel down the empty block to the silent building, forcing their way into a back entrance. They yanked the man up two flights, pulling him over steps his spine did not notice, picking a lock, drawing him into an office, dumping the shimmering wet mess on a pale grey carpet. The parcel of blood, somewhat contained by his suit, now had a field day, draining off the crumpled form, seeping luxuriously into the pale grey blotter, into a spreading silhouette.

His epitaph, "Messy little calling card, isn't it," was laughingly called out. It hung like ectoplasm in the quiet room.

The shapes walked casually out into the night.

Outside, down the dark streets, lights popped on one after the other: streetlamps, neon, headlights, a liquid pulse of illumination in the otherwise leaden black of city blocks. Night had arrived, lowering its thick cap over the seething beneath.

1

In New York it's a toss-up which urban attribute pushes you awake first. The icy balled-up sun, looking to soak up a little human warmth to drag itself through dawn, squeezing its way into the room through the blinds, sliding two-inch stripes of shadow over the room and its contents. Or the collage of sounds, the clash of voice and metal against air, brimming over the street, careening up to the windows. Today it was the city itself, the wailing child waiting to be picked up and held, that pulled Violet Childes out of a dream that had recurred nightly for months.

Barely conscious, she tried to catch the threads of the dream and yank them closer, tried to press the images forward. But the dream was always one step out of reach, demanding a clue of memory she could not find. She forced it aside, and to hasten its leaving shook her head sharply, whipping her disheveled mass of bruised-black hair into static electric peaks.

She propped herself up and reached for a cigarette. (The first Gitane of the day was one of her many rituals. In this instance it was Violet's interest in learning French by osmosis: the Gitanes and Gauloises, the Piaf records, the translations of Gide and Malraux, the bowls of *café au lait*.)

She smoked rhythmically, exhaling the rough smoke in long sighs, watching it play in and out of the hard shadows and sharp slats of light, the room so heavily lined it evoked a large hat box.

She was waiting for the mental haze to burn off into the string of morning acknowledgments, the Rolodex of checkpoints that got her out of bed. This morning it was filled with reluctance and a jet-lag hangover. Yes, all your limbs are whole, you're glad to be alive. Sure, you believe in miracles, you like small children and animals, you're cheerful, thrifty, and brave. On top of it all you are gainfully employed and in love. Who could complain? Then the odd one, the mean fact, appears. Father dead. Murdered. This slips in like a chilled hand closing over the heart. The trauma of this loss was intensified by its suddenness, because of its violence.

Victor Childes was a private detective. Read: he had a list of enemies as long as your arm. Private Eye: a rusty image from a novel or an old movie, but to Violet very real; he was her friend and mentor, the parent who had raised her. The grief scratched at her like crinoline; it was not yet saturated and released because of the violence of the death, because of its mystery. She was caught on that grief for a moment, allowed its fluttering pain, which resembled a panicked swallow trapped in a house, then forced herself to let it loose.

After the funeral her close circle of friends had turned a lot of Victor's insurance money into traveler's checks, filled suitcases, and sent Violet and her package of shock to Italy. She stayed with old friends in Rome, wandered the Borghese Gardens, sat on the Spanish Steps, and drank entirely too much. She rented a car and wound through Tuscany and Umbria, hovered in Florence and Assisi and Venice. Disoriented by sadness, estranged in her solitude, she left a trail of bright lights, a string of prayers, hoping something would find her, would catch up. Everywhere she went she lit candles. In large cathedrals, in small rural chapels, at bus stop icons with strings of Christmas lights and polychromed wooden Christs with gaping wounds. Each spit of light was a name—Victor.

Finally in Milan the shock and the obsession lifted somewhat. Violet looked up a woman she once worked with on a magazine in New York, a fellow photographer who was now editor of a design magazine. Gabriella had always been very admiring of Violet's work. After several days of catching up,

Gabriella asked her to accept an assignment, and then another one. Violet complied, with a series of abstract shots in front of De Chirico façades and empty slanting streets, pulling in all her recent and saturated visual references. One month in Milan became two, and Violet started to remember she had a profession, a context. Six months into her imposed expatriate journey, she also recognized that she was in hiding, wooing avoidance. She decided to come home.

Violet finished her cigarette in one deep drag, glancing around at the inventory of open suitcases, scattered clothes, tissued bundles of gifts—St. Francis night-lights, stolen ashtrays—and the steady throb of red on the answering machine. She didn't know where to start.

She threw off the covers and jumped out of bed, glad for the cold cheek of air rubbing against her. Stark naked and shivering (she relegated pajamas to the infirm), she squinted out the window at the welcome brawling beneath, sticking her tongue out at the city that taunted and charmed her, then ran off to the shower.

This was followed by her own casual pastiche of makeup, always applied in the nude in the bath before a large round mirror, wiped free of mist. In the bedroom she pulled on a comfortable outfit consisting of a large black dress with angular shoulders, patterned black stockings, and deep red cowboy boots. She glared at the blinking red on the machine, wishing she had given out a later date of return, and walked into the kitchen. In the spirit of reentry she jabbed on the radio, dragged in the morning papers, spread them on the large dining room table, made a pot of harrowingly strong coffee, and lit the second Gitane of the day. Habit was catching up, and she bent her head to read.

The Modigliani face housed dramatic eyes (she was named for their color) accompanied by assertive slashes of brows (borrowed from Victor), high-plateau cheekbones connected by hollowed furrows to a strong jawline, a slightly sharp angle of nose, and a dash of bowed lips. All of it was framed by an aura of unruly black hair, patent-leather shiny, its varying lengths and changing shapes always suiting her, but usually askew. Violet's beauty would have been intimidating but for two things: her personality of contradictions—part curmudgeon and cynic, part expansive heart; and her sense of physical unease in the world—her propensity to walk into doorjambs, skid down stairs, and drop Limoges plates. These took the edge off any attainment of seamless glamour.

Sometimes before tackling the headlines Violet would squeeze her eyes shut and try to imagine herself safe in Bergen County with a stockbroker husband and witty children, almost hearing their voices in the next room. In this post-feminist era, she wondered if it were a legitimate longing, or a means of escape, or merely sediment from growing up female in America, where suggestions continued to range from deodorizing every square inch of your body, to seducing your husband while swathed in Saran Wrap, to dancing the boardroom shuffle for eighty-nine cents on the dollar. The basic requirement remained limiting: to mate with an upright Hoover, to make your life's work throwing that cozy robe of womanhood around Him. The culture still insisted on a role that Violet could no more fit into than she could scale the Empire State Building with her teeth. Yet in weaker moments she wondered if she hadn't been hardened against certain possibilities.

Violet was addicted to topical information in any medium. This was a habit inherited from Victor, reinforced by the urbanite's need to stay on top of things, and was a particular project recently because she had been dating a famous reporter and was fond of provoking him with her daily examples of yellow journalism. In Violet's opinion, the physical act of reading was an anomaly that suggested the subversive; in the face of the latter half of the twentieth-century's visual blitzkrieg, it was an act approaching the meditative. Even if it was the *New York Post*.

Her lover worked for the *New York Tribune*, which Violet considered self-righteous and smug as well as politically questionable; his presence on the staff did not exempt it from her rather arch cynicism. Only when Paul really challenged her did she back down at all from her dismissal of what she considered half-truths, intra-truths, manipulated truths, and just plain bullshit.

The sight of the *Tribune* brought Paul to mind, as did thinking of the rest of the messages waiting to pour out of the machine she termed the "Box of Torture." She went to the bedroom, rewound what seemed like miles of tape, and punched the playback button as she began a slow, groan-filled wade through the clothes and parcels that were strewn everywhere, throwing outfits into a huge pile for the laundry, wondering why women couldn't have wives. The term "clothes horse" fit maddeningly.

The first message was from David, her devoted business partner and confidant, who had been holding down the fort in their studio-office while she was away: "Violet I hope you're back on time I swear the phone has been ringing off the hook since the Milan shoots were seen by people here I've had to fend them off with meat hooks everything is okay but I have to talk to you about the present assignment did you bring me anything I'll be in of course tomorrow please call if you're too lagged to show up I can't wait to see you did you bring me anything? I've missed you terribly. I hope it worked."

The verbal rush was pure David. The "it" was the intent of her clan, the hope that the time away would take the edge off her determination to find out who killed Victor and why. There were more messages, including one from her close friend Bernard, asking after his sun-dried tomatoes and their retirement villa, then suddenly the voice of Paul, which startled her into sitting down on the edge of the bed, a spasm of desire and confusion knotting her stomach. He sounded quiet and tentative, even nervous.

"Hi, Vi, I hope I have the return date right. I'm still sorry about surprising you in Venice, I wanted to know how you were, I couldn't stand another minute without you. I have not forgotten your need for separation, but God I miss you. Please call when you finish unpacking and—wait, don't do that—it could be weeks. Just please call soon. I love you."

Violet stopped the machine at this point, slightly wringing the dress in her hands. Paul Renault was the first man Violet had discovered whom she felt was appropriate to wake up next to. Paul was an economist in emotion and deed, streamlined. Lean stretches of virgin wool, sharp-edged cuff, silk sock, burnished alligator, smooth olive skin, hot blue eyes, ruddy cheeks, perfect teeth, pianist's hands, all slid together in a study of erudition. Paul was slick and self-contained, a continuous unbroken surface. This intrigued Violet immensely—as drawn as she was to run her hands over his cool marble veneer, she also wanted to abrade it, to crack it; she wanted to observe the inside. This was a large part of her attraction to him, something akin to a science project, which combined with his novelty, and perhaps with his evocation of her father. She closed her eyes, and the image of him ran through her; she gently dropped the dress, letting go only for the moment, and flipped the machine back on.

The voice that emerged was cracked and muffled. It seemed to stumble off the tape.

"Violet, it's Maxie. I heard you was due back right about now. I hope the trip was okay and you drank a lot of Chianti for me, like I said it's elixir. I miss him too, you know? Anyway I've been doing like you asked, and . . ." The voice trailed off into a hacking cough for several moments, then came back. "Anyway I got some stuff for you, I don't want to sit on it either, I can't put it on this machine, call me right when you get in, okay? I mean it, Vi. My number is 555-7070 as if you didn't know, okay? I been worried about you. When this is over maybe we could shoot a couple games, do that wake thing you was talking about. Don't make a move without me, okay? Call . . ."

The end-of-message beep was delayed enough to give the pause some drama. Once again Violet snapped off the machine. She was surprised to hear from him at all.

Max was a local numbers runner; he had done a lot of legwork and research for her father. A classically shady character, low profile but reliable, in constant limbo under the stick of the supposedly lawful, he had always had a soft spot for Violet.

Victor had entrusted Violet to his care on so many occasions that pool games during daylight and sips of Pabst Blue Ribbon were the closest Violet came to a day-care center. On the day of Victor's funeral, not at all satisfied with what the police had concluded, she had implored Max to look into the murder, to ask around.

Now she punched his number into the phone, trembling slightly with the anticipation of what he had to tell her. She let the phone ring a dozen times, then a dozen times more. With an impatient sigh she replaced the receiver.

The call from Max dropped a parenthesis that ended her episode abroad: post-travel, the kindness of distance was over. She wondered what Max's information was; his voice was such a reminder of that day. Whenever she thought of it she remembered the heat of that day. The continuing pain had been a shimmer that echoed the heat waves rising off the street, her eyes blurring with tears, the water running off her skin in the eight-block run from her apartment to Victor's. Heat in August in the city had its own brutal character, a layer of wet flames that teased and aggravated. She remembered the police on the street and the neighbors and the emergency attendants in white bursting out of the building with Victor in his shroud, bumping him down the steps with impatience rather than caution because he was already dead.

In the background Mr. Antonio made a sign of the cross as Victor was jerked by, and a line of children pressed forward, cursing at the fact that he was covered up, the whole scene bathed in the white-hot moisture in the too-bright light. Violet had mentally reeled back, the scene was underwater, she felt removed from it. Then, as Victor was dragged by, some part of his sheathed self brushed against her, all too real, and she fainted.

Violet sat on the bed once more, breathing deeply, pushing the image away. She stared at nothing for several minutes. She considered sending a message to the well-meaning: travel therapy hadn't worked. She felt scared and cut off, alone and dangerous. This morning it seemed that, assailed by memory and unease, it wasn't the forgetting that would release her, but that now life's reentry point would be to find Victor's murderer. It would be the tribute to her dead father who had painstakingly raised her, but who was now going to miss the better part of the payoff—the second act.

Violet lay back and looked at the ceiling, projecting a rerun of her travelogue: the bright green hills, dotted with sheep and cypress, the arches and stone paths and squares, the fountains and leaning lines of buildings, the dense mood of history, the provocative whir of people, the tactile sense of marble and rarefied enclosure and mystery, the light that was hot and cool at the same time, the glasses of *vinsanto*, the furtive conversations in expatriate bars, the Christs held captive in glass cases, all were swept into the design of prescribed wine, women, and song. She had done her best, dipped into all of it, but it was a wrong panacea. While it had been intriguing and seductive, and as much as this morning had become weighted and frustrating to the point that she wanted to go back, immediately, the entire adventure was now re-forming into the same concentrated mass she had held so tightly before being poured into the plane.

No, she hadn't been cured, she realized. The goal was still the same—to solve the mystery of her father's death. She was warned repeatedly, by all who knew her, not to pursue this. They should have known better.

2

Violet swung out on the street. The mean street, the big vaudeville of contradiction named New York; tragedy on one block, a miracle on the next. In fact, the street was an entity of its own—a battered tarmac with a questionable soul, grafting off all who moved on it, the keen and wicked and their miscarried dreams. Violet welcomed every inch she walked upon, the vibrato of the subway underneath starting her up.

Avenue B could not be mistaken for Park Avenue. Life in this part of town was a trial. This was the outpost, the annex, the Wild West in an urban sheath. Stick figures flailing under an umbrella of poverty and violence, doing a cracked dance to the beat of narcotics, Violet had seen too much of its misery to romanticize it. She had been caught in its crossfire.

Yet as she crossed over to Avenue A in search of breakfast Violet was reminded that she wasn't ready for uptown yet. Besides, uptown seemed to be speeding downtown at an alarming rate.

Violet had not missed breakfast since the early sixties. She bought containers of chinese noodles, croissants, cups of cappuccino, tangerines, Classic Cokes, and fortune cookies, all at the same store, and headed for her office building.

Violet's photography studio was housed in a dirty grey 1930s building. A relic even in that area, it contained floor after floor of small- to medium-sized office spaces, replete with prototype elevators and doors paned in frosted glass. Violet was aware that at least half of the businesses housed there—Limited, Unlimited, Associates & Partners & Sons Inc.—had only a tongue-in-cheek legality. One Import-Export company too many, a number of Spiritual Advisors, Transcendental Masseuses, the Monsignor Escort Firm, and a small Magritte-suited man who sold Tupperware of unknown origin, all resided comfortably with an increasing number of artists looking for cheap studio space. As diverse a group as it was, all were aware of the charmed life they were leading. Over the past couple of years Violet had noticed friendlier hello's and quizzical looks, a silent acknowledgment that the building was ripe for gentrified picking.

Violet ducked in through the side door, and in her usual avoidance of elevators, bounded up the stairway, heels scraping over the red-brown stains that did not catch her eye. She headed in the direction of her own office, but stopped at the door before hers and, without knocking, burst into the room.

"I'm back!" Violet announced, dumping her briefcase and breakfast packages on a nearby chair, and throwing her arms around the woman who was standing in front of the desk, speaking into a phone. Romaine Brookes was her closest, and one of her oldest, friends. They had been lovers in college, a small school in southern Ohio, the poor girl's Mt. Holyoke. They had gone through many adventures and permutations since then, and now, fifteen years later, had that deceptively easy intimacy, deep and without judgment, but hard won.

Romaine hugged Violet tightly with one arm while explaining into the phone that she was being assailed by a Jehovah's Witness and would have to call back. She put the receiver down to complete their embrace, and they stood clasped for several moments, laughing, both talking at the same time. Romaine grabbed Violet's hands and pushed her back a step.

"Let me look at you. God girl, I'm so glad you're back,

it's been so dull around here without you I've been having the masseuse twins in for tea—you look skinnier than ever, didn't they feed you over there? I'm so glad to see you!" Romaine hugged her again, and laughed her copyrighted laugh, a cross between an aria and steam heat. She pulled a chair up close for Violet and perched on the edge of the desk. Violet sat and looked up at her.

"Of course I ate. I ate constantly, didn't I write you that? I've never eaten so much in my life, I could author a cuisine tour of Italia, or a dictionary of pasta shapes you never knew existed." Violet began to make odd shapes with her hands.

"Yes, yes you did, the postcards and letters were wonderful. One of my favorite stories was the Texans drinking peach juice out of teeny tiny cans outside the Vatican, inviting, at the top of their lungs, all of Rome to visit the Big State that has grapefruits the size of the Pope's head. And of course I want to hear about all the rest of it, particularly Milan and Gabriella. Details!"

Romaine looked at Violet carefully. "But, honey, you look so pale. How are you really feeling?"

Violet returned the gaze, aware that this was the first of many assessments of her trip. She responded cautiously. "Well, I am exhausted, of course. And I am glad I went. If you all hadn't pushed me on that plane I would probably be swimming around in a bottle of vodka. But basically I feel the same way I did when I left. As if a major limb were severed—it's gone but the nerve endings are still there, with nothing to react to. It's a suspended kind of feeling, and it's not over."

Romaine picked up one of Violet's hands and stroked her palm.

"Vi, no one sent you away thinking you would be fixed. Grieving is pushing up from deep water. You have to look out for the bends. You have to come up at your own pace." Romaine's voice was low and musical. Violet often thought of a deep-toned bell when she heard it; it comforted her.

"Vi," Romaine continued, "the point is you had a long, hard year anyway, even before Victor died. Don't make him emblematic, don't hide there. And this crackpot idea of finding out who did it is no instant cure either. Well, you know what I think about that." Romaine squeezed her hand and released it, then walked around behind the desk and settled in her own chair. Violet crossed her arms and gave an exasperated sigh.

"For God's sake, Brookes, I haven't been back five minutes and you're already starting to lecture me."

"Okay, Vi, I'll let it go," Romaine said. "For now, anyway. And if you think that was a lecture just give me a few minutes on Paul."

Violet grinned and pointedly changed the subject. "Darling, how have you been? You look stunning as always."

Romaine was, in Violet's stringent and demanding opinion, the most beautiful woman walking the planet. She was a classic African beauty, a reference to Kenya rather than the south side of Chicago. Violet would have followed Romaine's countenance (flashing-dark seismographic eyes, a broad regal nose, full, precisely delineated lips, and an extraordinary configuration of elegant lengths of neck, breastbone, wingspan, and sweep of limbs) to the moon. Her carriage was that of a dancer (which she had trained for many years to become); her appointment that of an ancient soul called down one more time to dislocate the complacent. Which she did.

After an injury ended her dancing career Romaine went back to school and became a lawyer. Shortly after passing the bar she came to visit Violet and Victor in New York. Romaine and Victor were very fond of each other, after they got over the initial discomfort of Violet's first lover being female ("Violet, are you crazy? Exactly what do you expect Daddy to say when you bring a colored girl home to share your room?" "Well, he has to find out sometime. And for God's sake, where do you think I grew up? Scarsdale?"). It was Victor who suggested that Romaine start her fledgling practice in their neighborhood. She did, and Victor sent a lot of legal work her way.

Romaine shook her head. "I'll let you get away with that for the moment. And I'm fine, everything's been okay except for missing you. This week I've been busy trying to keep Zar's behind out of jail."

"Oh God, what now?" Violet asked. Zar (short for Rosa Cortazar) was a conceptual artist with an extremely political bent. She worked under the name Artemis, and her studio was on the top floor of their building.

"Actually a lot of artists are in trouble," Romaine replied.

"The city is enforcing an ordinance, for the first time in a million years, against posting bills. These artists have been doing it for ages—for some of them it's their major gesture—but I'm talking about announcements too, for readings and performances, et cetera. The thing is they're fining people left and right, a hundred bucks a pop, not per event, but for each piece of goddamn paper. We're talking thousands in fines. It's bullshit and a waste of all our time."

Violet rolled her eyes. "Oh Lord, I can just imagine how our resident hot-head is taking this. Do you think they're picking on the politics?"

"No, I wish they were. I'd have more to go on. Besides, I don't think anyone in the Mayor's office actually knows how to read. I don't know why the hell they're doing it, it's such penny-ante stuff. But that reminds me, I have to make several phone calls before Zar pops in for an update. Will you wait?"

"Sure. But what time is it?"

"It's eight-forty."

"Great. I don't think David is in yet. May I put out our ice-cold and congealed breakfast?"

"That sounds appealing." Romaine made a face. "Actually, please do if any of those bags holds a cup of coffee. You've been so captivating I haven't even started a pot yet."

Violet stuck her tongue out and retrieved the breakfast packages from the chair she left them in. Romaine pulled some papers out of a file, drew the phone next to her, and started her calls. Violet quietly started undoing the breakfast things, placing a not terribly warm cup of cappuccino in front of Romaine. True to form, Violet was ravenous.

She responded to most phenomena of significance, whether positive or negative, with hunger. When she was in this state, New York was suddenly reduced to a vast plain of concrete punctuated by eateries. Geography was the shortest distance between two favorite restaurants. She classified all social events by the quality, quantity, and character of food served. When Paul introduced her to the Mayor, she noted, "You would not believe it—he served egg salad on Wonderbread toast points and called it a luncheon." At a reception for an artist in SoHo the analysis was, "The paintings were okay, but they had nothing but herbed brie and crudités—and they call themselves avant-garde." In attendance at a cocktail party at a well-known tennis player's penthouse it was, "Well dear, she served exquisite carpaccio, bagna cauda, tapenade, and Veuve Cliquot. There wasn't a piece of puff pastry in sight and I asked for her hand in marriage right on the spot."

Violet could direct one to the perfect source for any variety of dining experience or culinary oddity, and was of the opinion that if garlic didn't exist she wouldn't bother eating at all. In fact, she would be hard-pressed to find a reason to get up in the morning.

While Romaine was on the phone, Violet consumed a container of now-cold noodles, a croissant filled with ham, and half a can of Coke. She lit a Gauloise and watched Romaine thoughtfully, running her free hand across the top of the desk in a silent piano scale. The morning street sounds were slowly growing louder, one on top of the other, merging into a steady blare. In contrast the light in the room was soft, regulated by grey blinds whose degree of slant was dictated by Romaine's mood.

Romaine hung up after her third call.

"Miss Vi, if you don't stop smoking those French suicide notes in here I'm taking you out of my will. It will be pointless, considering how much sooner you're going to kick it than I am." She took a bite out of one of the remaining croissants, exclaiming in the middle, "We have so much to talk about! God, I'm glad you're home."

Violet nodded in agreement smiling. "Yes, we've simply got to have dinner tonight or tomorrow. But I have to go see David, Mr. Reality Check, and I know you have a lot of work. Just one thing"—she narrowed her eyes in mock intensity—"you're glowing like a neon beer sign. What's up? Or should I say who is she? Sushi teacher? Your interior decorator? Divorce client?"

"Well . . ." Romaine responded reluctantly.

"Don't tell me, let me guess," Violet countered. "Tall, hopelessly elegant, highly literate, a lioness in bed, slight Midwestern accent—need I go on?"

"No, don't." Romaine was choking on embarrassed laughter. "Have I gotten that predictable? Actually we've been seeing each other for quite a while. Speaking of significant others, have you spoken to Paul since you returned?"

Violet shook her head. "No, I haven't called him yet, I needed to get a little settled first. And don't read anything into that either. I adore Paul. And before you make one of your usual cracks, shouldn't we be the first ones to say you fall in love with a person, not their gender?"

"Don't tempt me on that one, Childes. Don't get me started," Romaine replied.

Violet ignored her. "Anyway, Venice was definitely a strain. Sometimes Paul looks at me in the most concentrated, compressed manner, I get the feeling he's looking for something. Then I'm afraid he won't find it and will disappear. At certain moments he's my twin, then all of a sudden a stranger. You know what it's like when you get very close to someone, when you start slipping over each other's borders? It's scary. It's frightening to become that vulnerable. And—well, you know how I get when I fall in love. Positively unnerved. Disarmed. However," Violet leered, "we know how *you* are about love."

Romaine propped a clenched hand on her hip. "And just how is that?"

"Borderline mercenary."

"What? I'm a cupcake, a sweetheart, a regular Jennifer Jones."

"Yeah, right. You mean à la *Song of Bernadette*? Spare me. I can see it now, on your knees in front of a shrine. At least the on-your-knees part."

"Stop it. You're incredible. As for your present incarnation—"

"Look, dollface, I haven't joined the Communist Bloc. Okay, you know what it really is? Finally, after all these years, I found a pattern for porcelain in a Bloomingdale's catalogue—black and white, deco of course—that was worth getting engaged for and setting a date so I can register. And"—Violet was acutely aware this was an unresolved topic between them but it wasn't the time to pursue it—"the world is hanging by a thread, every waking minute is carcinogenic, there's no time to lose, and when you find love, the stupid, enchanted, cracked thing that it is, it's worth pursuing in any form. As you well know." She paused for air.

"Mm-hmm." Romaine crossed her arms.

"And what is that? I know, you think I'm just sideswiping normalcy for a change."

"Hardly," said Romaine. "That would be a long shot. No, really, I think you're corny as hell, but somehow always believable. I continue to be curious, that's all."

"You know I can't help it. It's the Sagittarian curse—they're all suckers for love." She held her hands together as though reciting a schoolroom poem, and intoned with a dramatic edge: "It's that exquisite pain of spring that derails the senses. It's a dare and a gamble, but you can never quite lose because love once given is indelible, irretractable. This is how it is—the heart jumps in with both feet. It's the universal salve, the stitcher of wounds, it's door Number Three."

"Yeah, and people in love should have warning flashers on," Romaine grumbled. Violet looked convincingly but falsely chagrined.

"Okay, okay, so I've been bodily invaded by Rod McKuen. Okay, so talk is cheap, love is only another form of currency. It's jumping out of a plane without a parachute, it's a straitjacket, a power play. An attempt to fill up spaces you should fill on your own. Okay, I've seen the flip side; it's the weakener, the enemy, the illusory. So—I still think it's the best thing ever invented and the point of it all . . . even if that makes me . . . Sisyphus." She played the last sentence out like a fishing line, daring the world to yank on the other end. She picked up her briefcase, and grazed Romaine's cheek with her hand as a good-bye.

"Later," she said and, arm extended, waved inwardly, Italian-style, to prove she had really traveled.

3

Violet ignored her own office door and let herself in to the rooms to the right of it. She felt a slight elation at being back. She enjoyed working with David, with whom she shared a similar workaholic intensity. They agreed on the pleasing symbiotic nature of photography: the balance of the technical and chemical with the artistic. Right now she welcomed the precision and demand of attention her business required. She needed the distraction.

The front room was used for the matting and framing of photographs and the sorting of slides. It contained simple work tables, light boxes, and filing cabinets of negatives and prints. The back room, behind a door covered with dire warnings and topped with a large red bulb, was the darkroom. This was the only room in the world that rivaled the kitchen in importance in Violet's realm.

Violet threw her things on the nearest chair. She noticed several strips of color negatives on the light table; next to them were bottles of retouching dyes. She wondered if this was the recent job David had been complaining about in his phone message. The lights were on and she could hear water running in the darkroom, which meant David was inside. She pressed a button under the table that lit up an amber light in the darkroom signaling she was there. The light had been installed because David spent most of his waking hours glued to a Walkman that emanated a level of sound no buzzer could get through. In a moment the door banged open, and a figure burst out, one hand shielding eyes against the bright light, the other waving a plastic sheet containing color slides, which David tossed on a table.

"Violet! Welcome home! *Come sta?*" He put his arms around her in a big hug and kissed both her cheeks. Violet heard dance music throbbing at his neck where the earphones were slung. He fumbled for the switch and turned it off.

"Darling, you got back just in time. I've had it with the help you finally agreed to let me hire, each one has been too precious for words, these students are beyond simple set-ups and developing, I could wring their necks. And this latest job is just—" Violet put a hand over his mouth, often it was the only solution. David's energy was best described as haywire, his physical movements were so skittish he was a blur most of the time—Duchamp's *Nude Descending a Staircase* in person.

"David! Just give me a minute to adjust, will you?" Violet

laughed and took her hand away. David bowed in an exaggerated fashion and stepped back.

"I'm sure Madam will find everything in order. I piled all recent correspondence and topical stuff on your desk yesterday, including a very healthy status report from the bookkeeper. You must be beat from traveling, I must know all—oops—I have something swimming in fixer I must rescue, I guess I'll have to wait for my present! You just go inside and get settled then we'll catch up"—Violet nodded, knowing better than to try to interject at this point—"I'm thrilled you're home, we all missed you terribly, I've even had the masseuse twins in for tea—" He squeezed Violet's arm, flipped his earphones back on, and sprinted into the darkroom. Violet picked up her things and opened the door to the main office.

The scene before her swung out like a left hook into a glass jaw. Slabs of light fell from the windows, and one of them pinioned the body, flooding it ruthlessly. Inventory: the pasty white mask, dull balls of glass protruding, the lips liver-pale, the whole eight pints covering the shiny suit, the monkey-paw hands, the done-in shoes, and the pale grey carpet. Final note: the crusted tracery of dried blood on the edges of the sliced throat, lipstick on an obscene mouth. The walls seemed to waver. Her heart slammed around in its cage. The contents of her hands dropped to the floor. Her jaw clenched. The gurgle in the throat was a trapped scream working to dislodge itself. Revulsion overtook shock and Violet stumbled into the bathroom, and was violently ill, confusion ringing in her ears. She threw cold water on her face and stood in the doorway, leaning heavily on its frame, alienated. She took a deep breath and staggered to the desk to call the police. She averted her eyes, but the scent of death is as vivid as its visual counterpart. She started to dial, and hand and phone were in midair when she could not help but glance at the corpse again. And recognize it. The receiver clattered onto the desktop, she murmured "Jesus Christ," she sat down hard.

It was Max. She was almost as shocked at the identity of the man as she was at the body itself. Immediately the morning's phone message jumped into her head. It had seemed intriguing but not desperate. She was breathing heavily. The horror of the mutilated form next to her sank in, and she realized the probable significance of the kill that had been literally dumped at her feet. He had information about Victor. He was in her office. He was slaughtered to keep from passing this information on to her. And was it a warning?

The world is full of loose ends, unsolved cases, unfinished business, all of it flapping around, nagging, pressing. Violet was accustomed to this, but she had made a pledge on the day of the funeral: she would find the person who had murdered Victor and she would return the gesture, as thoroughly and painfully as possible. This thought stemmed partially from the exaggeration of grief, partly from subterfuge. She had felt safe and centered while Victor was alive—after all, he had created that context for her in the first place. She had not quite gotten around to making it for herself.

Violet mentally pushed down continuing waves of nausea, staring at the former Max, involuntarily examining the physical intimacy of death as she had not with Victor or her mother. Lost in thought and feeling Violet sat unseeing as the door to her office opened and Romaine appeared, her mouth dropping open at the incredible sight, the bright bald light intensifying the scene, at the center of which was Violet, staring out, with clenched fists barely resting on the desk, her body rigid.

"Oh my God," was all Romaine could manage, rushing over to Violet, one hand over her mouth suppressing a gag, the other shaking Violet's arm. Violet broke out of her daze, looking up at her.

"Ro, it's Max," the words floated out, woozily. "He called me. Or he tried to. He left a message. He had something to say about Victor, some information. I guess you should call Donald . . ."

Romaine nodded, grasping Violet by the shoulders and pulling her to her feet. "Of course. But let's get out of here," she said, and they both stumbled through the door that connected the two offices. Romaine gently pushed Violet down on the chair behind her desk. She picked up the phone and punched a familiar number on it, tucking it sideways between chin and shoulder as she pulled a drawer open, retrieved a bottle and glass, and pushed a drink into Violet's hand. The phone connection was made, but Violet heard Romaine's voice only as a weird hum. At that moment it struck her that if he had been killed to stop him from seeing her, she was an unwitting accomplice to his death. Her heartbeat accelerated wildly in a feeling of guilt.

Romaine put down the phone and pushed the glass of brandy gently to Violet's lips. Violet swallowed and began to cry and talk at the same time.

"This is it, Ro, no more pretending it's a closed case, no more fucking around. There's Max to consider, too, now, he was killed because of his loyalty to Victor. Damn, I want the answer to this and I'm going to find it. Besides, I was weaned on technique, I probably know more by osmosis about tracking someone down than all those hammy detectives put together."

Romaine ignored this comment for the moment and sighed, shivering, playing along until Violet calmed down.

"Honey, do you have any idea what Max had to tell you?"

"My question exactly," interrupted a voice from the door. The two women looked up at Donald Cummings, who was a precinct police detective, Victor's best friend, Violet's godfather, and someone who disapproved strongly of Violet's amateur dabbling in solving the case of her father's murder. He was flanked at the door by two patrolmen, a photographer, and an assistant coroner. Cummings glanced at them.

"Do it!" He barked over his shoulder. He walked over to Violet and briefly smoothed her hair back off her forehead, then resumed a more official-looking stance.

"Don, it's Max, he was trying to get in touch with me, he had something to tell me about Victor, it opens everything up again doesn't it, let's—" Violet began.

"Let's nothing. Hold it right there." The detective shifted uncomfortably in his raincoat, raising a hand in a stiff salute of protest.

Looking up at him, Violet was reminded of the past occasions on which Donald had used the same paternal gesture, whether warning her off stealing second base, or dismissing her adolescent's plan to go into police work.

He had always reminded Violet of a lumberjack trapped in a three-piece suit. Well over six feet tall, his substantial girth was neatly distributed. His bright red hair had thinned appreciably, and was now substantially diluted with silver grey; it reflected light in a wispy crown. The wire brush eyebrows were unruly mustaches over the placid green eyes, and his cheeks and mouth were the same ruddy bruised mauve. His nose was a surprisingly delicate appendage on the strong wide face.

Donald saw Violet looking at him with an emotional appraisal, but he softened his demeanor only slightly.

"Vi, you know how I felt about Victor. But looking for his killer is very possibly going to get you the same thing he got. He would never forgive me for letting you loose on this case, which by the way is still considered closed by the department. I've told you that for months and I haven't changed my mind. How can you think of it after what just happened next door? That's the ugliest goddamn hit I've seen in months. Face it, your father made a million enemies in his life, and Max isn't far behind him in that area. Forget it, Violet—why don't you go home and think about a new hobby, racing cars or playing the market, like normal women." Cummings was bellowing, his voice belligerent but his eyes fearful. Unfortunately, his intent of intimidation had the opposite effect. Violet stood up.

"Listen, I'm going to find out who really killed him and when I do I'll cut his balls off and shove them down his throat and that's just to start. There is nothing you can do to stop me either, short of coming up with an answer yourself. And I don't get your reticence, Donald. At least use me up front as a lure. You're suspiciously soft on this one, noticeably hands-off"—she was baiting him now, testing—"Max didn't get his because he dressed badly. Why are you playing this down? Do I have to resort to a cover-up theory?"

Cummings looked ready to explode, then reeled himself in, merely nodding his head in a sarcastic reply, turning toward the doorway to Violet's office, abruptly brushing by the tall, intense-looking man who was on his way in. It was Paul, alerted by his police scanner on the way to a press conference, who gathered Violet to him, and looked with pointed dismissal at Romaine. She did not cooperate.

Violet felt herself collapse slightly, she wasn't ready for the reunion, much less under these circumstances, and she started to cry again, more from frustration than anything else. The tension between Paul and Romaine was old news; claustrophobia made her push his arms away and pronounce, "All right you two, this is the last time I'm going to say this. Victor was father and mother to me, and taught me music, gave me a trade, and the best pitching arm on Mott Street. And he was probably my best friend and he never once let me down and he was ripped out of this earth like a fucking turnip. And I don't care how childish you think it is, I'm going to find out who did it and why if it takes the rest of my natural life. Dig?" Violet folded her arms and glared. Romaine was silent. Paul correctly read the thin bravado, and punctured it.

"Violet, your sense of vengeance is refreshingly biblical but pointless if you end up like the lump next door."

Violet sank in the chair and put her head in her hands.

"Don't you get it?" she said softly. "Jesus, this is driving me crazy. I wake up at night in a cold sweat, I dream I'm in a coma, in a car with no brakes, in a house with a hundred rooms and nobody's home. I want to get to the bottom of this. I want some peace." Violet stared at the floor. Paul and Romaine looked at each other combatively.

"This is a scary little obsession, Vi. I want you to stop right now," Paul began, but was interrupted by Romaine.

"Damn it, why don't you take that Park Avenue smooth talk and—" Their eyes locked then released, acknowledging their shared concern, tucking away their usual and rehearsed hostility.

"It's part of her grieving," Romaine said to him.

"It's bloody dangerous," was his reply.

Violet was listening and was aware that they were talking as though she weren't there, and experienced a sense of acute déjà vu, sheering off into memory.

Was it Coney? Was it Fire Island or Brighton? Violet couldn't remember. It was a boardwalk, and the three of them were standing at the end, in front of a railing that sliced off the horizon in a neat half, and they were all holding hands. It was windy, but the sun was bright. Hot dog wrappers and bits of cellophane whipped against Violet's bare legs, stinging. She looked over her shoulder and watched what seemed like hundreds of red and white waxed paper cones, empty of their ice and syrup, bouncing around like pointy hats. The voices and the laughter that drifted toward them on the wind were muted and mocking. Why? The sounds of her parents' voices went back and forth in sad tones, meeting above her head. Why? Marie seemed to be sick all the time. What was different now? Violet was confused, and frightened that one of their favorite places suddenly seemed menacing and foreign. She felt excluded, which was unusual. She squeezed their hands and softly said, "Hey." They looked down at her, tears in both sets of eyes, yet they were smiling, and they pressed against her from either side. The group of three became a huddle.

Violet shook her head slightly, but the voices continued, as if over her head in a cartoon bubble. She was still looking at the floor.

"She thinks of him as some kind of hero, some perfect soul, which he wasn't, no one is. It's not healthy," Paul was saying.

"You got it, Chuck, and you're the replacement, which ain't healthy either," Romaine replied, and they seemed ready to squabble again, but Paul gave her an unabashedly imploring look, and Romaine gave in, and left the room, closing the door behind her.

Paul knelt in front of Violet and rubbed his cheek against hers.

"I'm terribly sorry about this . . . but thank God you're home." He held her hands in his own. "Let's start over."

Finally Violet raised her eyes. "You can't seduce me out of this one, Renault, I'm committed."

Paul was exasperated. "Why do you have to be so damn stubborn? What the hell do you have to prove? You know how much I love you, is it so hard to understand I don't want you to end up a pile of ashes in some Wedgwood vase? Why do you have to be so tough?"

"And why do you have to be so testicular?" She sighed. "I adore you, but I'm not helpless, and we don't have to revert to anemic role-playing. I need some room on this one. I'm grateful for your concern, but don't push me, okay? My trip hasn't erased any of that."

Paul was hovering around a reply when the door flew open and a familiar shape lunged toward Violet. It was David. He grabbed her shoulder.

"Jesus, Violet, what's going on? Who's in the body bag next door? I told them everything I know, which is absolute zero. Is it one of our clients?" His voice escalated in panic. "Did you—no, of course not, how could I say such a thing, I'm hysterical—" He was on the verge of babbling. Violet pulled him down on the chair next to her and quietly explained the circumstances. He was clearly shaken.

"Look," she said, "it's a shock, and if you want to get out of here, do. But if you can, keep working, distract yourself, we'll regroup tomorrow, okay?" He nodded jerkily in agreement and left the room, intimidated by Paul's presence.

Paul was torn between embrace and chastisement. He started in again.

"I've had it with this derailment of yours, grieving or not, it's beside the point—"

"Things that seemed in place have blown apart—"

"It's an excuse—"

"Things I counted on have changed into something else." Violet smiled bitterly. "It's just a little loss of faith—"

"You feel guilty because you weren't as close to him as you usually were when he died. Call me when you grow up," he announced, and left.

Violet looked at the floor again, familiar now with a certain square footage of the dark blue rug, a sector of deep space.

She pulled herself away and went next door. Max was gone except for the Rorschach blot of stain, and the blue chalk outline of his body. She sat at her desk in the lingering scent, with the aftermath detail of the violated carpet, the weary dread-blankness, the descent of drama into smaller, more regular concerns. Reluctantly, she sent Romaine and David to their respective quarters, promising to be in touch, announcing she was heading for home, and gave Donald's officer a formal statement. Sluggishly, with the languor of it slowing her down, she gathered all the material David had left on her desk, pushing it into the big pouchy briefcase. She left with the weight of panic reduced to a numbing anxiety.

• • •

Outside, striding under a viscous white sky, Violet plunged into the speedy horizontal of traffic, a dramatic contrast to the static verticals of the skyline, all of it shining in a recently sprung storm. The rain came abruptly, the hard staccato pummeled the skin, beating people into doorways yelling for cabs.

Violet walked right through the middle of it, seeking its cold cleansing. Okay, so the world is a tinderbox waiting for a match. Okay, so you're a dog walking a tightrope waiting to see which side you'll fall off. Okay, so you're in good company not understanding the phrase "happy as a clam."

There was the sound of a loud crack that wasn't thunder; Violet had heard it before. Now it coincided with a car sweeping up beside her on the street. Instinct made her dive behind a delivery truck while the bullet caromed off some object and skimmed very near in a deadly whistle. In that split second it took to roll toward cover, smashing her head on the sidewalk in the process, Violet noted: the black GTO, the massive hand with many rings holding the gun out the window, the sparks that flew out as the speeding car grated against a parked car and roared off, a red-gloved hand holding a red purse, some pointed white shoes, a striped awning, all assembled like a tilted sawed-off snapshot. Her head hit the pavement hard and a dark curtain lowered, pushing out light, sound, and finally even the rain.

A few minutes later Violet began to wake and pull herself through the layers of sensation that drag back consciousness. The rubbery brain took some time to clarify. She cautiously opened her eyes, aware of a painful banging hammer swinging back and forth in her head. She was in a small room, an office of some kind, which had dark red walls covered with photographs. She found she was lying on a fake leopard-skin couch. Surrounding her was a group of women, one of whom was pressing an ice bag to the back of Violet's head, another was holding a pool cue, another was pouring cognac into a small glass; the rest were simply standing and looking concerned. In a few seconds Violet realized where she was, and she closed her eyes again and said, "Honey, if that's not Remy Martin don't bother." The group laughed, taking the comment as a sign that she was all right. Then all but two of them wandered out of the room.

Violet was in Anita's, the oldest surviving women's nightclub in New York. Since the early forties it had been a meeting place of significance, a sanctuary for women of every social and economic background who were brought together by their status as sexual outlaws. There were many incarnations of these nightclubs; they seemed to change monthly, opening and celebrating, then closing for a variety of reasons, but Anita's remained the constant. As much as Violet claimed Anita's as her second home, she was distressed by its particular necessity, its sense of cloister, as if women agreed they should have a life apart in some dark bar. As far as Violet was concerned, nothing women did, including love other women, should be secretive or forced out of the mainstream. She also knew better than this, and acknowledged the need and appropriateness of this establishment. Violet looked up at Anita.

"Did anyone see what happened?"

"No. We heard all the noise, went outside to see what happened, found you of all people practically lying on the doorstep, and brought you inside. I thought you would prefer that," said Anita in her husky voice. Nearing sixty, Anita was still the penultimate hostess of lesbian nightlife. Her tawny attractiveness was inextricably bound with a stubborn life force and the smoothing calm of a faith healer's touch. She thought of the club as a spiritual bus stop. Christine, Anita's lover of eighteen years, just barely tolerated Anita's commitment to the nightclub, preferring a more austere line between home and work. Christine thought Anita was too involved with the bar's patrons, more social worker than businesswoman, which was true. To Violet, Anita was a surrogate mother, and Violet adored her. Anita leveled her sorrel eyes, her analyst's eyes, at Violet.

"Okay, sweetie, welcome home," she held Violet's face in her hands, "but what is this all about?"

Violet was aware of the other pair of hands, holding an ice bag to her head, and hesitated to respond; she flicked her eyes upward, unwilling to provoke further pain by moving her head.

"Oh, sorry," Anita responded to the glance, and the

woman in question moved into Violet's view. "Meet Dr. Lucy Brush, luckily here for lunch. She says you'll get away with no stitches, but, what do you think Luce, possible concussion?" The doctor nodded.

"Do you have double vision?"

"They've been saying that for years," Violet replied. Dr. Brush nodded.

"Anita warned me about you. But this is serious. Ideally I should check you into St. Vincent's"—Violet shrank internally, her entire relationship with her mother seemed to consist of hospitals, and she refused to step foot in one voluntarily—"but you seem to be neurologically sound," the doctor said, after putting Violet through several simple tests. "So go home and lie down, no drugs, booze, caffeine, or cigarettes, or I'll start taking lunch elsewhere . . . Or I'll repeat around town what Anita has told me while we were waiting for you to come around. Deal?" She grinned.

"Fine. Sure. Fine. Whatever you say. Your last sentence did it," said Violet with mock sincerity. Dr. Brush left the room smiling. Anita focused once again on Violet.

"Spill, baby."

Violet filled her in, concluding with the shooting ambush that had just occurred, which, as far as Violet was concerned, fit right in with everything else.

"So," she finalized, "Max knew something and someone knew Max knew something and on top of it they think I know whatever it is he knew. Or, they've decided to discourage me from looking into it further. What the jerks don't get is that this stuff makes me more curious and more determined, not less so."

Anita started to say something then stopped, and sat thinking for a moment.

"Vi, I know better than to try to talk you out of anything, and if anyone understands what this means to you, I do. But do me a favor, just don't try to take this on all alone. I loved Victor, he helped this place out of a lot of tight spots, but I swear to God if I have to bury another Childes I'll never speak to you again." She touched Violet's forehead briefly, then stood up and walked to the door.

"On the other hand," she continued, "I'd love to be there when you catch him. And don't repeat that sentiment. Cummings is out front. Do you want to rest for a while and talk to him later?"

"Thank you for the sanctuary, but I'll see him now. I want to go home. And Anita . . . I'll save you a ringside seat."

Anita nodded at her solemnly and left the room. Violet gave Don a brief statement, ignored his warnings, put off a meeting with him until the following day, and dragged herself home. She was immensely grateful for the sight of the disheveled bed. She pulled off her clothes, swallowed some aspirin, and threw herself down, sinking very quickly into the erasure of sleep.

4

When she woke up it was nearing five-thirty. The pounding in her head was complemented by the honking clamor of rush-hour traffic. She lay quietly for several minutes, thinking about Max. Her final image of him was pathetic, the length of his stained trousers, the pointed shoes crossing each other at the tips but at an odd angle, the rest of him cut off by the door to Romaine's office. Mannequin legs. Props.

Violet had seen plenty of violence, on the street and off, while she was growing up. Her mother's illness had seemed a long, slow courtship with death, then finally the obvious marriage. But the aspect of violence added to loss found in Victor's killing and repeated in Max's slaughter were a different and jarring manifestation of death.

Thankfully her headache pulled her away from thinking about Max for a while. She put on coffee, swallowed more aspirin, and took a quick shower. She pulled on her favorite white linen pajamas, retrieved what was left of her pack of Gitanes, poured a large amount of coffee into a mug (while mentally apologizing to Dr. Brush), and dumped the contents of her briefcase on the dining room table.

In the array were logs of the work done while Violet had been away, David's excerpts of recent bookkeeping stats, small boxes and plastic sheets of slides, and various catalogue pages, brochures, and advertisements that the work resulted in. Most were pedestrian, some were amusing, and Violet pored over them all, looking for the edge-work, as she and David called it, that took the standard commercial assignments and twisted them slightly and, they hoped, toward the artistic.

Violet had always, with frustration, tried to balance the obvious income-producing work, and the time and energy it took to put out, with her own personal photography. Often it seemed a losing battle. After hours or even days of production over some bacon strip or waterproof watch shaped like a sports car, the last thing she wanted to do was delve into her own work; she wanted a beer and a video like anyone else. The challenge to switch gears was continuing and acute, and her own work had evolved into a challenge of what she thought was the sterility of the sleek commercial transparency. For the last several years she had concentrated on the classic—nudes mostly—using view cameras and platinum printing and some of her own made-up chemistry, pointedly moving as far away from modern technical formats as possible.

On bad days she thought of chucking the business and doing anything—car repair, dog-walking—to keep the art separate, not connected to how she supported herself. On good days she recognized that she was a photographer to the bone, and, while ambivalence reigned, she got a kick out of the perfect lighting of the dumb bacon strip, had fun placing the waterproof watch on the wrist of an up-and-coming actress, submerging both in a room-sized aquarium filled with pink-tinted water and plastic sharks.

She sent away for her first camera at age seven, a genuine official Lone Ranger model called the Silver Bullet. She cut her teeth on a Weegee style of urban photojournalism, found weekly in *Life* magazine. Further influence included her father's police photographer friends with their array of shiny equipment, and harrowing accounts of subjects relayed casually at the kitchen table as well as billboards and tabloids—as a teenager she roamed the Lower East Side seeking the lurid, and found it. At college she studied the masters, and discovered the Zone system, light meters, and women, all at the same time.

After graduation she returned to New York. Victor helped get her a job with a friend of his, and her first commercial photos were food shots. Hamburgers/fries, tuna/cottage cheese diet plates, for signs at Lamston's all over town. She was hooked. After the requisite years of developing someone else's film, photographing friend's weddings, indexing slides in a stock photo house, and doing a short stint at Playland complete with Alice-in-Wonderland stage flats that you stuck your head through, Violet saved enough money to open a small studio with a high school friend who had taken the same route she had.

Violet was impressed and grateful that David had kept up so well without her. She left a message on his machine to say so, and affirmed a plan to catch up and reorganize their business the next morning. Attention to work made her feel slightly settled, temporarily relaxed. She walked into the kitchen and removed a waiting and ice cold Dos Equis from the freezer, returned to the living room and flipped on the stereo, and sounds of Billie Holiday swooned into the room as she lit a Gitane. She sipped some of the beer and listened to the music, the mourning of the voice a contrast to the bright lyrics and upbeat slides of shiny brass notes.

She was wandering through this sensation when the ring from the lobby phone interrupted her. It was a messenger, and she buzzed him in. Probably more work from David, she thought. Moments later the doorbell rang, and she unlocked and opened the door. The young man in purple high-tops thrust the package toward her, looking tense and irritated. At the same time Paul popped out from behind him. Violet gave the guy five bucks, pulled Paul into the room, and closed the door. At the same moment she accepted his embrace, Violet saw the handwriting on the package, as she tipped it onto the table behind Paul. There was no return address, but Violet's name and location, scrawled in tall lean letters, had come from Max. She stiffened in surprise. Paul felt it and pulled away from her slightly.

"Honey, what is it?" he asked. During the second she was considering a reply, Violet decided to keep it from him, beginning to be wary of constant censure of her continued inquiry.

"Just more work to catch up with, when I thought I had all of it here." Her fingers traced gently down the lengths of his sleeves, running into a hand filled with roses and another with champagne (which Violet had no use for unless shot through with Guinness Stout).

She grinned. "As always, Renault, you look like an extra from *The Philadelphia Story*."

Paul smiled back, cocking his head slightly. "I came to apologize for leaning on you so hard this morning. The last thing you needed was some ham-handed lecture. I'm just here to observe, to tell you I'm thrilled that you're home, to tell you you're a beautiful, stubborn, idiotic fool and I love you." He held her face for a moment and kissed her gently. It was a sweet reminder that there was a place removed from the Victor pain, the shock of Max, the jet lag, the fear. And it was standing in front of her.

"Apology accepted, come on in."

Violet disappeared into the kitchen to put the flowers in a vase and returned with glasses, placing them on the table in front of Paul. He poured some champagne for both of them, they touched glasses, then Violet sat down and looked at Paul in anticipation of trouble after their confrontation that morning. But he simply ruffled her hair and gazed.

"You're really back. You're home. Thank God, I was starting to take up weird hobbies."

"Like what?" Violet challenged.

"The crossword puzzle, juggling, and a lot of weird writing."

"On the novel?"

"Yes and no. You know me, I dance around it any way I can. Shopping lists, letters, journal stuff, notes to the plumber, then finally a line or two." He was gazing again. Violet felt slightly overwhelmed. She grasped one of his hands.

"I'm very glad to see you, but—"

"But you're starving and would I perch in the kitchen and babble while you cook, right?"

Violet nodded and grabbed his hand and her glass. He followed with his into her favorite room. She pushed him into a chair, trying hard not to rush out, hide herself in a closet, and open the package Max sent. Instead she started to prepare dinner.

"Peel these. And tell me everything," She had thrust a small plate holding many cloves of garlic at him, accompanied by a knife. He complied; she cooked, he talked.

The black-and-white-tiled floor, the soft green deco canisters, the refrigerator plastered with *Post* headlines, the 1939 World's Fair clock—it was her cherished room. Surrounded by a minimum of carefully chosen utensils, battered pots, every herb and spice ever grown, and wielding a paring knife or whisk, Violet felt cut loose and creative. She loved to feed people, it was such a direct and simple way to please them. She wanted to open a restaurant, a soup kitchen, a hot dog stand. The Peace Corps had appealed as a franchise wielded against starvation, but they turned her down.

Paul talked about work and gossiped. Violet listened, finally feeling she was home, and, becoming serious, removed cream, Parmesan cheese, butter, and prosciutto from the refrigerator, a box of baby peas from the freezer, delighting in the jazz floating in from the living room, listening to an argument in Spanish on the street below. She stopped Paul at seven cloves, chopped them, cut the prosciutto into small strips, and placed them both in a pan on medium heat in some olive oil. While that was cooking slowly she drained the peas in a colander under cool water, and grated a hunk of Parmesan.

"Vi," he started. "I called your office this afternoon, then checked in here, I was worried about you. In tracking you down I heard about what happened. It certainly escalates things, doesn't it? I won't pretend I'm not concerned; getting shot at is no little cease-and-desist love note. How do you feel?"

"I'm fine except for the gong bashing around in my head. I received some great treatment at this little backstreet restaurant, no Blue Cross needed."

"Yes, I know, you were at Anita's with the guys," Paul said with sarcasm. He never bothered to hide his distaste for Violet's involvement with women. She wasn't sure if he was intimidated or insecure or just being a jerk.

"Oh Paul, shut up." Violet shook her head. Paul got up and walked to the sink to rinse his hands, standing next to her.

"Sorry, pal. That's really a false issue at the moment. I'm annoyed at your voluntarily endangering yourself."

Silently, irritated herself, Violet dumped the container of cream into the prosciutto and garlic, added the cheese, adjusted the heat to low, and put on water to boil.

"Don't move," she said, and left the room, returning in only a moment. She pulled Paul to the table and pushed him in a chair. She was holding a book.

"Last night I had the dream again. It woke me up. I was overtired anyway, strung out from traveling. I couldn't get back to sleep, so I picked up this Edna St. Vincent Millay book you gave me—you know she's never been my favorite, but she's growing on me—anyway, I found this poem in it and it explains perfectly how I feel about Victor. I'm going to have it blown up and put on billboards all over Manhattan until you guys get the message and stop with this harangue. Okay?"

Violet flipped through the pages and stopped. Paul folded his arms and propped one leg over the other, looking at her curiously. Violet started to read.

" 'I am not resigned to the shutting away of loving hearts in the hard ground. So it is, and so it will be, for so it has been, time out of mind: Into the darkness they go . . .' "

At the start of this line Paul was speaking it too. Violet let him take over: " '. . . the wise and the lovely. Crowned with lilies and with laurel they go; but I am not resigned.' "

Violet had started softly crying. "Do you know the end?" she asked. Paul nodded.

"Down, down, down into the darkness of the grave
Gently they go, the beautiful, the tender, the kind;
Quietly they go, the intelligent, the witty, the brave.
I know. But I do not approve. And I am not resigned."

They were quiet for a moment, then Violet spoke with a quaking and false briskness.

"Now, as you know I prefer Valéry and Apollinaire and Sylvia and Ann and Emily, but this states exactly how I—"

Paul pulled her into his lap and finished the sentence with a kiss. He lifted his hand to trace a soft line on Violet's face, over her forehead, down her cheek, up and down the long neck, and ended pulling gently on one of her ear lobes, drawing her face toward his. They kissed, tentatively. Paul looked at her intently.

"Let's get married."

"Oh brother," was the reply.

"Okay, then let's mate."

"Oh God." Violet was emotionally on edge and open to suggestion. They kissed again, deeply, with an accelerating heat, tongues entwining, ribbony, vibrating. Paul stood up, pulling Violet with him. He shut off the heat under the pasta water and the sauce, grabbed it and the rest of the food and shoved it all into the refrigerator. Paul swept Violet up and carried her into the bedroom, where clothes were shed like unwanted skin, and they mated, with great pleasure and variety, finally falling asleep in each other's arms.

5

Somewhere a siren screamed, puncturing Violet's sleep, interrupting the ever-present dream. She woke up remembering more of it than usual.

A woman, surrounded by flapping white shapes, gestures or dances, forming a pattern of movement. The woman has bright white hair and dark skin, although the exact features of her face are vague. She repeats the movements over and over. There is a sense of extreme anxiety and violence, all of it a step beyond Violet's grasp. The dream taunted and distressed her.

Turning her head she gazed at Paul, curled up like a child, flushed, hardly moving. Paul had exceedingly long eyelashes, and thick hair as black as Violet's. It annoyed her that he slept so soundly through anything, while she was a classic insomniac, jealous of anyone who trusted the world enough to surrender so totally to sleep.

The consideration of Paul was confusing to Violet, who was drawn to her own gender on all levels. In fact, she pointedly avoided the examination of his presence in her meta-feminist life, her context of women. She was fond of saying she had no objection to the appendage itself, it was what went with it that was problematic. Further, she felt you could combine the integrity, honor, and sensitivity of the majority of men and barely wallpaper the side of a dime. (However, during the break-up of an affair Violet had been known to make exactly the same statement about women.)

Violet was introduced to Paul through Victor. During the year before Victor's death, Violet had been going through the agonizing dissolution of a six-year relationship with a woman who had disappeared so far into the haze of heroin addiction that Violet could no longer recognize her.

During this excruciating period, Violet found herself drinking many cups of coffee at Victor's red Formica table, or lying on her mother's side of the bed while he was out on a case. At some point she focused slightly, and noticed Paul, who as it turned out had been there during much of that time, as he and Victor were working on a project together. In an oddly visceral way he had slipped into her emotional landscape; he was inside the acreage of grief and intense pain.

While reeling around in this surfeit of emotion, Paul presented Violet with distraction; she was drawn to his otherness, his alien status. Slowly this situation translated into tentative dating. This consisted of Violet dragging Paul to her favorite *film noir* theatres and dance clubs, and Paul dragging Violet to The Four Seasons and revivals of *Man of La Mancha* or *Guys and Dolls*. The anachronistic choices were a clear reminder of her father. Frictional, at odds, combustive, Violet forgave Paul his stuffiness (she thought of it as a challenge), and Paul forgave Violet her engagement with lower Manhattan. Violet loved her life shot with romance, even, apparently in this case, with a man.

This liaison caused a minor earthquake and major scandal in Violet's community. Her friends thought Paul was a weird oedipal reaction to Cindy and said so. Romaine thought it was a vulnerable time to get mixed up with a new species and said so. Violet decided it was fate, and was going to see where it led, and she didn't give a damn who thought what about it. She was not going to offer the information that Cindy's presence and effect had not gone far; it lay closely about Violet, one aspect a smooth muscle layer of hurt, the other a necklace of bones, rattling and poking into her.

Violet shook all of this out of her head and glanced at the clock. It was four A.M. She was wide awake, dying to open the package from Max, and, of course, hungry. The sounds outside were as quiet as they became, muffled and subdued, a blanket wrapped around a radio. Violet peered out the window at the sky, her faithful oceanic sky. Tonight it was a furry saturated black, so dark the massive amounts of city lights could not reduce or soften it. Violet gazed at it as though reading a palm, then quietly slipped out of bed.

She pulled on an oversized sweatshirt and, closing the bedroom door behind her, went into the kitchen to make fresh coffee and construct her favorite sandwich, roast beef-and-horseradish-with-artichoke-hearts-and-pickled beets-on-pumpernickel. She ate while waiting for the coffee, located her cigarettes, put on Bach cello pieces for company, and headed to the dining room with Max's package.

It was wrapped in cut-up pieces of a supermarket bag; inside was a shoe box from May's. Violet opened it gingerly, from emotion rather than necessity, trembling slightly in anticipation. On top of the contents was a folded piece of lined paper, a letter from Max.

> Violet—No time to explain much. Hope I'll talk to you soon anyway. I've been doing what we talked about at the funeral. You left to soon for me to tell you—2 points for me because I figured it would take them awhile to get around to Vic's car. I took some stuff and left the rest but I don't think I fooled them. Since then in the past few months my place has been wired and twice gone over totally and some slick has been tabbing me. I went

to Don but he clammed. Your due home in a couple days but just to be sure I sent this stuff. I cant make anything out of it but maybe you can. The tail is pushing hard. I ought to know a squeeze when I feel one. Call me and be careful.

Max.

Violet looked at the printed scrawl and thought of his scarecrow weightlessness and slanted smile and his devotion to Victor. This was replaced immediately with the image of Max on her office floor. She shuddered.

Bringing herself back to the subject at hand, Violet was impressed with Max's insight. She had forgotten entirely about Victor's car, the brown Dodge Dart called Theo that functioned so rarely it was more meditation hut than vehicle. Victor used it as a moving file cabinet; materials pertaining to a case at hand were always strewn inside, along with a variety of health foods, his self-styled stakeout kit, and the St. Christopher gaud hanging from the mirror.

Violet could wait no longer; she dumped the contents of the box on the table and spread it out. It did seem that Max had been in a hurry, since the bundle included racing forms and phone bills and take-out menus from Da Silva's Noodle Emporium.

Floating around on top was a snapshot of Victor and Marie, the colors faded into pastels. They were in a tropical setting. She flipped the photo over and found an inscription, in her mother's petite exquisite handwriting: *"Lovers on the Lam, Borneo, 1943."* They were waving. Violet wanted to wave back.

She sifted through the pile several times, finally pulling aside three objects of interest. Two were paper-clipped together. One was an article from the *Village Voice* on product-dumping in Third World countries. The other was a sheet that held typing and Victor's printed scrawl. The typed sections were columns of initials on either side of the page. In the middle were shorthand phrases of commentary. Taped to this sheet was a torn piece of lined paper, the ink faded, the paper yellow with age. In Victor's handwriting was a name and address: *"Lt. Bill Aragon, Greencourt Rd., Medford, Mass."* None of this meant anything to Violet.

These two items were stapled to a manila file folder which was stuffed with clippings which Violet spilled on the table. Some of them were old, some were Xeroxed, others were relatively new. Looking through them they appeared to have two subjects. One was the Well-Dyne Corporation, and the clippings covered a variety of financial moves, stock quotations, general business stories, and a few items questioning actions of various subsidiary companies. The other subject was a man, John Maxwell Yardley, who was represented with articles on a slew of social functions, grand philanthropic gestures, quotes about humanitarianism, greed as the enemy, and the positive use of the power of money.

Clipped to the articles were two photographs identified as John Maxwell Yardley. One photograph showed the elegant face of a 1930s movie star: cleft chin, elegant hairline, deep blue eyes just slightly out of focus, distinctly set off by laugh lines that looked like complimentary echoes rather than wrinkles. The other photograph, obviously catching its subject off guard, was a very different view. There was a grimness to the mouth, a barely repressed sneer. His eyes were cold and his appearance as a whole was slightly seedy, decayed around the edges. Violet was fascinated by the split personality and wondered why this man was so significant to Victor.

Violet separated the papers by subject, then casually glanced back and forth, reading a random sampling of both. The subjects were miles apart, and she could make no connection between the two groups beyond the fact that they were residing in the same file.

She returned her attention to the article from the *Voice*. It was a heated and critical essay on the government-sanctioned selling of knowingly defective products to Third World nations. Two of the more controversial examples were Barker I.U.D.'s and flammable children's pajamas: the former because of millions of dollars' worth of lawsuits pending in the U.S. as a result of infertility and death, the latter for obvious reasons. The article described government regulation changes that caused liquidation due to the obsolescence of huge quantities of products on short notice, after which the companies would sell their stock abroad in silent bailouts. Inexplicably, to Violet, the regulations did not apply to exports. It was further suggested that with such an outlet, large companies were less than committed to caution, knowing that if they were caught with substandard items, or if a regulation was changed or created, they were free to unload goods. The author of the article pointed out that there were no requirements for warnings about the potential hazards of an item, noting that there was a full-scale recall for Barker shields in the U.S. while hundreds of thousands of them languished in dangerous states in wombs abroad, and then stated in a sarcastic tone that perhaps a million children were incendiary in their sleepwear.

The article and its contents was the type of material that always got Violet revved up. Irony is alive and well, she thought. This is the sperm of capitalism, how the free world's profit margin is kept intact, ketchup is a vegetable, unnecessary hysterectomies buy BMWs, the men running this show have their brains below their belts . . . but her internal muttering was short-lived. She was trying to place this information in the context of Victor's sheet of initials, and it wouldn't fit.

Violet noticed a note in the margin of the top page, "*copy to R.,*" and recognized this as Romaine. She wished it were a decent time to call, thought of doing so anyway, decided Romaine was probably entwined with her latest conquest, and resigned herself to calling in the morning.

Violet placed the article and paper carefully to one side, and picked up the only other item of curiosity in the pile.

It was a record, square and thin as cellophane, the grooves barely discernible. Violet examined it, rippling the black shape slightly as she walked over to the stereo to put it on. It was one of those records children make at the top of the Empire State Building, in a booth like a pay phone, shouting to be heard over the wind. She had made one herself once.

She turned on the stereo and stepped away to listen.

Immediately a loud collage of scratches, aural hatchmarks, filled the air, and yes, the sound of the wind was there, and faint sirens, then two voices laughing (one was Victor's, and Violet's heart started beating uncomfortably), then Victor's voice announced "Live from the Empire State, on top of the world, with Bayonne in view," then two voices hummed a musical introduction, and finally lyrics that Violet knew by heart, one of her mother's favorites, the cadence unmistakable, a loony sort of polka . . .

"If your blonde won't respond when you flatter'er, tell her what Tony told Cleopaterer / If she fights when her clothes you are mussing, what are clothes, much ado about 'nussing' / Brush up your Shakespeare, and they'll all kow tow . . ."

The voices erupted into laughter, there was thunder in the background, the woman's voice said, "For our next num—" and it was over. The needle stuck in the last groove; scratching, it was the sound of a thousand petticoats rustling into a microphone. Violet waited until it irritated her into movement; shutting it off she flopped into Victor's red armchair.

It was a silly stupid thing, an excerpt from someone else's private life, but it caused in her a large knot of jealousy and pain. It was a distressing combination of gibes: to hear Victor's voice and laughter, joined intimately with a strange female voice that was not her mother's, singing a song that had belonged to Victor, Marie, and Violet.

Violet felt confused and chagrined. The box Max had sent was looking like Pandora's, with strange, meaningless fragments residing next to an explosive one, none of them an answer, or even a coherent question. She decided to put it all on hold until conferring with Romaine.

She walked over to the window, cracking the blinds to see what time it was. Mid-dawn. The city gathers light differently from any other place. The veil of smog inhales it, splits it into fractured beams, then sucks it up entirely. As Violet looked out, the sky was a steaming hot pink and orange crush, it rested for a moment on her face, then all too quickly subsided into grey, every shade of it—gun-metal, slate, silver—wrapping the city in a saturnine gauze.

Violet took a deep breath and tried to push the memories aside by starting her morning routine.

She went to the front door and retrieved the sheaf of newspapers from the other side of it, and slumped on the couch to read. GOD MADE ADAM AND EVE NOT STEVE/HOMOS GO HOME was the headline on the top paper. She went on to the next one, which proclaimed, MAN FOUND FROZEN TO SIDE OF BUILDING/PREZ SEZ HOMELESS ARE HOMELESS BY CHOICE. Violet decided this was a keeper and tore it off. She had started in on *The Wall Street Journal* when she heard Paul running a shower and humming and rustling around, and in a minute he emerged from the bedroom.

"Good morning, you gorgeous thing," he said, walking over to her, slipping a hand down her front and around one of her breasts.

"Your hands are cold and I'm nobody's thing," Violet replied testily.

"My, aren't we cheery this morning. It's rather like sparring with a snapping turtle. I must remember to count my digits before I leave the apartment. But I have to say you look fetching this morning."

"Fetching? I thought that was a dog trick. You, on the other hand, look like a refugee from J. Press."

"God, you're in a cozy mood."

"Name someone cozier."

"Alger Hissssss."

They both laughed.

"Actually the problem is obvious, you've been reading the papers again. I swear to God, Violet, there should be a city ordinance against you reading the papers. I'm going to mention it to the Mayor the next time I see him."

"Don't push me, Renault. I've been up since four working and now I have to deal with your colleagues and their busy little hypertrophic typewriters hammering out their budgeted disinformation—"

"Wait, what's 'hypertrophic'?"

"Vocabulary word for the day. It means an appendage or organ that enlarges because of constant use."

"I have a great comeback line, but maybe—"

"No, maybe you'd better not. I haven't had my coffee, I'm hungry, and I don't even know who's on the 'Today Show' this morning."

"And your eyes are like the Berlin Wall."

"You stuck-up Calvinist prick," Violet yelled, springing off the couch, lunging for where Paul sat. She unknotted his tie and unbuttoned his shirt enough to grab a handful of his chest hair and yanked hard. Paul yelled and Violet was propelled backwards, falling on the Oriental rug with Paul on top of her. They wrestled, ending up in a bundle of clothing, in the middle of an embrace.

"Paul," said Violet, "you use sex as a distraction more than any female in history." Paul did not reply. His eyes were closed, he was hanging on tight, breathing in her scent as if this would pull her still closer.

"Shut up for a change," he growled. They sat up to look at each other. They pulled each other's clothes off, laughing, cracking their heads together, untangling themselves, tangling themselves, and made love in the middle of the laundry pile on the Oriental rug.

They took turns being on top. They traded kisses and bites and hair-pulling. In between heats, Paul traced messages on Violet's body with his tongue; the moisture and friction made Violet feel like a tuning fork, all of her nerve endings vibrating in one chord, aching to be plucked. Violet drew her fingers through Paul's chest hair, rubbing his nipples with her palms, her cheek, her tongue. She plied his long elegant flute with teasing licks into an altogether different instrument. This game was known as divining rod. When they were both hysterical and taut, trembling and swaying like two drunken soldiers on leave, the inevitable consumed them; they became two swimmers, two eels, glistening. Flesh skimmed against flesh like a hydrofoil picking up speed, plunging into the dark light of orgasm, like slamming into deep space, like a tropical storm, and finally in an extended sigh.

The Oriental rug, backdrop turned into a field of prickly stars, was silent. They lay in their tangle and sweaty comradery, having made a pact, a treaty.

They showered in the pink-tiled bath in silence, keeping the secret intact. They put on robes and met in the kitchen, ignoring the heap of clothes on the rug, in a conspiracy against order. Paul was the first to break the silence.

"Don't tell me, let me guess. You're hungry again. What shall we have?"

"Well, I've been dying to start trying out the recipe I picked up in Florence. There's this breakfast thing, with mashed chicken livers and anchovies and garlic—"

"What?"

"Then there's last night's pasta—"

"Hold it right there. Are you crazy? How can you eat food like that at this hour? Haven't you ever heard of sunny side up? Frozen waffles? Toast and jam? I'm gagging. Let me cook for a change."

"You cook? Watching you in the kitchen is like watching Kate Hepburn in the last ten minutes of *Woman of the Year*, when she tries to cook breakfast for Spencer Tracy, mangles every appliance in the kitchen, and makes waffles with two cakes of yeast."

"How could I forget. It was ridiculous, totally unreasonable, the guy was a bachelor sportswriter with a huge bowl of yeast cakes in the refrigerator. Totally implausible."

Violet laughed in exasperation.

"Only you are capable of watching a seamless movie like that and harbor resentment over one crummy little detail."

"Sure, laugh, but attention to crummy little details like that is what makes me an excellent writer."

"Mm-hmm. Modest, too. Okay, fine, cook. I'll read."

Violet retrieved a selection of papers and noisily spread them out on the kitchen table, noisily not noticing Paul's movements. She became absorbed in what she was reading, propping up the *Trib* headline so Paul couldn't miss what she was reading. He couldn't resist.

"So, what?"

Violet narrowed her eyes.

"Don't get me started. I'm reading your very own paper, and women politicians are still on the style page. Now I'm reading a story about the four-hundred-plus-pound man who raped his daughter, but who won't be incarcerated because he's so fucking fat he needs breathing apparatus and the state won't pay for it so they're letting him go. This story is on page eighteen hundred. On page one is the D.A. proclaiming bigger than huge numbers of convictions. If you don't mind my saying so, things are bad enough without you considering a job with that ultraconservative bozo from New Zealand who's vacuuming up newspapers right and left. I don't know if I can stomach you working for him. It makes me nervous."

Paul rolled his eyes: "Have you ever thought of transcendental meditation? And notice the stories you choose to quote, and your leftover feminist ravings. But I'm sorry I interrupted you—let's hear the rest of the tired speech about how horrible men are, how they're responsible for all the problems in the world . . ."

Violet collected herself in several deep breaths.

"Paul. Call me pedantic, call me a whiner, but as long as the largest group of impoverished people are women and their children, as long as criteria for employment includes cleavage, and as long as raped and murdered women are blamed for crimes they are the victims of—and, because you turn flapjacks so well, I'll leave out 'as long as I hear slit jokes in the elevator of the *Trib* building'—I'll be a feminist." She looked at him carefully. "It's not a matter of blaming men. It's a matter of how we treat each other, how all of us treat each other, which should be with honesty and tenderness and as precious beings. The distaff side is as culpable as your own. In fact in reviewing the history of feminism, if you must bring it up, it's as fraught with missteps and flailing as any other political movement. When I get depressed about it I equate the whole complicated gesture with Israel—in a contemporary political sense both can be their own worst enemies.

"However, I'm talking about something else and that is this job you're considering. To me it's about a political tool disguised as journalism, and it scares the shit out of me. Because if one man owns all the papers then it's one man's editorial line. Don't you see that I'm afraid of you being a part of that?"

Paul was rattling utensils, trying to control his anger. "Don't you trust me? At least I recognize that this media shift is happening, and I can have some effect. If I can jockey around a certain set of newspapers and editorial lines, God, Violet, the power. Think of plunking down a certain approach to things, from Poughkeepsie to Laredo . . . Of course it has a political effect, I'm counting on that."

"Oh Christ, you sound like Huey Long. Paul, do you expect me to okay it because I might support your views? What happened to the press as witness, reportage as neutral? Power is power. It's seductive and very hard to control, and if you impose a certain type of power into a realm long considered immune to that type of influence, well, you're nothing but an arm of the State, even if the State represents supposedly progressive liberal politics. Give me a break."

Paul was overtly angry now. "You're so naïve. The bottom line is that in that position I can have more effect than all your raving polysyllabic speeches put together. You can't go fifteen minutes without pontificating on something."

"You're the one who insisted on turning breakfast into a summit confrontation. And what approach would you like in the morning? An organdy apron, a weather report, a little sangfroid, some fresh-squeezed? Lucy and Ricky play house?"

They glared at each other.

Violet mulled over the exchange while getting dressed for work, ruing the direction the morning had taken. She had a shoot scheduled with David later that morning and dressed accordingly in a black jumpsuit with red piping and red cowboy boots with black details. She knew Paul was right, Romaine had noticed it too, a spoken version of a continual anxiety attack, but the neurosis had a life of its own, its momentum increasing due to Max's death. She had no idea how to tame it. Violet retrieved what she needed from the photographic materials, and pushed that and the clippings from Max's box into her briefcase; returning to the kitchen, she placed a gentle kiss on Paul's neck.

"Truce, dollface?"

"Later," he grumbled.

She passed by the pile of clothes on the Oriental rug. Out on the street, feeling rattled and angry after their fight, Violet reinstated the ritual habit she had formed in Italy. She ducked into a storefront chapel, this one reminding her of a Frieda Kahlo painting. In the window was a female department store mannequin dressed as the Pope, an electric fan blowing ropes of gold paper chains out behind him.

6

Violet simultaneously knocked on and opened Romaine's office door, and was greeted with the sight of Romaine barely visible above mounds of briefs and open law books. The air was filled with haunting music. Violet knew better than to say a word, but Romaine held up a finger to her lips anyway, saying "I'm waiting for the miracle part. If you say a word you die." Violet gently placed a cup of cappuccino on the only clear spot near her friend, and stood listening to the piece.

Romaine heard music everywhere. In between the catcalls and the urban din Manhattan sang to her. The rhythms of subway clatter, the cantata of shouting voices in different languages, the collage of sound enchanted her as much as any Mozart piece. A bona fide urban mystic, she would find in herself a less particular awe for some rarefied chunk of Tibetan scenery. The perception of good, of mystery, of spiritual ardor, was so much more elusive in the city atmosphere that the spasm of recognition was in turn more appreciated, more dramatic and keen.

Violet did as she was told and simply listened, aware that the piece was building in a mournful way to a very gentle and complicated crescendo. As it started to fade away a series of bells sounded, one after the other. The music finally stopped, and Violet waited for Romaine to break the silence. Music during the workday usually meant trouble.

"What did you think?" she finally said.

"I thought it was beautiful, but sad enough to make you want to crawl back under the covers. Who was that anyway?" Violet replied.

"Charles Ives. Insurance salesman slash genius."

Violet studied Romaine, and spoke cautiously. "The mood in here is distinctly volcanic. Do I dare ask?"

Romaine's mouth drew sideways in an annoyed line. "I decided to come in early and catch up on some work. I was greeted in the hallway by reporters in an absolute feeding frenzy. They were looking for you, of course, but apparently I would do. They were accompanied by nine-tenths of the building's residents looking for a gossip fix. It took ages to drive them away. I can't get Max out of my mind—the sight of him. Can you?"

Violet shook her head. "No. I'm still in a state of shock. And if all the N.R.A. jerks and violent-movie lovers saw him as we did yesterday . . ."

Romaine rolled her eyes. "Vi, could we skip the issue of the day for a change, and jump to the lecture on the era of the child-on-the-milk-carton, or your impersonation of Eartha Kitt singing 'Love For Sale'?"

Violet was hurt. "I'm sorry, I'm obviously intruding, I'll go . . ." She walked to the desk and placed four out-of-print Nino Rota albums, brought back from Italy, in the only other clear space she could find. Romaine caught her hand and squeezed it.

"I'm the one who's sorry. Sit down. I had a bad night, that's all." She smiled broadly at the records. "These are incredible, I wish I had a turntable here. Thanks, Vi."

Violet sat. "Miss Milwaukee?"

Romaine laughed ruefully. "Yes. But you needn't make it sound as though I'm dating a representative of the dairy region. And by the way, while I was at Anita's I heard about what happened to you yesterday, so fill me in. You *were* going to tell me about it, weren't you?"

"That was such an obvious change of subject that I won't harass you by asking any more questions." Violet gave her the details, then told her about the Max box and its contents, and pulled the materials out of her briefcase, placing them as close to Romaine as she could, pointing out the notation referring to her.

"Okay, let me look at these a second."

Romaine studied the files, while Violet studied Romaine.

"God, you're beautiful," she had to say.

"Really?" was the reply. "I thought you pined after the Y chromosome these days."

"A droll way of putting it. But that's not really the problem, is it? You just don't trust him, do you? I can feel that."

"No, I don't, not any further than I could throw that arrogant white carcass of his, which isn't far."

"I'm going to change your mind."

"Good luck."

Violet sat quietly while Romaine read through the material and nodded in recognition.

"You've read all this, right? Here's what happened. Victor asked me to look into whether or not lawsuits could be filed—from these countries, personal or class action—against one individual here in the States."

"What did you tell him?"

"The answer was no. In many cases the materials were simply donated to the countries for huge tax benefits, and the circumstances of sales of the items were subject to whatever regulations each of the governments did or didn't have. In both cases the plaintiffs would have to deal with their own governments for allowing the imports, supposedly with full knowledge of their effects. There is present litigation, a kind of international class action suit, but it is addressed against the insurance company of the American corporation. There is no way to target an individual, which is what Victor seemed to be asking about."

Violet took a deep breath. "So, was he working on this when he died? Do you make anything out of this Yardley file? I mean, the fact that it all was sitting in the car . . . and Max . . ." She couldn't bring herself to specify.

Romaine shook her head confidently. "No to all of the above. But the sheet of initials—that's weird. Listen, I have a client in five. Could we talk about this over lunch?"

Violet was chagrined. "Of course. I'm sorry I'm so self-involved these days. Lunch would be wonderful. But only if we can talk about *la dolce femmina* too."

Romaine walked Violet to the door, her arm around her. "You know that therapy would work a lot faster and would be a lot less dangerous than this sleuth bit, don't you?"

"Listen, Dr. Solano and I—"

"Don't start with the radio psychologist stuff, will you?"

Violet held Romaine tightly. "Honey, the way you look, you could use some radio therapy yourself. You seem to be in a bad way—do you want me to punch her out?"

Romaine relaxed finally, and laughed. "No, I don't think that's necessary, at least not yet."

Violet cradled Romaine's cheek in her hand. "I may be obsessed, but I'm still your best friend. Call me when you need me—I'm still better than Oleo versus Featherbane anytime, even in my present state. Promise?"

Romaine promised. Violet turned to leave, but Romaine stopped her. "I just thought of something. Odd as it is, I sent Victor to Zar with his questions. At the time she was working on a poster project, her 'Status of Women' series, which included information on economic status, where genital mutilation still occurred. The posters included miles of statistics, so I thought she might help."

"I remember that. I still have the posters hanging in my apartment. They make Paul very nervous."

"They should. They make me nervous too. Now beat it, will you?" Romaine closed the door to her office.

Violet glanced at her watch on the way into the studio and saw that she was late for her appointment with David. Upon entering the room she noticed that someone from the building had removed the pale grey wall-to-wall carpeting. The furniture and equipment looked odd on the hardwood floor, but Violet decided to leave it that way.

At one end of the studio David had started to prepare for their shoot that morning. He had hung a large, mottled, putty-colored cloth backdrop on the wall, letting it drape on the floor, and had placed a glass table on top of it. Standing around like extras on a movie set were lights waiting to be placed. In the corner under a tent of heavy plastic sheets David was spray painting something gold. Violet went to see what it was, and found many bags of toy plastic soldiers sitting outside the tent. David looked up and saw her, put down his paint can, removed his mask, and stepped outside the tent.

"Well, you're a couple days late for the jet-lag excuse so don't try it. Judy with the endless limbs will be here in twenty and we're not ready. May I expect an engraved announcement concerning your actual return to work?"

Violet feigned a slightly coy air that she knew wouldn't fool him. They did have to talk about work. She had given up running the studio when she left, with total trust but without much discussion.

"Have I told you how impressed I am with what you did while I was gone? And have you really gotten your hello hug yet?"

David looked exasperated. "The answer to both questions is 'Not sufficiently.' "

They hugged each other warmly, and Violet was effusive with praise. She held his shoulders and regarded him seriously.

"David, I know we have to reassess everything, I'm just adjusting a little, okay? A lot. Please be patient." He nodded with an annoyed toss of shoulders that implied she should take that for granted. She grinned. "You're still just waiting for your presents."

He nodded again, in the same mode of sarcasm.

"So what are we starting with, and why are you spraying plastic soldiers gold?"

"We're starting with the trade show catalogue. Of course, only we would contract for fifteen straight pages of the avant-garde and bizarre, which means there will be a parade of loonies in and out of here."

"Would you rather we went back to shooting glow-in-the-dark water piks for *Dentist's Monthly*?"

"No. And actually we're not as rushed as I'm making it seem, it's just that Renée darling insists on using Judy and Judy is leaving the country tomorrow. And by the way there was a call from Don's office confirming an appointment for ten-thirty this morning which you just might make if you do the tech setup while I finish this specialty artistic work."

"Okay, I will in a moment. First show me what Renée is up to this season."

David grabbed her arm and pulled her over to the glass table, opening several black velvet cases that were sitting on top.

"These, believe it or not, are eighteen karat casts of the same plastic soldiers you see strewn around you. *Mucho au courant*, no? You must read the literature that comes with them, it sounds like one of Zar's pieces."

In the boxes were bracelets, earrings, and a necklace that held so many soldiers it looked like the breastplate in a suit of armor.

"Hmm," said Violet. "Bold. Tribal. Primal yet retaining the proper amount of feminine—"

David laughed. "Save it for Renée."

David went back into his tent, and Violet went about setting up lights and filters, filling film holders with eight by ten film, and interchangeable film backs for the thirty-five millimeter and two-and-one-quarter cameras. She set up tripods and the Polaroid, thinking, with amusement, as she worked about the parade of ant-farm ties, fur-and-fruit belts, and ionic-column hats that would move in and out of the studio in the next few weeks.

They finished work at the same time, and met in front of David's now substantial pile of soldiers. He pulled off his respirator with a flourish and gave a slight bow.

"Voilà. For this I went to Cooper Union."

At that moment Judy with the endless limbs arrived.

Soon she was swathed in camouflage cloth and inundated with soldiers. David painted one of her arms with camouflage-colored paints to set off the bracelets. An hour and a half later, every conceivable arrangement and angle, lighting design, and film type had been used, and the perspiring trio stopped for coffee.

Violet went to wash up before going to see Don, noting that she had spent a luxurious morning away from the matched set of pain, and aware that it was masking an indulgence she could not afford. No one could.

She returned to find Judy and David laughing uproariously at some of the items to be photographed for the catalogue. After teasing the two for biting the hand that fed them, Violet told David she would check back with him later, and left for her meeting with Don, in a confrontational mood, filled with questions.

7

Violet burst into Don's office and closed the door. Quietly. Don was standing behind a desk in a rather wary stance. He waved Violet toward a chair and sat down. Violet pulled out the file of clippings, steadied the article and sheet of initials on top, and placed them on the desk. She started right in.

"Don, I'm not blaming you personally, but I think the case was closed too soon and I think this stuff has something to do with it."

Don tried to head her off.

"Honey, let me review it for you again. The case is closed with good reason, with all leads followed up, and with as much research done as possible. For Christ's sake, Violet, I wasn't in charge of the investigation, but you know what he meant to me. I paid fucking close attention to it—excuse my language. When Victor died, he was working on a high-profile, blue-blood divorce case, involving millions and claims of child abuse; he was working on an extortion case at a major insurance firm; he was doing his usual gig with a thousand clients who couldn't pay him; he had a missing person or two; he was working for us, et cetera. And sure, that"—he pointed to the material on his desk—"was probably on his mind as well.

"On the day he was murdered there were at least five people accounted for, arriving and leaving Victor's apartment. Max, an assistant D.A., an unidentified woman, an executive from the aforementioned insurance company, and one Todd Leimenster, known as the Harvard hit man. Bullets found in Victor's body matched those found in Leimenster's gun found on Leimenster's body found hung by the neck in his apartment. Everyone agreed this was too damn slick, everyone dug deeper, nothing more of significance was found, and you know all of this already."

"But Don, what about Max? He sent me—"

"I saw what he sent you. He came in with it weeks ago. It's meaningless. Sit down . . . please?"

Violet sat down, crossed her legs, and lit a Gitane, her top leg swinging nervously, the cigarette waving like a mad baton.

"If it was meaningless, why was he tailed, why was he wired, why was he murdered and left in my office?"

Don folded his arms and shifted back into his chair so far it looked as though he was trying to lean out of the room.

"This is all privileged information, as you know. The truth is, Max was working for us. He was set up as a drug courier in a particularly vicious outfit. If he thought he was being tailed he probably was—we're certain he was killed because they found out he was a plant. We lost touch with him for a few days—he missed several regular contact points, he just wasn't to be found. The assumption was they were suspicious and he had to be put out of communication."

Violet thought this over.

"Even if that is so, Don, again—why my office? And why was he convinced this stuff was important?"

Don shrugged. "I have no idea what his thinking was. The autopsy showed a lot of coke in his system, which surprised me. He missed Victor terribly; he was on a mission you started him on; I don't know . . . Violet, I don't doubt that he was coming to see you, but the truth is whatever he thought about this junk, he was not killed trying to get in touch with you about it. I'm sorry he died that way. I'm sorry you had to see it. Are you satisfied?"

Violet shook her head. "You're rushing me, and I don't get it. Don, this stuff was found on the front seat of Victor's car. That was his open file. It means he was working on this case the day he died, that it's possible this Yardley has something to do with it, and you're downplaying it. Why?"

Don reached for his coffee, swallowed some, and placed his hand on top of the file, pushing it away from him.

"That case, as you call it, has been going on for years," he said quietly. "There was nothing particularly topical about it at all. Okay?"

Violet got up awkwardly, lit another cigarette, and started to pace.

"No, it's not okay. You're being mysterious, you're not answering my question about the connection of the clippings to Victor's death, and this information is the last link I have to him. If you want to get rid of me you'll have to do better than that."

Don rubbed a hand across his eyes. "Damn," he said with frustration. "Violet, it's not my story to tell. If Victor wanted you to know he would have told you. There are a lot of things he didn't let you in on. You worshiped him so, he was such a hero to you, then when Marie died you became so attached . . . I think he was afraid to alter your image of him even the slightest bit."

Violet sighed and relaxed slightly. "There were a lot of things we didn't talk about, but there are a lot of things I was aware of that no one thought I was. So. Talk." She returned to her chair.

Don rocked back and forth, uncomfortable but resigned.

"Okay. But I'm telling you, this is the stripped-down version, I mean shorthand, and don't ask me about this again, because it's not our business, and because I need something a lot stronger to drink than this lousy coffee to tell the whole story."

His face had become cloudy and troubled, almost as though a shadow had moved across it. He pulled open a drawer in his desk, yanked out a book, and placed it on the desk in front of him. Violet recognized it as one of her father's journals. Don placed his hand on top of it and began.

"Look, Violet, some people got over their war experiences better than others, some didn't get over them at all. Victor was one of those people, and Yardley had a lot to do with that.

"You know the basics. That Marie and Victor met in Borneo, that in 'forty-three they were interned with the rest of the civilians, first at Berhala, then in Kuching." Naming the names and places, the year, seemed to startle Don, or remind him of that time in his own life. He closed his eyes, and his delivery sped up, as if to rush past the words before having to hear them himself. He closed his hands into fists and rested them on the arms of his chair.

"You know how extraordinary their love was for each other, and I believe that's the key to this. But the fact is, Marie was with Yardley when she met Victor. Yardley brought her to Borneo in the first place. Yardley didn't take it well, Victor and Marie, and that's putting it mildly. Then they were picked up. Victor and Yardley were in the men's compound, with other civilians and some British soldiers. Marie was down the street with the women and children.

"At first it wasn't so bad, although they were all starving to death, and as Victor said, both the guards and prisoners were so far from the fighting action that it all seemed abstract, like playacting. Then they were moved to Kuching, and things got very bad. Rations were even less, the camp's commander was replaced by a demoted lieutenant who was bored and sadistic and encouraged the guards to abuse prisoners. The stories that came out of the women's camp, which were somehow communicated to the men's side, were incredible. Victor of course was going nuts worrying about Marie."

Don stopped for a second, opened his eyes, noticed Violet's presence. He stared at her blankly.

"When they moved the prisoners from one place to the other Victor was beaten badly. His wounds weren't healing, and he became addicted to morphine. Morphine he got by helping Yardley run a very lucrative smuggling business.

"Then the new lieutenant decided to get rid of a lot of prisoners. He started forced marches to fields down the road, in the sun, on empty stomachs. Supposedly they were harvesting food for themselves, only the prisoners were dropping like flies. Anyway, on one of these marches Victor sees Marie pass by in her group, clearly suffering from malaria, and although she was so emaciated it was kind of hard to tell, he was certain she was pregnant. The next day the women's group passes by again, and Victor watched Marie collapse, beaten back on her feet by the guards.

"He said he knew, the way you just know certain things, that she would not last another day, that she would die in the sun on the road and be kicked into a ditch."

Violet was stunned at this image of her parents. During

Don's recitation, the wall behind his head had become a projection screen; the slide of the softly tinted photo of her parents in Borneo had jump-cut to this horrific view. As Don continued to talk the nightmare images seemed to flash, a hideous home movie.

It was clear Don wanted this over. The rest came out in one long push.

"Victor went to Yardley for help. In a perverse way, prison was no different than being on the outside for Yardley. He was in the Borneo area making a small fortune from various schemes, and drug smuggling was among them. He was as brutal as any of the captors, fearless, and well protected by the Nipponese guards, who played a large part in his activities. His attitude was business as usual. Victor was painfully aware that Yardley was the prisoner with the most power and effectiveness, really the only one Victor could turn to. When Victor approached Yardley, Yardley laughed, thought about it, said it would cost a fortune to get Marie out, what did Victor have to offer. He said nothing. Yardley repeated that it would cost a lot; he asked Victor to kill a certain Nipponese guard, a man who was asking for increased kickbacks and was someone Yardley thought was about to turn him in.

"Victor agreed. Victor did it. He felt he had no choice; he was stoned and desperate and not thinking clearly except with regard to saving Marie. He was a little nuts at this point, if you ask me. Yardley and Marie escaped that night. Victor was left to assume they were all right. Weeks later he heard that they were.

"Now things get sketchy. Victor was sprung early, under circumstances he never explained. Marie had had a miscarriage. Yardley had disappeared. Victor and Marie go home. Marie never gets over her illnesses from the war. Victor never gets over Yardley. Victor is haunted by what he did, haunted by Yardley getting more rich and famous and powerful, by tactics not much different than those he used in the war.

"Then you arrived. A reprieve. A charm, they called you, their charm. So things improved and he let go of it. For years. When Marie died it snuck back in, slowly, and in the last year it escalated a lot. Yardley's Well-Dyne was in the news often and was getting bad press. Victor never said anything about it. But I know he was looking for something, some big bad illegal thing to pin on him, to make him lose face—to ruin him, basically. Marie was gone, you were grown, he had nothing to lose.

"I'll tell you this," Don said quietly. "I understood a great deal about what motivated him. And I think that missing piece was somehow retriggered this past year. Victor was obsessed, and his hatred for Yardley is pinned on something that isn't in his journals, that he never revealed to me, and you and I will never know what it was. It won't change the fact that he is dead. The End. Okay?" He sounded pleading, as if the telling of the story should pacify her and send her on her way.

Violet stood up, meaning to go, meaning to get away from the weird melodrama, the rapacious fluorescent light that was splashing on them, meaning to escape the way his words were editing her memories. But the floor was moving underneath her in linoleum waves, and she sat back down. She became aware that she had to hold this story, let it drift up into her diaphragm to wait for later examination. The intensity of feeling seemed dangerous: she was dismayed to have the vague landscape of her childhood, with its fuzzy trees and suggestions of hills, become paint-by-number clear. "Later," her head was saying to the chest cavity.

Violet looked at Don in a new way. "I know you loved him. But why was talking about that time so hard for you?"

He looked at her condescendingly, as if she had insulted him. "Because I was there," he said curtly.

The two were silent for a while: Don looking guilty for telling a story he had promised not to, even if it had been in shorthand; Violet trying to fight against asking further questions. If she were going to crack up over it she wanted to be flooded with detail. At some point they relaxed into a truce.

"Don, I appreciate your telling me this. But doesn't everything you just said confirm what I've been saying about these?" She pointed to the papers on the desk. "Doesn't it suggest he found that missing piece, and was killed over it?"

Don nodded. "Yeah. Sure. And after months of fine-combing all of the details there is no way, I mean none, to connect Victor's death to Mr. John Maxwell Yardley, and that is why I've been pushing you away from it. There's nowhere for it to go."

Violet stood up—the floor had stopped shifting—and pushed the papers back into her briefcase. She wanted to embrace Donald, but it was clear by the look on his face that he wanted to back away from the memories, to retreat, and now by telling her she was part of them, too. As close as they had been over the years, she had never seen him retreat this way. He would not meet her eyes. She got up and walked to the door. She turned to look at him. "But wouldn't you say, when you wake up at night, or when you're walking the dog, when you're alone with your thoughts, that Yardley was responsible for Victor's death, that he had it ordered, that he might as well have pulled the trigger himself?"

Don nodded. "Yes. The way you just know certain things."

Violet nodded back, slowly. She felt acutely clear and cold, like ice-water aspic: she had turned a corner and something had chilled inside.

"Well," she announced, "I think I'll take up where Victor left off."

Violet fled the room; Don did not try to stop her.

Walking back to the studio, Violet experienced a perverse sense of relief. There was something to attach the grief to, somewhere to place the increasing series of small electric shocks. Instead of going back to her studio, instead of running to Romaine, she would start a quiet hunt. She was retracing steps now, starting her research. She headed for the studio of one Rosa Cortazar.

8

As Violet approached the door to Zar's studio, she heard loud music emanating into the hall. It seemed to be a combination of phrases of sound placed at right angles to one another, the soundtrack of a disturbing dream. Violet listened for a moment, while reading a few of the pronouncements, poetry fragments, and excerpts from Zar's work that were pasted on the door, including the slogan, "Plantation days are over, it's time to be a soldier not a slave." It took a lot of pounding on the metal-sheathed door to get a response. Violet had almost given up when the door flew open to reveal the very flushed and wild-eyed Rosa Cortazar.

Hovering above the skyline at six foot three, eyes focused in a glare, nutmeg-colored skin defining statuesque bodybuilding, a flood of dark curls barely contained by a headband, tight black T-shirt announcing SPERM FREE across her chest, matching tight black running shorts introducing mile-long legs—all of these were caught up in a defiant stance, with *"What!"* shouted out of the middle of them. Her features—eyes so dark they absorbed light like black velvet, slightly crooked nose, crushed-currants mouth—were set in an elongated face, an El Greco painting, self-contained and brooding. It took a great deal of anger or mirth to alter her composure. With her propensity to eat with the same voraciousness that she consumed everything else she might have been slightly heavy, but all of her was so regimented and pounded into muscle that the result was an impressive density. Because her scale was so large she gave the impression of one who didn't know how much strength she had—a storm in a glass menagerie.

Violet observed the countenance that frightened and baffled many others, and simply smiled in appreciation.

"Sorry to bother you."

"Childes?" Was the reply. Zar swept her into a hug and twirled her into the room, kicking the door shut behind them. She placed Violet back on the floor.

"Childes, where the fuck have you been? I've been so bored I've had the masseuse twins in for tea, and they can't talk art. Their idea of art—have you seen their "offices"?—is flamingos painted on black velvet. My God, you and David are the only other artists in the building." She stopped for a moment, leveling her ferric gaze at Violet.

"Ro told me you were back. How are you?" she said less loudly.

Violet was surprised and somewhat touched at her effusiveness. Claiming that she saved language for her work was a polite version of the fact that Zar abhorred small talk to a near-violent degree. Violet calmly waited for the change. Zar did finally act as expected, she ruffled Violet's hair, said, "Coffee!," and all but disappeared into the corner of the huge room that was designated as the kitchen. Violet took the opportunity to wander around.

She was always amazed and often somewhat jealous of Zar's studio. It was a huge, extraordinary warehouse of ideas, and Violet was in awe of how completely it consumed any other aspect of lifestyle. The room was filled with tables, some empty, some overflowing. It was also filled with shelves of books and paints and chipped pieces of cornices, silk-screening equipment, recording equipment, broken statues, easels, hot-plates with cans of wax sitting on top, file cabinets, video monitors, keyboards, and, sprawled on every wall, all overlapping, were versions of many of her works, pages from magazines, spray-painted slogans ("If they can put a man on the moon then why can't they put them all there?" caught Violet's eye), photographs, recipes, souvenir plates. It was a media explosion. Violet, for reasons of dust and personality, kept her workrooms separate, at home and at the studio; for her, Zar's place was a sumptuous array of raw materials.

As she looked around Violet noticed four large tables pushed together. On top of them were over a hundred bottles of various sizes, standing in neat rows—half of them were painted black, half were painted white. Curious, she walked over to look, meeting up with Zar on her way back with two cups of coffee so thickly black they looked like squid ink. She placed them on the edge of the table in front of Violet, then removed stacks of things off the tops of two stools and pulled them over. Perched, Violet gestured toward the bottles.

"What's this?"

Zar looked at her sternly. "Later. I'd rather hear about the Milan shoots. I was as impressed as anyone else. Otherwise, tell me why you're here."

"How about both?" Violet replied.

Zar nodded her okay. Violet filled her in on Max's box and its contents, explained Romaine's recommendation, and expressed her general dissatisfaction. Zar already knew Max had been found in her office, and she was happy to comply with what little she had told Victor about Yardley. Shaking her head to dismiss repeating what she thought was basically irrelevant to Violet's concerns, she added her own opinion.

"Sure, I had stats for back up on the not-so-secret but not-very-publicized name John Maxwell Yardley, head of Well-Dyne. I gave Victor what little information I had about the Jekyll-and-Hyde nature of Yardley. The nasty Mr. Hyde is never revealed in the press, at least not in a way you would connect with Well-Dyne's lily-white deeds. The mainstream press seems to love him; he's always good copy. You have to dig into the more left-wing journals to find anything that isn't in a favorable light. I gave him some Xeroxes, including the *Village Voice* article you just mentioned, and I went back to work.

"I think the conclusion about Victor's death sucks, and if you're inclined to continue looking into this, count me in. It's just a sensation I have, it's nothing concrete. I must say Victor seemed torqued about this Yardley thing. He wasn't forthcoming about it, but I thought he had it in for this guy."

Zar looked at Violet questioningly. Violet felt reluctant to elaborate. Repeating the story Don had just told her would be to solidify it, something she had no interest in doing.

"For the time being can we just say that I've got it in for him, too?"

"No problem," was Zar's reply. "I know you'll give me the scoop when it's time. And I'll keep an eye out for more dope on Yardley. Now what about Milan, and all those girls masquerading as rock? Explain."

Thankful for the support and the contrasting opinion, Violet didn't press her luck, and moved on from the subject she had come to discuss.

"You're the last person I would expect to need an explanation on this subject. You know how I feel about women portrayed as paragraphs of body parts; I just did one of those this morning. The way I look at it, in this business they're already reduced to those elements, angles parading as sex, so I decided to take it one step further and make them so abstract that you would never mistake them for comeliness. An arm, yes, a leg, a collarbone. I was also spending all this time wandering around stone—armaments, fountains, streets, walls, chock-full of patterns of granite and marble, veins, beauty-mark speckles, flashes of light, and then there were all of those statues. There's a chill in the Florentine air and it comes from stone—the overriding element in Florence is stone.

"Then in Milano this series started, and suddenly and with no conscious effort, the limbs and jawlines merged with different patterns of stone. It was a cold thing, I was immersed in the coldness. I simply, well, not so simply from a technical point of view, transposed the stone-coldness, the patterns and texture, on top of the limbs they shoved in front of me. Hopefully it was a good disguise. But I'm making that up as a description for what I did by rote, by response to the muddy place I was in. Cynical, hopelessly vague, and terribly hungover. Should that worry me? I don't want to think of our art as vulnerable to cheap emotional topicality."

They both laughed.

"Honey, I don't think you should worry about it. We all create in a kind of sleep-walking state—anyway, we can be didactic about it later. Speaking of which, how come we don't hang out more often?"

"The truth is I'm afraid I'm not political enough."

Zar thought this over for a moment. "But, Violet, the truth is we're all fighting our own fights. I don't have any judgments to make. We're all making our own gestures; the focus is different for each of them. I wasn't born a media freak or an activist.

"I'll tell you exactly what happened. Several years ago I was making very primitive structures out of sticks and striated aluminum. So, I'm waiting for something to dry and I turn on the news. There was a story on about a Nicaraguan woman; she was slightly politically active, mother of many, et cetera. Well, she was arrested and disappeared and there was this big stink about it and finally she reappeared. Dead as a fucking doornail, and photographed big as life. The broadcast had a live shot of her, it seemed to hold the camera on her forever.

"It focused on her upper body. The woman had been beaten incredibly, she was all swollen and bruised and purple. But her eyes were open. And her arms were placed across her chest, carefully, in a praying position. Her hands had been severed, and in this fucking tableau they were replaced, an inch away from the arms; you had to look close to see that, but you had plenty of opportunity. There were flies buzzing around her head. In the corner of the frame was a soldier's boot, nudging her arm. The voice-over continued for what seemed like hours. And there she was, breasts exposed, eyes open and pleading, and the voice-over continued, and I thought I was going to lose my mind. But I kept staring. And staring, and the inch between her hands and her arms kept growing in my head. It became huge. It was the space where violence against women is casually sanctioned, where human dignity is shredded, this evil place where a soldier kicks at a dead woman's arm while Mr. Potato Head recites a defensive line about American caution—all on live TV, a thick dead space of silence where rage should be, where tears should be."

Zar shifted on her stool uncomfortably, remembering.

"But I've never been good at crying. So, instead, I get galvanized, so to speak. I become a media-hog, a media-vacuum. I start studying how we ghettoize information. Stuff like that. I'm paying attention, I'm gathering things. So this is what I'm working on now. It's a news broadcast that is just as ghettoized as the rest of them." She paused. "But this is all women's news. I want to show a clear assessment, in numbers, of the status of women. It's an update of the posters. I think that, simply stated, with no rhetoric but out of context, the viewers will find the facts shocking.

"The idea started a long time ago when I was dating an anchorwoman at WLBS. God, if they knew one of their major well-coiffed anchorpeople was a dyke, and only one of many . . . Anyway, the things she told me about general station policies toward stories she brought in about certain women's issues made me fucking furious.

"You know, one of the things I'm after as an artist is to gather an enclave of images that are distinctly female in a male-saturated world which is becoming more destructive every day. The culture is imploding and it's pushed in that direction by the male agenda. Fuck now, pay later, ejaculate everywhere you can. Colonialism with a new name—multinational corporation. I know, I know, there she goes again.

"So anyway she brought home some friends from the

station and we starting jamming about it. It was just a fantasy at the beginning, Beaujolais-induced and totally wild. Then several meetings later everyone blinked at each other and said, Why not?

"So we're going to take over a news broadcast. I mean, countrywide. Nonviolently, of course. We have most of this in place. Then we'll just convey what's happening, state the facts, give the numbers, in a way you wouldn't otherwise get to see. Powerful in its concentration, don't you think? I've got a whole mock-up, and graphics. It's slick as hell. In the middle of your normal broadcast—and we've got the technology to do it—women are going to appear and tell some truths."

Zar stopped abruptly. "I can't tell you any more. It's supposed to be a secret. Forget I told you, okay?"

Violet nodded. Zar was being so unusually verbal that she decided to take advantage of it. "How's Madeleine?"

Zar grimaced. "Madeleine left on a noon tide called Julia. About a month ago. And yes, I'm wild with pain."

Violet spoke quietly. "The last time I saw Madeleine was a couple of weeks before Victor was killed. We had coffee. She seemed unhappy, so I asked how things were going between you two. She said she felt as though she was being chewed up by your machine in the same way you devoured and digested all the rest of your material, with no more and possibly less significance."

Zar slammed her hand down on the table so hard all the bottles rattled together in a chorus of tiny chimes. The sound was so dreamlike it chastened Zar's mood. Immediately she seemed to regret the gesture. She replied in a tone rarely heard by Violet, one softened with pain. "But the opposite was true. She was the first lover I ever had who pulled me away from the machine, from the obsessiveness and rigidity of it. She irradiated me, just seeped right in." The large hands, which each spread wider than an octave on a piano, were stretched in a fan in front of her. She appeared to be examining the empty space in between her fingers. "Damn."

Violet knew the room would soon be flooded with sarcasm, and she wanted to stave it off; it was so rare for them to speak intimately. "I'm sorry, I know . . ." but that was as far as she got. Zar stood up in dismissal. "Fuck romance anyway, a ride on the IRT lasts longer. I'm glad you're home, Childes-babe. I have to get back to work."

Violet was hydroplaned toward the door by Zar's intense energy.

"Come around more often," were her last words, emerging as the huge door swung shut. Standing in the hall Violet felt suddenly orphaned. She wondered if Zar would allow her to move into one of the dusty corners of the studio. She sought apprenticeship in Zar's baroque collage and compelling female bastion.

9

Emotionally drained, Violet dragged herself back to Romaine's office, moss looking for a rock to cling to.

They did cling together on the way to a very late lunch, Violet pressing her head lightly against Romaine's shoulder as she told Donald's story, which was her story, too. She wept cautiously, trying to hold off a deluge. They walked blocks farther than necessary, Violet speaking about the sensation of having your worst suspicions confirmed, Romaine countering with the notion of survival and transcendence. Violet thought Romaine was being purposely opaque in order to distract her and complained. Romaine said to get outside yourself for two seconds, work for SAGE, take a night course, grow up. Violet feigned punches; Romaine threatened to kiss her in the middle of midday downtown and did so. This surprised Violet into a silence that lasted long enough for Romaine to get her foot in the door, to express what she had known of Victor, to interject some positive, some light-filled reminiscences. These helped Violet pull herself together. As they swung into Anita's, Violet was promising to work for SAGE, and Romaine was hoping she could start worrying a little less about Violet.

Anita's at lunchtime was unusually subdued compared to its evening character, which made the reception for Romaine and Violet unexpected. Riotous greetings, whistles, and applause rang out up and down the bar.

"I guess it's been a while since we've been here together, hasn't it, or maybe they think you've come to your senses," said Romaine quietly, then said more loudly to the group, "Ciao, pink things!" Violet propelled her toward the main room, knowing that if she didn't they would be there all day. As it was, the effort to pull herself away from Donald's story was a strain.

The Hall, as it was known, was a large room with black walls, the ceiling a complicated network of lights. In the center was a dance floor, oddly dull at noon without its flashy underpinning of lights. Around the floor were tables covered with pink cloths and candles. There were usually paintings on the walls, which changed monthly; the present exhibit appeared to be expressionist portraits of rather aggravated nuns.

Anita had emerged from her office to see what the commotion was about, and walked over to the table they had chosen.

"Well, you two certainly liven up the place. You've obviously been missed—I haven't seen a reaction like that since Cher came in looking for a pay phone," she said, laughing, and sat down to join them.

"Thanks," said Violet. "I should visit more often, I miss it. On the other hand, I hear Ms. Brookes has to be bodily removed every night."

"And how would you know? You start showing up here again and Paul would have a fit, and you would probably give in to him," Romaine said.

"Oh, that tired subject again. You know I don't care what Paul says about this place."

Anita refereed. "I've met Paul on several occasions, he seems all right."

"You're in good company, I like him myself," Violet replied. "Romaine is the only holdout. Why, I don't know."

"Childes, why don't you change the subject before I get overtly rude."

At this moment Christine approached the table, bending

down to press her cheek lightly against Anita's. Violet had not seen Christine in a long while, in fact ran into her rarely, and when she did was reminded that even after all these years they had never really connected with each other, considering Violet's close relationship to Anita. Christine with the mysterious Argentinian background. Christine with the saturated chestnut eyes, with the blushed henna-brown skin. She wore an air of privacy so concentrated it threw off a force field around her. She was an architect of high standing, consumed with her work. Violet felt a loss at not knowing her.

"Hi, it looks like a family reunion," Christine said. "We really should have dinner sometime soon. We've missed your theme dinners. What was the last one called? Oh yes, the American Classics—Cheez Whiz on crackers, tuna–potato chip casserole, TV dinners, Whip and Chill for dessert—"

"Christine! We've finally found our joint métier. No one ever remembers what I serve—"

"Violet, how could I forget? I dreamt about those little tin trays and their corrugated compartments for nights. Don't tell anyone, but if you look closely at one of my projects since then the influence is obvious."

They were both trying; the strain became less noticeable every year.

"So, Christine, why don't you and Anita join us? We could plan the next feast. I picked up a lot of ideas in Italy. Any country that canonized a patron saint of TV is my kind of place."

Christine smiled but shook her head. "I'd love to, and we wouldn't talk about food either, Violet, we'd talk about the Milan shoot and your architectonic approach. That's our joint métier, but I'm afraid I just came out to retrieve Anita, the natives are getting restless."

"What's up?" asked Romaine.

"We're being audited again," Anita explained. "The third time in three years. It's part of the new strategy to intimidate gay bars into closing. Four did last year. You know I'm immune to intimidation, but I do want to keep an eye on them, the creeps. It certainly is revealing—men seem to get very nervous at the thought of women getting together without them."

"And let's face it, queer-hating is fashionable again. The scent of reprieve has evaporated. Don't get me started on the pathology of this, but when the majority resumes beating on the minority that liberated itself with approval, something's eating them," said Romaine somewhat bitterly, then added in a lighter tone, "Personally I think lesbians are charming. I don't find them threatening at all."

The other three laughed.

"Yes, we know you do, dear," said Anita. "I'll send someone over for your order. We really should get back—the T-men are getting an education they didn't bargain for, surrounded by my gallery of famous dykes in history, some of whom even surprise me."

After promises of meeting soon were exchanged, Anita and Christine left, replaced seconds later with a young woman in her early twenties, barely contained in a black leather miniskirt, a tight white T-shirt spelling ACT UP across the front, crucifix earrings, and black leather high-tops. Romaine and Violet looked at each other ruefully. The woman whipped out her order book, popped her gum, and grinned. They ordered.

When the waitress left, Violet turned to Romaine. "Jesus, every time I come in here the women are getting younger. She makes me feel like a matron from Larchmont."

"There's a solution to that," Romaine replied.

"What? Retreads? A total makeover?"

"Free weights, darling. Nautilus isn't enough anymore."

They received several other visitors from the bar, and lunch arrived: pasta with pesto, a rare New York strip steak, salad, and Chianti for Violet; a Caesar salad for Romaine. Lunch passed under an aura of reminiscence, in a pleasant haze of wine and shoptalk, Violet deeply grateful for the vacation from her pained and stressful state. Finally, with a pot of coffee on the table, a Gauloise lit, Violet withdrew the now familiar group of items from her briefcase and put them on the table. Romaine looked disapproving.

"Just let me babble for a second," Violet began. "I know you think I'm childish or obsessed or looking for a reason to hold myself up—well, think whatever you like, they're all probably true. I can't quite justify it or explain it, I'm a late bloomer. I'm still trying to put some things in place that everyone else did years ago. Maybe you're right about therapy, maybe you're right about Paul—no, wait, scratch that.

"Anyway, Don convinced me that from his point of view the case is closed, that they exhausted their leads and options. But let me say two things. First, it wouldn't be the first time that someone got somewhere on a case that was supposedly closed, someone who could work freely outside the bureaucracy. Second, I think Don has as many personal reasons to let this thing go as I do to continue. Which I am going to, whether or not you help, though I know you will. So look at this sheet of paper again, okay?"

She pushed the paper of initials in front of Romaine.

"I would also like to point out that, as I told you, Don is convinced that Max's gruesome death was not connected with trying to get information to me—but what about the weird scene outside of Anita's? We didn't talk about that, but was it a coincidence or what? I don't think so. Well, are you in?"

Romaine sat thoughtfully for a moment, looking carefully at the old friend who was on her way to unraveling.

"I'm in. So let's start."

Violet grabbed her hand and squeezed, then pointed at the sheet of paper.

C.H.C.	E.M. T.T.H. M. NJ. 09876
P.N.Y. 15990	D.B. H.M.F. H. DE. 33445
Kate Patient Same Capacity?	S.S. Y.M.C. R. KY. 99889
cross/ miss. per.	A.P. H.M.C. P. KY. 97877
FBI?	N.C. A.M.H. L. AR. 23343

Lt. William Aragon, Greencourt Rd., Medford, Mass.

"So, what do you think?" asked Violet.

"Well," Romaine mused, "it's not exactly deeply coded, is it?"

"No," replied Violet, "and as I said to Don, the fact that it isn't seems more significant. Again my sense that it was an open file, topical as hell, material he was working on that very day. Although it's unusual that he would leave it in the car. But I can't connect it to this Yardley stuff at all."

Romaine shook her head. "Then don't. Let's stick with this for the moment. Now, 'Kate Patient Same Capacity?' Unless it's a comment on her temperament, Kate is a patient at some type of facility in New York State, and whatever else is going on, the last two initials on each line are also clearly states. The zip codes make it easy. It's possible the first two initials in each group are names, but we have Kate spelled out, so perhaps she is more significant so we start with her. What do you think?"

"I think you're fabulous. If you weren't here I don't know what I'd do. I've stared at this stuff for so long it's turned into hieroglyphs," Violet said excitedly. "So now what?"

"So now I see if Anita has a directory, which she probably does because of their mailing list for club events, and you go and call Mr. Aragon."

They both left the table, Romaine heading for the club office, Violet for the bank of pay phones in the back hall. She got his number from information, stood thinking for a moment about what she would say, and dialed. After many rings, a man answered.

"Lieutenant Aragon?" Violet asked.

The man at the other end of the line laughed. "It's been years since I was called that, and it usually wasn't by a woman, but yes, that's me. What can I do for you?"

Violet jumped right in. "Lieutenant Aragon, I'm calling from New York, my name is Violet Childes. My father was Victor Childes. Did you know him, by any chance?"

The voice on the other end sounded reluctant. "Yes . . . I did. I'm sorry about what happened. I, well, I thought he was a great fellow."

"Thanks. Listen, did he call you recently—by recently, I mean last summer?"

"Yes, he did, and it was odd too, because he was calling to ask me if someone else had called. Why, Miss Childes?"

"I guess you could say I'm tying up loose ends."

"And I guess I'll just have to buy that, considering you're his kid and all."

"So," Violet continued, "who was he asking about?"

"Oh, some broa— I mean some woman. Her name was, uh, Karen, no, uh, Katherine, or maybe Kate, who called. Yeah, that sounds right."

"Which?"

"Kate, I think. Listen, is that all, honey? The Celtics are on and—"

"Just one more thing—what did she want?"

"She asked some questions about the war, did I know Victor then, stuff like that."

"Please let me ask you just one final thing. Can you remember the date he called, or when it was in general?"

"Sure, I remember when he called. It was a couple of weeks before the Sox dropped four games in a row and ruined their chance for the playoffs. That would have been early August."

"Well, I'll let you go then, you've been a big help, thanks a lot." She returned the receiver and walked slowly back to the table, where Romaine was sitting with an open directory and a quizzical look.

"What is it?"

Violet sat down. "Well, this name keeps popping up all over. We have Kate Patient. This Aragon guy says a woman named Kate called him last summer, then Victor called him to ask about her. Also—do you remember the Empire State record I was telling you about?" Romaine nodded. "Well, the two, Victor and the mystery woman, were singing something from *Kiss Me, Kate* . . . I was so rattled at the time I didn't really think of where the song came from. I'm beginning to think he was having an affair."

"Not the most startling revelation, Violet," Romaine said cautiously.

"No, of course not. It took years to get used to the idea of Victor with someone besides Marie, but that's not what I'm getting at. He always shared that kind of thing with me, that's what makes it unusual."

"Vi, I don't mean to be critical, but you were kind of consumed with Cindy during that time. You were rather out of it. Doesn't it occur to you that if all this information is so easily obtainable, it's not particularly significant—or mysterious? Maybe Don's right, maybe you should leave it alone."

Violet shook her head emphatically. "No. First of all, I'm going in the opposite direction—he was killed because he found something he could use on Yardley, and the Yardley material was in the car on the day he died. This sheet of paper, this Kate person, is practically pasted to him. And we think Victor was dating her, and furthermore have you forgotten that on Don's list of people going in and out of the apartment that day is an unidentified woman. My God, if anyone knows any more about Yardley or the day Victor died, it's her . . . Jesus, she might have killed him herself," she added with a slightly crazed look.

"Hold it, Vi. Don't go overboard. And what about Leimenster?"

"Fuck the Harvard hit man. I have to call Don." Violet sprang from the table, calling over her shoulder, "Did you find anything?"

"Yes!" was the reply Romaine called after her.

"Don, it's me. Who's Kate?"

"Honey, I'm kind of busy. Kate who?"

"Let me start another way. Was Victor seeing anyone romantically last summer?"

"Well . . ."

"Come on Don, give."

"Yes, there was someone. But he was very secretive about it, and I respected his privacy. I thought maybe she was one of his clients, and they had gotten involved. I don't know. Anyway, something happened, and he did say at one point that it was over."

"Name?"

"I never knew."

"Well, Don, what about the unidentified woman coming out of the apartment the day—"

"The word was she was a client, and she was wrapped in scarves and wearing sunglasses and impossible to identify. And that's not what the killer was wearing, if you get my meaning Violet. He was wearing his trademark two-hundred-buck pinstripe—"

"Thanks, Don," Violet interrupted his description of Leimenster and hung up, hurrying back to the table, sitting down, and lighting another Gauloise.

"Okay. He confirmed Victor was seeing someone. What did you find?"

"I worked backwards from the zip. It seemed clear we were looking for a hospital, so I went through the four

P-towns in that area, and came up with this—Cobb Hill Clinic, Pinehurst, New York. It's the only one that fits."

Violet leaned over and kissed her cheek. "Brilliant! Wait, did you say Cobb Hill?"

"Yes. Why, have you heard of it?"

"Well, oddly enough Cindy was there for rehab, at least for a while. That's what I was told anyway."

"Do you know any more than that? What kind of place it was, what her treatment was?"

"No."

"I hate to ask this," said Romaine, avoiding further discussion of Cindy, "but what next?"

"That's obvious," Violet said dryly. "Kate seems to be the key, she's everywhere we look, and even if she can't explain the Yardley business, she was around those last few weeks or months before Victor was killed, so I've got to talk to her."

"Earth to Vi, you smug thing," Romaine said. "We have a first name only. It's just a hunch that she's in that hospital, and they certainly aren't going to let you roam around looking for her."

Violet sighed. "Okay, Miss Rain-on-My-Parade, what do you suggest?"

"First of all, I have to get back to my office, you freelancers and your all-day lunches slay me. When I have time I will call Cobb Hill, and . . . hmm, I'll say that I'm a lawyer settling an estate, trying to locate the beneficiary of a huge inheritance and I believe she is in Cobb Hill under an assumed name and the first name might be Kate. What do you think?"

"I think it's the fishiest story I've ever heard, but if anyone can pull it off you can. I, on the other hand, will track down Cindy and see if I can get a line on what this place is about."

Romaine frowned. "Do you think that's wise?"

"Wise? No. But I've wanted to check in with her for a long time, and I just couldn't bring myself to do it. A neutral topic will make it easier."

Without further comment they gathered their things and paid the lunch bill. Violet threw her arms around Romaine and held her tightly.

"Thank you. You always go one step further than even a best friend would."

Romaine stepped back, grabbed Violet's hands and squeezed them, then picked up her briefcase and walked toward the door. "That's because I love you, even though you are an unstable, neurotic, crackpot, spoiled—"

"Will you be the maid of honor at my wedding?"

"—bitch!" she finished, and strode through the doorway.

10

Climbing the steps to Cindy's apartment, Violet realized it would have been appropriate to phone first, but had a good idea of why she hadn't. She did not want to hear her voice, did not want to see her. The hammering heart said it all. Ultimately the door appeared in front of her. Ultimately it opened.

"Oh my God," said the apparition.

"You took the words right out of my mouth," said Violet, moving past her inside. The apartment was one very large room, with high ceilings and not much else. The walls and floor were painted white, as were a huge Marlowe bed, several chairs, a bureau, one long table, all but lost in the gaping space.

The effect of the white and the density of emotion made the dimensions of the room seem to tilt and lift away. The effect was blurring to the senses. Violet swallowed and turned around to face her.

Cindy was quite a bit shorter than Violet; her appearance was a study in contradictions. Well-toned muscles were bathed in porcelain skin, which held up an equally porcelain face, gaunt cheekbones that seemed permanently rouged, a shock of blonde hair that seemed permanently ruffled, and fluorescent blue eyes that seemed permanently fourteen years old, on the brink of discovery.

Violet could not resist her. Their eyes met and held; neither could speak. Cindy was clearly at a loss. All of a sudden so was Violet. She walked over to her silently, taking up both of her hands. An unexplained current, to Violet a damnable one, ran between them. The rush of feelings was palpable. Their gaze fell into a vortex: car crash, A-bomb, two unstoppable trains. They had not seen each other for almost a year. Or was it yesterday?

Not a word was spoken as they half-dragged each other, half-ran to the bed, as the jumpsuit and boots appeared in a heap on the floor with Cindy's white robe, as they sank into deep memory-racked kisses, splayed on a field of white. Melancholy split in half; two bodies remembered once-familiar terrain; the air between them charged with a desire that out-foxed time; two halves speeding toward a whole. Breast slid against breast, thighs that were milk-smooth grazed, electrified. Two planes of taut stomach pressed tight; the precarious balance tipped then dove into ripe flame; delirium reigned; a parade of sensations let loose in a cool white room. Tongues danced on pink velvet; trembling sheaths of silk skin traveled, speeding up to the apex where they hung, suspended in dazzle, in a jagged diamond spasm, then fell together, one mercurial dolphin, collapsing in a near faint. It was always that way between them.

Violet watched as Cindy made coffee in silence. She wondered whether the source was anger or fatigue. The room itself implied silence, a blank page, an airless white container filled with cotton. Cindy flipped a switch and nervous-sounding jazz slipped out into the room. Freezing rain began to tap an irritated telegram on the window. Violet pulled on the jumpsuit and sat at the table. Cindy placed the coffee in front of her, shifting her weight from foot to foot as if ready to sprint. Violet sipped some of the coffee before speaking.

"Do you really despise me that much?"

"That's hardly the point." Cindy walked to the window, pressing her hands on the hot cup, as if seeking a physical manifestation of the internal jarring.

"Well, what is the point?"

"The art of emotional geography. You know, how we fill each other up, ease into those hollows, then just as easily vacate. The temperature of emotion moves from hothouse to tepid to freezer burn in arbitrary flicks, in eye blinks. In elevator stops. One stop love, the next stop loss. The human is not to be trusted, *n'est-ce pas?*"

Violet almost smiled. She had nearly forgotten that Cindy had a tendency to speak like an unpublished poet.

"If you are referring to us, you are leaving out insurmountable problems in your accounting, not mere rejection on my part."

"One problem too many? One over the prescribed limit? Not up to Childes standards?"

Violet winced. "Do you really want to go through all of this again? Your addiction and the obsession surrounding it sucked up all the air around you. There was no room for anyone. If I had agreed to make the buys myself, if I had stood around and watched you die, if I had arranged the funeral, would that have proved my loyalty?"

Silence came again, the tape stopping on cue. The room was steady as a still life. Cindy closed her eyes and dug the heel of a palm into one of them as if to press back memory, then opened them and continued gazing out the window.

"No, that's not it. I just don't understand the rule that says you have to go through the hardest parts alone. Who the fuck made that up anyway? What difference does it make, what does it prove to face things alone? We don't exist as separate continents."

Violet held up a hand. "I don't know why you're bringing this up. But if you hadn't run into that wall alone, at breakneck speed, would you have cornered yourself; would you have realized you were craving to die and then changed your mind if you had someone wrapping you up in some hopeful fiction? You were the one who had to say no, who had to fight back, however unarmed."

"Unarmed?" Cindy walked over and placed her coffee on the table, picking up a lighter and cigarette with jerky stop-time movements. Violet lit one of her own. Bouffants of white smoke hovered, still another white in a gallery of whites; snow white, fluorescent white, marble white, aspirin white. The curtains moved balletically, like big linen handkerchiefs. Violet felt as though she were slipping around on an ice floe. They smoked for several minutes in stark gestures, in abbreviated truce. Cindy spoke again.

"Do you know where I got the money to go to the hospital?"

"Yes, that supposed art patron who had a crush on you."

Cindy stared at her. "It was Victor. Even he thought enough of our supposed devotion to contribute to making me whole or at least more acceptable to his precious issue. What a bad investment. A Band-Aid over a bullet hole."

Violet was startled; they were clattering now, two dice rattling in a box.

"I don't believe you."

"I don't fucking care if you believe me or not. The point is he didn't walk away."

Violet slammed her cup on the table, the splash of brown a grin leering at no one.

"I did not walk away, I ran," said Violet in a near shout. "Because you pushed me away, you drove me away, you flung me away. Jesus, your editing skills are remarkable. What about the side-line liaisons, the disappearing for days, the glazed look, the embalmed body, the attempt at elegant lies, the mood swings that slammed back and forth like a berserk metronome? And the beatings, the tantrums; it was like being force-fed a nightmare. I didn't leave, I was jettisoned. And not without trying, not without spilling every drop of love and sanity until I was bled dry. Alone? Who was really alone until those last days when I left? Was it you, with your elegiac drug, your swan-song entourage, your protégée lovers, or was it the witness, who had to live with the flopping, grinning skeleton? Tell me. Who was alone?"

This was almost a wail. Cindy was visibly shaking, hugging herself into an anguished arch. Slow tears traced down the cheeks of a vibrating ghost.

"Stop," she whispered, sinking down into a chair. Palms slid across the table and fingertips touched, another minor truce.

"I'm sorry, Violet," the words came out like a slow rosary, evenly spaced notes of pure pain. "I do know, now, what I did to you. I know it was horrible, I know I sent you away. I will never get over the loss. I just don't understand why you're here."

Violet told her about Cobb Hill. Visibly relieved at the change of subject, Cindy shook her head. When she spoke her voice had hardened.

"I don't buy it, Vi. You could have gotten that information in a hundred other ways. I think you're here to check up on yourself. I think maybe you're not sold on this new life with Paul," she said in a challenge, meaning to hurt. Violet narrowed her eyes in surprise.

"How did you know?"

Cindy allowed herself a slight and bitter grin. "When a favorite child of the order switches allegiances, it gets around." Violet drew her hand away and leaned back, suddenly very weary.

"God, I'm sick of hearing that. Loving Paul has nothing to do with loving you or anyone else. I'm tired of being treated as though I'm deserting ranks. It's irrelevant." She was quiet for a moment.

"But I am sorry"—she sagged down farther into her chair at the thought—"if you're right about this exchange." Cindy's hand lay open on the table, pallid, slightly twitching, like a lone trout on a bank. In a wooden voice, she quietly recited what she remembered about Cobb Hill. A cloud released the sun, which in turn fled into the room, making the white vessel surge with new insistence. The white was prodding, it was enervating. Violet felt compressed, frantic, she had to try again.

"I really am sorry. I would never have believed myself capable of using you as a barometer for my feelings. I do love Paul, at least I think I do . . . I will always love you. But we are wreckage. And you know that." Violet shivered and started to cry. Cindy was swaying slightly, lone hand still extended. She folded it neatly into a small, resigned fist.

Violet finished dressing and gathered her things. She noticed a photograph she had given to Cindy a year before, when she was still trying to get her attention. The photograph was of Cindy, taken years earlier. It was mysterious and vague; Cindy looked as though she were under water. The mat around the photograph was round; Violet had burned the edges into a ragged circle. Printed beneath it was a poem

Violet had written to augment the photograph. It was the only instance in which she had ever used words to accompany an image. Violet picked it up.

"May I read it?"

Cindy shrugged.

"'The light started around her head, fluttering like wings without the bird, then became a stutter, cold jags of light shedding off in glass pleats. The light poured out of her eyes like rushing water and I saw that she was leaving, moving off, but I could not reach her. Once we were like two palms pressed together, wed, stitched into the same secret lining. Now she was leaving, moving off, and I could not reach her. The light moved down around her in a sheath, a cloak of nameless music that was calling her away. I pressed the skirt of light against my face but she was gone. She I could not reach.'"

Violet gently placed the photograph back where she found it.

"Why do you keep this around?"

Cindy stared at her. "As a reminder of a place I never want to go back to. I'm new at this game. Some days that stupid picture is the only thing that keeps me clean."

Finally a small understanding was passing between them. Violet tried to enlarge it.

"I don't know why it has to be this way. You are the center of the best of my memories."

"Yes," replied Cindy, still as a stone in the white cocoon, already withdrawn. "And most of the worst. I hope I never see you again."

The white covered them.

"Please don't. What is the point in that kind of finality, we're all we've got, all of us."

Violet looked at her one last time, knowing they would meet again, wondering whether it would ever be any better between them. The white room had triumphed, parading their failure in bas relief.

"Good-bye, then." It was all there was left. She turned and went, closing the door behind her.

It was a long walk home.

11

As Violet let herself into the apartment, she could hear the phone ringing. She answered it, collapsing into the nearest chair. It was Romaine.

"How did it go?"

Violet sighed. "I should have known better; I don't know why I didn't send you. It was like ripping stitches out of a wound."

"I'm sorry, Vi," Romaine said quietly.

"What is it they say? Whatever does not kill you makes you stronger? God, people say stupid things. Forget it."

"Of course. But did she say anything about Cobb Hill?"

"Yes. She said it was the Betty Ford Clinic watered down to a trickle, not at all what she needed, and she didn't stay long. I'll tell you the rest later. What happened when you called?"

"I'm afraid they didn't buy it. The nurse I spoke to said rather sarcastically that they did not have any mystery patients; their roster was confidential information; and why would someone leave a fortune to a first name?"

Violet laughed ruefully. "She's right. Damn. Amateur girl detectives strike out. Now what?"

"It's going to take some more thought. Even with a full name, we wouldn't have much luck without a court order, which we don't have much chance of acquiring."

"Oh, Romaine, what should I do?" Violet grumbled. "Sublimate? Drop the whole thing?"

"I think we have a couple of choices. But at the moment," she said firmly, "I say we just sleep on all of this and I'll talk to you tomorrow."

Violet knew when to quiet herself and follow Romaine's suggestion. "Will do, reluctantly. And thanks for everything you did today."

They said good night and hung up. Violet stood up to pursue a drink, then sat back down, picked up the phone, and dialed David's number.

He started right in. "Do I get to lecture you now or would you rather I do it in person?"

"How do Judy and the soldiers look?"

"Pointedly bizarre, just as planned."

"David—can the trade shots be put off for a week or so?"

"I suppose so," he answered slowly. "Why?"

"You know I'm thrilled to be back working with you, but I still have these loose ends . . ."

"No need to be euphemistic with me, Violet," he said, more gently than usual.

"Thanks. Then how about this? Give me a week to see what I can find out. Pretend I'm not back yet. If you want to get the trade stuff out of the way, hire anyone you like. I just hate this in-between jazz and I'm of no use to you. At the end of the week I promise I'll be back full time. How does that sound?"

David was quiet for a moment.

"Sounds fine. There's a ton of work right now besides the trades, as you know—but there always is. And I'd just hate to have to call gorgeous Mario at N.Y.U. for night work, but a man must do . . . I guess I know better than to suggest that throwing yourself into work would be the best thing for you."

"Yes, you do know better."

"Well, don't disappear."

"I won't. I'll be in a lot. But a woman must do . . ."

"Got it. Good night, Vi. Stay safe."

"Thanks. Bye."

Violet hung up the phone, splashed a judicious amount of Scotch into a glass, and made her way into the bathroom, stripping off her clothes and drawing a very hot bath. Violet slid into it, then balanced the glass on one of her knees.

Violet was not fond of baths, she felt embalmed and restless in one, but tonight it was purely therapeutic; she needed to be forced into a relaxed state. Romaine had brought up a subject it was time to address, namely Paul, and what, if anything, she would tell him about recent events. The obvious answer was everything—Violet believed in full-disclosure relationships. But Paul had been so negative about her continuing fixation on Victor, and while she agreed intellectually that it all belonged in the past, another part of her would not let her put it there. The question was which would do more damage, the erosion caused by her continuing inquiry or the later revelation of it. She sipped her Scotch and ruminated, poised between the rock and the hard place. Her thoughts had drifted to Cindy when the phone rang. It was a classic French phone, gold and white with a bell-shaped mouthpiece; it was next to the tub where the previous tenant left it; it was Paul.

"Hi, Vi. If I didn't know better I'd say it sounds like you're taking a bath."

"I am."

"How was work this morning, is it good to be back?"

"It was wonderful." Violet recounted the soldier story.

Paul sounded relieved. "That's great. I was beginning to think you were going to take a header into that silly notion of play-school detective."

Something clicked in Violet's mind at the word "silly." Inadvertently, he had just made the decision for her; she would let him think she had given up. As childish as she knew it was, she wanted to prove something to him.

"Right," was all she could manage at the moment.

"So, what drove you into the tub?"

"Various oddities—life's squalor, our fight this morning, sheer fatigue, et cetera."

"Will we survive this morning?"

"The distaff side has."

"I have the perfect antidote to all of this. I'll be right over, I can minister to your mood with the famous Renault touch. Shall I describe it to you?"

Violet laughed. "No, don't, I might break down and

change my mind. I'm exhausted and I have every intention of crawling from here directly into bed."

"Are you sure? My bedside manner is beginning to throb."

"Yes, I'm sure it is. Please keep your largesse in your pajamas."

"Okay, I give up. What's the plan for tomorrow's date?"

"I'm just checking. It's my turn right?"

"Yes."

"Then I'll tell you tomorrow when you arrive."

Paul groaned. "Oh God, another mystery date. I haven't gotten over the last one. What should I wear, a clown suit?"

"Anything but madras, dear. See you at ten."

"Right."

Violet hung up and got out of the tub, dried off, ran into the bedroom, and jumped into bed, pulling the covers over her head. She had had enough of the entire day; she wanted to slip the whole thing under someone else's door. She lay thinking about what to suggest for the following day's outing.

To vault the distance between their two lifestyles, Paul and Violet subjected each other to trade-off dates on alternate weekends, in preparation for uptown marrying downtown. Two weeks earlier Violet had switched turf and taken Paul to the Metropolitan Museum, after promising not to yell "Tradition in the absence of culture" as they walked up Fifth Avenue.

The Met was a favorite place of Violet's, the setting for some of the very few memories she had of her mother outside of her sick bed. The scenes remained vivid. The small mittened hand in the larger gloved one, the big-skirted coat that swelled out against her and slightly pushed her away. Her mother's face so pale and faraway that the child convinced herself that holding that gloved hand was all that kept her from floating off. They moved through the large chambers, stopping at Marie's favorite paintings and objects, through rooms papered in a precursory silence. The lunch next to the pool, the bus ride home, her musical laugh, all were treasured vignettes.

Marie was often vivacious, and always presented her warm side to Violet, but children's perceptions are prismatic, snaky, able to dart around and catch the hidden temperament. Years later Violet became aware that Marie was dying the entire time she knew her. In subsequent consideration it seemed she knew all along, somehow—had seen the specter hovering, making itself felt in the tremble of the gloved hand, in the pain of the white-plated face.

During the last passage, the bedroom became as still as one of the halls in the Met. Victor's boisterous carriage had narrowed down into a series of devotions. At age eight Violet understood sensation more deeply than fact; that the source of pain was pulling her mother away from them, separating her into layers that peeled off into death one by one, until her mother was taken away.

After Marie died Violet returned many times to the Met. It was a notably haunted reverie until she discovered a room they had not visited together, which presented a chance to get out of the tomb the apartment had become. This is where she had taken Paul.

The room that housed the Met's collection of musical instruments seemed to be a well-kept Manhattan secret; most of the time Violet could count on it being empty. For a dollar one could rent headphones attached to transistor radio handbags. Stopping in front of a case of instruments, the handbag triggered a tape loop of sound from each one. Violet thought this was the best invention since the garlic press; Paul wasn't quite as sure. She could not resist moving from case to case to create a cacophonous musical collage. On the day in question Violet discovered a group of kids from uptown who had splintered off from their youth group and looked bored. Violet rented them all headphones and taught them the collage trick. While it lasted, this futuristic dance troupe, led by Violet, leapt from case to case in a mime version of a Balinese-Zulu wedding march.

A logical progression occurred, and the nine children and Violet began to vocalize their own interpretations of the sounds of the instruments. In the melee that followed (as they were being thrown out), the department head said he had never witnessed such undignified behavior at the Met before. The woman who ran the desk and passed out the handbags said it was the most fun she had had in eleven years of doing so. The tracked-down social worker from the Bronx offered Violet a job. Paul, who decided that from this point on he would carry a pocket disguise for occasions such as this, commented that maybe uptown wasn't all it was cracked up to be and he would be just as happy to limit their adventures to Violet's own neighborhood.

Violet smiled to herself under the tented covers. She was riled with thoughts, they became circuitous, she was asleep in seconds. She dreamed of Warsaw.

12

It was Saturday morning; Manhattan's uproar was muted, almost demure, the chaos was diluted into the near-acceptable.

Violet woke up in pleased anticipation of spending the day away from her cage of anxiety. She lit her first Gitane while rummaging for a dance tape, did some tentative stretches, then showered and dressed for the day. Saturday clothes consisted almost entirely of voluminous black leather, today broken up only by red leather high-tops and red-framed sunglasses.

Paul arrived as Violet was finishing the last of her breakfast. He put his arms around her, avoiding contact with the fried-egg-bacon-tomato-and-anchovy-paste sandwich.

"I love you, in spite of your diet."

"Well, you only live once, pal, and what else is there besides good works, sex, and food?" she mumbled through the last of her sandwich.

"Good works, that has a quaint sound to it. It implies folding Red Cross bandages—"

"That's hardly what I have in mind," she replied, as Paul brushed the crumbs off his speckled black blazer. "I know you all think I'm a self-indulgent brat, but it's just a phase. As soon as I get some of my art ideas out of the way, because if I don't they'll just bug me for the rest of my life—I'm serious, it's like being pregnant with a child that keeps talking to you—well, then I've got big plans. It's good works till the end."

"I don't doubt it for a minute. Any room for a husband in all of that? Have you decided what form this gesture is going to take?"

Violet grimaced. "Ooh, that word makes me shiver. I guess we'll just have to see, won't we? As for the plan, it's called The Bridge. I'll tell you about it sometime."

Paul glanced at her outfit. "Ah, the dominatrix look. If you had only let me know, I would have dressed appropriately. What's the plan?"

"A quiet day, if you don't mind. Perusal of every local gallery. That okay with you?"

"Fine as long as you protect me. Wait, what word makes you shiver?"

"*Husband*, dear. Now come on, we have to get going. Did you see the spread on the Lower East Side in *Town and Country*? How to experience the cultural edge from the safety of your stretch limo? We have to get out there before they rope the whole area off and start giving house tours."

Out There was waiting, the urban polemic in a swathe of concentration. Travelogue notes: Close to the edge, the air and light are dense and sulfurous, suetlike, and there is a grey, the grey of the diaphanous drug haze, a grey that settles on many in a fine Hiroshima ash. Tourist views on downtown: The man on Houston and Broadway, with his large collection of bright white socks that he washes daily and displays, who delights in announcing that the money you give him will be spent on vodka, not his family or hard rolls. The man around the corner who leans on the hood, making a half-swipe at the windshield with a filthy rag, threads of spittle gleaming; money is heaved out the window to get the shaking skeletal fingers off the car. The black man, who sums up the racial progress of the twentieth century, seen jumping out of the way of a taxi speeding straight for him, shouting "Don't hit me I'm really a white man." The thirteen-year-old girl in a thin shirt in freezing air, pacing back and forth, feeling her own breasts; eyes, nose, mouth running—so stoned she is cross-eyed. The tourist flees, the resident takes it for granted.

Flip side: Close to the edge, a band of cultural miscreants, turning the ruins into plots of the avant-garde. The air is hopped-up, the air is raining images. The street speaks. Inflammatory. Close cover before striking.

Paul and Violet started their tour, stopping first to visit Maria, a local street person and friend of Violet's who was reading a beaten-up copy of *Pride and Prejudice*. Maria had no use for Paul, who in her eyes was suspiciously clean-looking. Violet chatted with her for a moment and gave her some Twinkies and a copy of *The New Republic* (she would accept no money from Violet), and Maria gave Violet a copy of *A Room with a View,* and asked her for a tape of Aaron Copland, which she had no way of listening to, which she wanted because "He is the Babe Ruth of twentieth-century music, know what I mean?"

As they walked away Paul was shaking his head.

"I don't know how you can stand living down here day after day. It's so depressing."

"If you lived here day after day you'd know."

"And those packs of Marlboros you hand out with a dollar inside—it just encourages them."

"*Them*? Who is *them*? Anyway, I'm distinctly cynical about it, Paul. I give money away to smooth the passage, know what I mean? I would also like to point out that I receive more harassment, particularly of the sexual variety, uptown in your area from men whose suits look uncannily like yours."

Paul ignored this. "That reminds me, where are we going to live after we get married?"

"Hmm, that's becoming your leitmotiv, isn't it? Well, if the day ever came, would you consider . . ."

"No way. Would you . . . ?"

"Nope."

"How about a compromise, say a condo in midtown, just a cab ride away in either direction?"

"Yuck."

"What, then?"

"Let's start someplace else."

"Chicago?"

"Paris."

"L.A.?"

"Belgrade."

"I want the ring back."

"Fine."

There was no ring, but they had clearly moved into a test pattern, pushing at each other's expectations.

They proceeded to sample the New Wave. Many of the galleries were the size of airplane bathrooms, some looked like pawn shops; the streets were lined with names like Cell Block H, New Science, and Gallery X. After emerging from one particularly extreme gallery called Target, which was filled with polyester casts of animals hit by cars, Paul finally protested.

"I've had just about enough of this obscene flotsam."

"Well, I wouldn't term all of it brilliant, but it takes chances, it's out on a limb. I love it."

"It's sheer random detritus merged with television. If you haven't grown up attached to one surgically this stuff is incomprehensible. The most profound subject it touches is the Jetsons."

"It's a new iconography, strictly American for a change, not watered-down European."

"It's post-neo-garbage."

"Honestly, Paul, I've got your number. You want the living room filled with Leroy Neiman, right?"

"And you want to bring home one of these reproductions of a road pizza. Please, I can't stand any more," he said in mock desperation. "Take me to the Madison Pub for repairs, before our differences drive me into a monastery."

"There's just one more stop we have to make. I promise it's the last." Grabbing his arm, she dragged him toward First Street, while he grumbled and covered his eyes—both of them secretly acknowledging the fact that acute appreciation of their differences was their main attraction to each other.

The last gallery on the list was in an ancient, boarded-up building next to a men's shelter. Usually one or two prone forms had to be stepped over to get to the door, which lacked sign or handle. To enter one banged loudly on the door and hoped someone heard.

Someone did, and they were ushered inside by a tall, gaunt white-haired man and left to their own devices. The gallery had three small main rooms. The wood floor was so rotten it had broken through in places. The walls were crumbling brick halfway up, crumbling plaster the rest. The show was a group of eerie oil paintings, a cross in style between Thomas Hart Benton and the covers of 1940s cheap drugstore paperbacks, each a narrative mystery. They were rendered in a bluish palette. They were provocative and sensual, with such a strange aura that most of the observers were silent. Even Paul was impressed. They moved hypnotically through the rooms several times, continuing to return to the same painting. In the same bluish cast of colors were hacksaw fragments: the corner of a woman's coat, leg, high-heeled shoe, the coat red, the shoes blue, blurred with movement. A gnarled tree, light splashed on it by an orb shining like a car headlight. On the left side on the ground was an emerald green shoe attached to a brown trouser leg, veering out of the frame. Paul and Violet nodded to each other and went into the back room where they paid for the painting, slightly shocked at their first shared purchase. Maybe things weren't impossible. Violet talked to the gallery owner asking questions about the artist. Paul was transfixed by the atmosphere, he was staring out the window.

The room had two doors opening on the courtyard, where a group of people were standing around in the dusk, deep blue lapping up around them. Someone was projecting a movie through a window of the gallery onto the back wall of the courtyard; in the increasing darkness the black-and-white image hovered inexplicably, the skyline above it dissolving. The windows of the shelter next door were softly lit, filled with shadows of the men inside, some of them pressed to the window to observe. These shadows were thrown in relief on the cement courtyard, mingling with the harder outlines of the standing figures. The scene mimicked the tone of the painting they had just bought. Paul tugged on Violet's arm gently, pointing outside.

"Is that a film or a movie?"

"Damn. Just when I think we're getting somewhere you start up."

"I'm just kidding, I like it here very much. I'll never be able to top this next week."

"That's another thing, this competitive bit—"

He put his hand over her mouth. "Will you shut up?" He removed his hand and kissed her. "You are going to marry me, aren't you?" he said in a whisper.

"Oh, that again. Yes, if you insist. What was your name again?"

"Stop it. You promise?"

"Sure. Today if you want, or we could just live together and have a lot of children out of wedlock."

"Fine, as long as I'm in charge of their eating habits."

"God, you're stuffy. Forget the whole thing. Let's go."

They linked arms and left the building. With a sudden rush of affection for Paul, Violet considered seriously for the first time throwing her lot in with his. Her present feeling of comfort was blurring her thinking, perhaps it was time to let it go. It was getting colder and had become dark. They stood discussing where to eat.

Suddenly they were startled by the appearance of two tall, heavyset men with identical hats who brushed closely by Violet and Paul. As they moved past, a tape cassette clattered to the sidewalk next to Violet. One of the men stopped, picked it up, and handed it to Violet.

"Hey, lady, you drop this?"

"No, it must be yours."

"Belongs to you, lady, take it." He put his hand over hers, pushing the tape toward her. The hand was wide and strong, with several rings holding huge stones on it. He turned to join his companion. Violet frowned. Something clicked.

"Paul . . . Paul, that's the guy who shot at me, I'm sure of it, hey you—" she yelled, starting off after him.

"Vi, don't—" Paul began. It was too late. The men returned instantly, and not so politely this time. One of the men yanked Paul's arms back behind him and held them there. The other man put an arm around Violet and pulled her to him. The hand without the rings produced a switchblade and sprang it open, carefully placing the point against her neck. Half a block away was a streetlamp, whose anemic pool of light barely grazed them. The street was empty except for their group of four.

"Listen, lady. This. Is. Your. Tape. Put it in your fucking pocket and take it home." The man's face was a dim white blur under the brim of his hat. Paul was struggling to get loose. The man pressed the knife point inward, the skin dimpled then pricked open, a small trickle of blood started down her long neck. He took the knife away, wiped the single drop of blood off the end of it on Violet's jacket sleeve, popped the blade back in, motioned to his friend, and they walked off unhurriedly. Paul rushed over to Violet.

"Are you all right?"

"Yes," she said, slightly dazed. "I'm fine." Paul pulled out a handkerchief and put his arm around her, gently dabbing at the blood, a wet line of burnt umber in the weak fluorescent light.

"Paul," she said in a perplexed tone.

"What? Are you going to faint? Should we go back inside?"

She pushed him away slightly. "No . . . Paul, that was no chance meeting. How would they know where we were unless . . . they followed us all day?" She shivered. "It's creepy."

She drew herself up, taking Paul's arm. "Let's go home and listen to that tape."

Paul shook his head, marveling at her ability to switch gears. "I'll get a cab."

Violet, though trembling, laughed slightly. "A cab on First Street? We walk, boy." They walked off, clinging to each other, striding in and out of the cold disks of light, their figures illuminated in hacksaw pieces.

The tired pair arrived at Violet's apartment a while later. Silently, Paul gently dabbed antiseptic on Violet's neck and, retrieving ice from the kitchen, fixed them each a Campari and soda. Violet sat on the couch sipping the drink, absently turning the cassette over and over in a shuffle on the table in front of her. Finally, she got up and shoved the tape into the cassette deck and punched the button, returning to the couch. The tape was silent for a full, nerve-racking thirty seconds. Abruptly the next sound was a man speaking, seemingly in mid-sentence, in a low tone, ". . . can't believe it's you," followed by a section of hissing tape. Then again the man's voice, lower still, and sounding vague, limp, drooping over a cliff of panic like a Dali watch. "Kate . . . Violet . . ." The tape hissed again, then popped back into play, two loud sounds, explosions or gunshots, then the tape hissed again.

Violet let it do so for what seemed like an interminable length, to see if there was more. Finally Paul went over to the stereo and violently stabbed the OFF button. Violet stood up and slammed her glass on the table so hard it smashed, its contents and chunks of glass flying.

Violet was wide-eyed in disbelief and shock; she was shaking with it. "Those bastards those fuckheads—" the words spit out like scattered buckshot. "I don't believe it. Paul, am I crazy, am I losing my mind, or did that sound like the last five seconds of . . ." Her eyes shot the question at Paul, who nodded in a dazed way. She collapsed on the couch, tears pouring down her face, rough sobs beginning. Paul joined her, holding her tightly. The crying was short-lived, and as Violet began to breathe deeply, she began to stiffen with anger. She drew away from Paul to look at him as she spoke, her tone a question mark.

"Again—this Kate. We're in his last sentence. Together. Why?" Her voice was thick. Violet ached to tell Paul about Kate and Cobb Hill. But hearing the tape erased any remaining ambivalence about finding Kate and talking to her. She was so convinced that Paul would try to stop her that Violet bit her lip hard. Instead she became accusatory in spite of herself.

"Paul, who is Kate? Was Victor seeing her last summer? I don't know why I didn't think to ask you this before. You two were so close those last months. Did you know about her? Did you?"

Paul shrugged. "Maybe. I guess so. I mean, I didn't know her name was Kate. I knew Victor was seeing someone, but he was mysterious about it. I would almost say he was obsessed with her. But toward the end he was brooding, and then overtly changed. He let me know rather vaguely that the relationship was over. That's all I can tell you."

Violet was frustrated. "How the hell is it that everyone knew about this woman but me?"

Paul said, with slight impatience, "Violet, your closeness with Victor is legend. I'm sure everyone assumed you were aware of her. Doesn't that make sense?"

"I suppose." Violet felt she was on the verge of babbling, still shocked by hearing Victor in such a cruel setting. It seemed that the time since she'd returned from Italy had consisted of a series of electric shocks, jerking at her emotional stays.

"Okay, Paul. If the case is so closed and the consensus is that I should just get on with things, what was that nightmare on the street for, and why was that tape forced on me? For God's sake, Paul, it was sadistic."

Paul placed a hand over Violet's forehead as if gauging her temperature, and gently moved it back and forth.

"Actually, I do have a theory about it, and it applies to the shooting in front of Anita's as well. Did you talk to Donald about that?"

"Sure I did, and Donald has a theory, the doorman has a theory, Maria has a theory. What's yours?"

Paul took a deep breath. "You know Max was undercover for Don, right?" Violet nodded. "Victor was working on the same case concerning this drug syndicate. Now . . . the day Victor died you were yelling some rather bold claims about finding out who killed him and what you were going to do to them. You were heard by a lot of people. This may be a metropolis but it's got its small-town side, and word gets around. In this circle you're not exactly unknown as his daughter.

"I'm convinced that these gestures toward you—and as ugly as they are, in their vocabulary they're as common as a note passed between desks in the fifth grade—are simply a matter of scaring you off. The assumption is, you have access to Victor's personal files; the assumption is, you'll go poking around. They got Max, they got Victor, and if you resume a low profile, and give it all up, this will stop. If you don't, there is a possibility they will dispose of you just as easily."

Violet considered all of this for a moment, thinking he was right, that perhaps both she and Don were off-base. But a series of small holes were appearing through this resolve.

"Paul, I've heard all of this before, I don't know if I buy it. If it *is* just a matter of intimidation, if the police know who killed Victor, where did they get this tape?"

"Leimenster," he replied, beginning to sound impatient. "He was part of the group." Paul cupped Violet's face in his hands. "You've been through a horrible time and I'm terribly sorry. Stop fishing. Let Don and the rest continue."

She stared at him, primal, myopic. "Okay" was all she

could manage. But it was an utterance that resembled a stone skipping across water, destined to sink back into the sea it emerged from.

Violet shook her head sharply and stood up. "Please take that piece of filth and get rid of it, take it to Don if you want, I don't want to see it or hear it again." She went out into the kitchen. Paul knew enough to leave her there. He cleaned up the smashed glass, poured another drink for himself, and paced slowly around the room, listening to Violet slam pots and pans and cabinet doors. She was threading her distress in and out of culinary panic, a familiar course of relief; the knives were flying, the wrists frantic.

An hour and a half later Paul sat down to the products of despair, Violet-style: braised endive, the famous heart salad (hearts of lettuce, palm, celery, and artichoke), pasta primavera, and sautéed veal in a reduced Madeira sauce. For the most part Paul pushed his food around on his plate, Violet ate all of hers and some of his. They cleaned the kitchen together in silence, they undressed and showered together—they who had more profoundly become a we that day, an us. They slept entwined, grateful for the dubious peace of sleep.

A few hours later Paul's snoring woke her up. Violet jiggled him until he stopped, noting to herself that this went on the con list in regard to marriage. She lay thinking of the tape, feeling alone and terribly sad. Donald's story made Victor sound isolated in his strange quest after Yardley. She wanted to talk to him about it. She thought again of his panicked and private farewell to herself and Kate; she felt like an invader. The tape made Kate all the more significant. She had to go to her, and that was all there was to it.

Even if she knew nothing that would help Violet solve the murder, it seemed that Kate had been close to Victor during the months before his death, during Violet's time of twilight removal from everything. Contacting Kate would be getting back in touch with Victor during those lost months.

Violet slipped out of bed, threw on a shirt, and wandered into the kitchen. She poured out a cup of coffee, put it in the microwave, simultaneously slammed the door and punched several buttons on it, and stumbled out of the kitchen backwards to the relative safety of the dining room, her forefingers making a sign of the cross. Thus protected she waited for the beep. David had given Violet the machine a year earlier with the hope that it would help get her to work on time, but Violet didn't trust it for a minute. After a certain incident with a lobster, use of the microwave had been limited to reheating coffee.

When the beep sounded, Violet flew back into the kitchen, opened the microwave door, grabbed her coffee, slammed the door, unplugged the machine, and covered it with its usual camouflage of St. Francis tea towels.

She went into the living room and settled into Victor's chair, sipping the coffee and pondering the various options regarding Cobb Hill. At the moment there didn't seem to be any. The structure of the hospital and understandable protectiveness toward its patients simply did not allow simple contact with them. Logical exceptions—a visiting doctor, or some kind of state official—were on a level of subterfuge far more extreme than anything Violet had ever attempted.

Violet wandered back into the kitchen, thinking over the various things Cindy had said about Cobb Hill. In what she thought was an inspired moment, Violet drew the phone toward her on the counter, meaning to call Cindy and ask her to return to Cobb Hill as a patient. They would arm her with information about Kate, and questions to ask if Cindy found her. But Violet knew neither the phone call or her outrageous request would be welcome.

Violet's fingers drummed the counter next to the phone. She considered making Napoleons from scratch, or a few dozen tortellini. Something to occupy her hands and jittery thoughts, and allow room for some true inspiration.

But the idea of Cindy returning to Cobb Hill, impossible as it was, kept creeping back into Violet's mind. Who would have better access to a patient than another patient? There seemed only one clear solution. One that Violet let amble around in her mind until it settled. She picked up the phone and dialed Romaine.

The phone was picked up and banged around, but the voice that finally spoke was not Romaine's.

"Hello?" the voice whispered.

"I must have the wrong number, unless you're Miss Mil—"

"I'm sorry what did you say?"

"Forgive me for disturbing you. Is Romaine around?"

"Yes, of course she is, but she's sleeping. Do you have any idea what time it is?"

"No. Do you want me to go find out?"

The voice on the other end laughed softly. "This must be Violet. Hang on a second."

A moment later Romaine's sleepy voice came on the line.

"Is this your one allotted phone call? Don't you know any other lawyers in New York?"

"Actually I'm working on this new recipe . . ."

Romaine groaned. "Childes, *cut it out.*"

"I'm really sorry I woke you but I couldn't sleep and I had to talk to you." Violet told Romaine about the tape and Victor's mention of Kate. Tears were rolling down her face, but her voice remained steady.

"Violet, that's disgusting," was Romaine's reaction. Violet went on to explain Paul's theory.

"So we're back to finding Kate. I've been up all night thinking about an answer, and I've found one. It's the only effective thing to do. We have to enter me into Cobb Hill as a patient. Then I'll have access to Kate."

"What do you mean *we*? Someday I'm going to tire of playing Ethel to your Lucy."

"So. Until you do—"

"Wait a minute. Not so fast. The other half of the Kate mystery is the initials for the rest of what we think are hospitals. If Victor was working on a case involving something troublesome or illegal at these hospitals, then Cobb Hill is part of that, and you could be in some danger."

"Spoilsport. Let's go back to the focus-on-Kate part. I simply want to talk to her. Forget about the rest. How's this for a scenario—you call up and present yourself as my shrink and say I need therapy in a restful environment—"

"—and we put me on retainer as the permanent straight man for your schemes."

"Just think about it, will you? The sooner we get this thing solved—"

"Okay, okay, I'll think about it, but you need some work on the passive part of your passive-aggressive mode—"

"See what I mean? That's back-of-the-matchbook-trade-school shrink talk if I ever heard it."

"Before you start pandering, I have to go. But because I love you and because you're right, the sooner we get this resolved the better. I'll think this over, and maybe make some calls tomorrow. But, Violet, don't count on this as your next move. Cobb Hill is not a Ramada Inn that you simply check into and ring for ice. And, Vi, some aspects of what you're suggesting have a very tenuous relationship with legality. I do have a code of ethics to—"

"Helping me find Victor's murderer doesn't make you Roy Cohn," Violet interrupted, "but I do respect your position."

"Honey, I just want you to be aware that there are some limitations to what I can do. I'll talk to you tomorrow. I'm hanging up now. Say good-bye."

"Good-bye, Ro darling friend and shrink imperson—"

Romaine hung up at this point. Violet went back to bed, exhausted but feeling slightly better after talking to Romaine.

Not much later but still early in the morning, Paul got up and left, placing a note on the bedside table. Violet woke up at the sound of the front door closing. She noticed the message and read: "I hope last night sunk in, I hope you're finally committed to letting go of this. I love you." Violet put the note down, vowing to show him a thing or two, and fell back to sleep.

13

Violet woke up with a headache, a hangover from the previous day's drama, feeling pressed into a flat slab of malcontent. A certain level of tension had sustained itself so long she was bored with it. She wanted out. A small miracle arrived in the form of a message left on the answering machine, the flashing light ignored by the languishing Violet until she could stand it no longer.

"Ciao, Violetta, this is your betrothed. I know it's not our regular day but I must have lunch with you or expire. One o'clock. Just come. Holiday a must. See you then."

It was the voice of Bernard, her closest friend besides Romaine. "Holiday" referred to their tacit agreement, on occasion, not to mention the controversial or painful, an arrangement of escape. It was just what she needed.

When Violet arrived Bernard was setting the table for lunch. Because they both had the same passionate attitude toward food, they were terribly competitive as cooks. Over the years they had quietly developed a truce; they rarely cooked together, as when they did it posed a threat not only to their relationship, but physical danger to anyone within throwing distance. The game, therefore, was to have the meal basically completed before one or the other arrived. The last time they met Violet made the mistake of not preparing the salad dressing before he walked in. The ensuing argument over the proper amount of Dijon mustard and the use of dried tarragon was so heated and drawn out that they ditched it and went around the corner to eat tabouli. Violet thrust a huge bouquet of gladiolas into the middle of their embrace; one of his favorite flowers, he said they looked more artificial than real plastic. He took the flowers from her smiling, his wide cheeks flushed with the heat of the lunch preparations.

Bernard's appearance was always a combination of the rakish and the formal. His tightly curled black hair often included sprouting strands; his green eyes looked slightly sleepy but never missed a thing. His elegant nose tipped up slightly at the end, and his mouth was beautifully defined. He had the most expressive forehead Violet had ever seen; the changing configuration of lines and articulate eyebrows was impossibly eloquent, and often spoke in contrast to what he was actually saying. He could keep no secrets from her.

He bowed with the flowers in his arms, the pink and red flowers against his black apron, hair and eyes a vibration.

"Sit, sit, these are gorgeous."

Violet complied, sitting at the 1950s white enamel table, set with black linen napkins and pink Fiesta-ware plates.

"For you I have cream of fennel soup, lobster ravioli with black bean sauce, radicchio salad, and pear sorbet. And I hope you appreciate that I will be dining on dry toast and gruel for the rest of the week. This has emptied my wallet and drained my imagination, I won't be able to paint for days. Not that I'm complaining. I love the effect hand-rolling pasta has on my forearms. Nothing in the gym compares with it."

Violet removed her gloves, poured herself a glass of the Orvieto in front of her, noticing the moody jazz piano on the stereo, noticing his slight tremble. She took a deep breath, and suddenly she had the feeling their "holiday" theme was evaporating. "Who is it this time?"

"Is it that obvious?" he said softly, arranging the flowers in a martini pitcher and placing it on the table.

"It was a friend from the health club. No, he wasn't my *homme du moment* either. I've given it all up. I've been seeing Scott again occasionally—you remember him—but most of the time we blow kisses at each other and write wonderfully filthy fantasies and exchange them." He lowered his head and stared at a spot on the table. "It's turned into a nightmare, Vi, it's sick, it's the Catherine wheel that just keeps spinning and spinning and we're all stuck to it, pinned to it like paper dolls.

"Anyway this guy lost his lover last year. He was excruciatingly lonely, not out at work. We used to hang out drinking those God-awful health drinks and talk. We had such different lives it was like two worlds colliding. It happened very quickly, the progression of symptoms I mean, and yesterday he died. The whole community is in a state of mourning. I mean, it's a perpetual wake. It's an abstraction of war where men come home in boxes at a perversely young age—if only they would treat it like that." He looked across at her, eyes filled with tears. "I'm afraid," he said simply. "They're folding up around me like card tables."

Violet pulled her chair next to his and put her arms around him and they both cried. Violet had never been more aware of the threat of losing him. She was frightened, too, and felt her love for him in painful stabs; her chest hurt, she wanted to fold him inside her until it was safe.

Finally Bernard pulled away from her, dabbing at both

their eyes with a corner of his apron. His voice wavered. "You know this whole era is pure Emily, at least that one poem, 'After Great Pain a Formal Feeling Comes.' Do you remember it?" Violet shook her head.

Bernard paused to recall the lines. " 'This is the hour of lead, remembered if outlived, as freezing persons recollect the snow—first chill, then stupor, then the letting go.' "

Violet felt as though she had stepped into a cold spot in a haunted house.

Bernard stood up abruptly, squeezing one of Violet's hands. He served the soup.

Suddenly, from the building next door came a huge wailing, a midday service from a religious group of unknown denomination. The combination of the quiet jazz, the street sounds, and the dubious singing next door was so absurd they both laughed in spite of themselves.

"You're not here five minutes and I break the rules. Eat, and tell me everything, and I mean all of it. Do I have to hear this stuff on 'Nightline'?"

Violet told him absolutely everything, ranging from Milan to her conversation with Donald, and including her decision to take up where Victor left off. They ate while she talked, the food was fragrant and exquisite and soothed them both.

Finally, sorbet in front of them, Bernard responded.

"I know the party line is that you're poised on the edge of some breakdown and that you're endangering yourself." His tone was bitter. "But in my own present state I don't think anyone is safe, so fuck caution. I say go get the little bastard; he's a slimebag anyway. I know this doesn't apply to Victor's search for something to hang him with, but Well-Dyne owns a huge pharmaceutical firm that holds, and is sitting on, patents for two experimental AIDS drugs. They're way behind on testing, but that hasn't stopped them from getting a production setup going to make them, at a cost of two thousand plus a month. Put that in your clippings file—the man is a corporate hydra, the ultimate cliché of business villain. I don't know how he holds on to his image as Mr. Philanthropy, and why the press keeps sucking his weenie. Well, actually I guess we both know why."

At that moment the phone rang; it sounded muffled and

Bernard explained he had hidden it under a pile of pillows on his bed. He went to answer it and returned.

"It was Romaine calling from the corner announcing her arrival. That Diva approach—it's hard to resist."

A few moments later he buzzed her in and threw open the door. Romaine walked in, looking flushed and excited. Bernard and Violet looked at each other, then threw their arms around Romaine in a sandwich hug. They held each other closely, murmured news and vague threats, a cluster of affection.

Parting only slightly, Romaine spoke. "This trio gets me so pumped up I don't know if we should get together more often or less." She placed a hand on her chest, slightly breathless.

"I love you both, but I've got to run." She turned to Violet. "Does he know everything?" Violet nodded. "Well then. I am now your psychologist of the rich, Dr. Anthony, and you are now one Sheila Haverhill, under the weather and over-the-edge, soon to be a new patient at Cobb Hill. I still do not approve, but we have an appointment tomorrow afternoon. This is making me nervous. I'll talk to you about it later, I have a meeting in ten." She narrowed her eyes at Violet. "You owe me a big one, Childes, a big hard one. I'm going to have a ball figuring out just what it will be." Romaine kissed both of them and left so quickly she seemed to dematerialize.

Violet and Bernard discussed the finer details of both their lives while washing the dishes, including the prospect of Violet entering Cobb Hill. Bernard was openly skeptical.

"Vi, usually I'm the one you call flighty, dashing after some wild enterprise. At the moment it's you. You can't just casually impersonate someone, waltz into a well-known institution, one of whose aspects is legal commitment, and play Miss Marple, Lady Detective. It's so implausible it sounds silly, you make it seem like a parlor game. It's not."

Violet nodded aggressively. "I know, I know. You're right. And Romaine is right. But think of everything I've told you so far, realize that my point of view comes from this weird shaken place. At one point my life was very clear, now it's a bunch of abstracts. Victor's death started pulling a thread that just keeps unraveling. The result is, I feel like I have nothing to lose.

"I was thinking about all this last night before I called Romaine. So I get caught trying to impersonate a patient, so I get caught trying to find Kate. So what? That's all I kept coming up with. Trouble? So what? I know it sounds crazy, and it's not the healthiest thing in the world or the wisest. Be my guest. Call me reckless and I'll agree."

"You're being exceedingly reckless."

"I agree. Okay?"

Bernard decided to park the subject for the moment, and moved on to a subject that was more controversial, but safer to discuss. Paul.

"You know the odd thing is, as far as this damn disease goes, I'm in the most vulnerable group, while you, you dyed-in-the-wool dyke, are in the least vulnerable, except, of course, for this recent journey into the, shall we say, straight and narrow—or are you more comfortable with 'revoltingly conventional'?"

Violet scowled in exaggerated defense. Bernard continued. "As far as I'm concerned you've been gay since birth, but you have this passionate insistence on the anachronistic, ergo, Paul." He threw out his arms, palms up, and shrugged.

"Well, you're right about one thing. Paul is very much the opposite of everything I know and am attracted to, but that's part of his appeal. And I do have serious questions about the whole thing. It was a chance meeting. It's turned into something else. And you're just jealous, and if you want help with the dishes, you'd better shut up."

"I just want you to be happy, and Paul is still a question mark—"

Violet was staring over his shoulder out the window.

"What are you looking at? You're not paying attention."

She pointed. Bernard screamed. It was snowing, which was one of Bernard's favorite world events besides sex.

Violet agreed with his sentiment. She thought snow in Manhattan scraped against the miraculous, with obvious magical properties capable of the instant covering of the city's residual grime, throwing up a cottony screen that filtered out the dinginess. The snow-veil damped down the usual roar, made everyday sounds seem arcane. It capped the streetlights, it took the razor edge off the buildings, blanketing their angles into curves. The sky dropped down, the air was coldly sweet; the feeling was one of containment, the city felt like a big snowy room filled with murmurs. The big, visual slam was diffused into a subtle diorama.

Bernard whipped off his apron and tossed it on the table.

"Forget the dishes, there's only one thing to do."

"And what would that be?"

"What else—shop."

And they did. The flakes were huge and wet; Bernard's first purchase was a large garish scarf, an Indian print, from a street vendor. They held it above themselves umbrella-style; it streamed out behind them, ballooning in the cold breeze. Underneath it they were a cult of two. They enjoyed the snow in silence for several moments.

"Vi, why don't you dump that old rag and marry me. Every day I will kiss your fingers and read from Simone Weil and we will bake pear tarts and shop and kick people in the street who are mean to their children. I'm sure that dreary old thing has never even heard of Simone Weil."

"It may be news to you, but a lot of people have never heard of Simone Weil, fool. And Paul is not the slightest bit dreary. Maybe if you spent some time getting to know him . . . What do you mean bake pear tarts? If we lived together we would have to eat every meal out and you know very well why. I would probably die of monosodium glutamate poisoning. Besides," she slowed her gait at the thought of it, the scarf swirling down around them, "you know I want to have a child, maybe several." The words seemed to surprise both of them.

Their vision blocked, the ensemble smacked into a pole and stopped entirely, forcing rearrangement of their tent. Bernard considered what Violet said as he raised the scarf around them again.

"We could adopt. We could eat Stouffer's or canned vegetables. Or," he lowered his voice into a seductive tone, "maybe I should spend more time with Monsieur Renault." He batted his eyelashes. "You know—protective brother interviews prospective groom. I'm convinced once you delve into matrimony I'll never see you again. I'll be reduced to Uncle

Bernard at Thanksgiving, doing card tricks for little Paul, an aging spinster, nothing but a name on your Christmas card list. I'll die of boredom from safe sex and lack of Violet."

Violet gave an exaggerated sigh and drew closer to him. "And I thought Tallulah was deceased. You know how much I love you, we'll never be far apart, and I take back what I said about you spending time with him. You keep your liquid green eyes off him. You could turn Clint Eastwood into a fairy." She pulled him into a hug.

"So stop whining. Let's shop." And the spectacle moved off. Bernard bought three pairs of shoes for his impending trip to Bali, grant-provided, and Violet bought him the tackiest St. Christopher's medal she could find. They gathered numerous amounts of Americanized items Bernard was convinced he wouldn't find abroad, and when they could carry no more they dragged it all back to Bernard's. As she got ready to leave Violet grabbed him up in one last hug.

"Now, Violet, I want you to be careful about this revenge business, this vendetta—"

"Who said anything about a vendetta? I want the thing arrested, that's all. I want to kick him in the nuts. Did I say anything about revenge?"

Bernard leaned forward and narrowed his eyes, imitating Vincent Price. "Beneath the civilized skin, under the sheerest sheathing of temperance, looms in us all the hoary primordial, the bestial, the base, the instinct to steal, to cover your neighbor's loins, even to kill."

Violet laughed. "What is this cover your neighbor's loins bit?"

"Lust."

"It sounds more like gardening."

"Seriously, Vi, maybe I shouldn't be leaving the country with all of this going on. Maybe I should postpone."

She shook her head vehemently. "Forget it. You'd lose the fellowship if you did. I'll be fine except for missing you."

He kissed both of her cheeks tenderly. "Same here. Just be careful. Now go, I despise good-byes."

"Me too. Don't forget your money belt, and your dental floss"—he was pushing her out the door—"and your decongestant, and don't get your head turned by some Balinese dancer and miss my wedding."

He pressed the scarf into her hands and waved her down the hall. "I won't, I promise. So long." He waved.

"*Addio.*" Elated with their afternoon, she turned and ran down the stairs to avoid the impending emotional display.

Once inside her apartment the buoyancy faded slightly; the obscenity of the tape and its message had lingered, the rooms felt alien to her. Violet called Paul who wasn't home, and left a message on his machine. She called Romaine who wasn't home either, but she knew where to locate her.

Anita's on Sunday could be found in alternate moods. Some weekends it was still jumping until last call, patrons wringing the last vestige of community before returning to the masks they wore at work; other weekends it was quiet and introspective, the way Sunday nights are. Tonight it was peaceful, which Violet welcomed. She sat at the bar for a while, gossiping with the bartender, gathering herself before looking for Romaine. Twenty minutes later Romaine appeared out of the back room in search of change for the pool table, spotted Violet, and slipped into the seat next to her.

"Hi, sweetie. Are you becoming a regular again?"

Violet nodded her head. "Why not? You think my husband-to-be doesn't indulge in cronyism on his own time? So, where is she? I came over to spy on you."

"I haven't been that mysterious. Just say the word and we'll all have lunch together."

"Where is she now?"

"At home."

"With her husband?" Violet guessed.

"Well, yes, if you must know."

"Mm-hmm, I thought as much." She wagged a finger at her. "You know what my radio shrink says about these kinds of relationships, the safety of the impossible . . ."

"Does she explain mutual attraction? Head over heels? Fate?"

"Well, as a matter of fact—"

"Never mind, I don't want to hear it."

"Then how about Cobb Hill details?"

"Absolutely. I spoke to a Dr. Shelby, who was very reluctant to waive the usual procedure, which calls for two meetings with the prospective patient, one with the patient, their attending psychologist, and Dr. Shelby. However, after a lengthy conversation, coupled with the fact that I was unfazed by the fee, he offered a hearty invitation."

"I continue to be amazed at your array of talents. Please go on."

"Thank you. He requested a preliminary meeting before actually entering you into Cobb Hill; a combination of the two meetings that are the customary process. I explained that I felt your level of anxiety and emotional discomfort were so extreme that I wanted you in a situation where you could be properly monitored. He agreed to admit you contingent upon a lengthy interview between the three of us."

"That's it?"

"That's it. I rented a car, and I suggest we leave by midmorning. On the way up we can discuss what our exact approach should be."

Violet was silent for a moment. The proximity of the trip made the fantasy aspect of the whole charade suddenly evaporate. She stood up. "I guess I'd better go pack and practice hyperactive mumbling," she said with a falsely casual air.

Romaine joined Violet with her own bravado. "What practice? I'd better get back to the pool table. Do you want to join?"

"No thanks, not that I wouldn't mind dethroning you. Speaking of which, maybe you shouldn't be the last one to leave for a change, since you're playing chauffeur."

"I will, there isn't the usual impetus to stay late anyway."

"Clearly. We're going to have a little chat about this."

"Listen baby, if you're going to go around marrying men, my affairs are out of reach of your comment, and furthermore—"

"And furthermore I'm leaving."

On the way home Violet tried to think of some reasonable tale to give Paul. She was still ruminating as she entered the apartment; the phone was ringing and she was unprepared but she answered it anyway, anticipating correctly that it was Paul.

"Hi, Chuck. What's the password?"

"Umm, ribald? Transcendentalism? *De rigueur*?"

"That's it. Speak."

"How did you know it was me?"

"You have a very masculine ring."

"I should hope so. By the way, what in hell is a 'chuck'?"

Violet laughed. "We really shouldn't call you that, it's a leftover homegirl word. It's the generic term for man."

"Sounds highly insulting."

"Usually it is, but I say it with affection. Besides, there is nothing remotely generic about you."

"Thank you for noticing. I called because I have to go to Chicago tomorrow on business, and thought perhaps you would like to go with me. Get out of town for a few days, hang out at some blues clubs. What do you think? Also, I don't like the idea of leaving you alone with everything that's going on."

The coincidence was too much, it was too easy. It panicked her. Sure, now she could slip off to Cobb Hill, he would never know. She could be tortured and killed by a mad psychologist and Paul would never know. It felt like bad luck, from a karmic point of view. Violet stopped talking to herself and returned her concentration to Paul.

"Paul, I would love to go with you, I really would. But we have such a heavy workload this week, and I've been gone for so long already I just can't let David down." ("And I want to present you with Kate and a signed confession from Victor's real killer," she wanted to add.)

Paul sounded annoyed. "I shouldn't have sounded so casual about this. Actually, it's a very important trip. It could affect our future radically."

"Aren't you being a little pushy? And do you think you could explain somewhat? Exactly how it affects our future, for instance? And is this the McKinley deal by any chance?"

"I'll tell you when we get there."

"Oh, is that an order?"

Paul's response was to slam down the phone. Violet replaced the receiver and waited. The phone rang.

"I'm sorry I pressured you. I guess I'm moving a little too quickly. I'll probably be in meetings the whole time anyway. Just remember we have to have a long talk when I get back. Shall I come over so we can spend our last night together?"

"I would love to see you, but I'm half-asleep as we speak. You'll just have to spend some time in abject longing. It will be good for you."

"Not even a good-bye kiss?"

"Not even. Have a good trip."

"Thanks. Take care of yourself. The office knows where you can reach me. Bye."

"Good night."

Violet hung up the phone with relief mixed with fear at how he would respond when he found out the truth. She was too tired to think about it. She skipped packing, undressed, and flopped into bed, mercifully exhausted past worry, and dreamed of Savannah.

14

The next morning presented itself all too quickly. When the front door buzzer sounded, Violet jumped. She let Romaine in, and waved her toward the kitchen for coffee, returning to her bedroom while continuing a sentence begun before Romaine's arrival.

"Ro, do I take neurotic-rich-girl clothes or will I have to wear some horrible standard-issue hospital garb? You know how I look in green. I don't think I can go through with this," Violet shouted toward the kitchen.

"Do calm down," was the loud reply, "and you might have to get out of that place in a hell of a hurry, *sans* wardrobe, so stop packing for Rio."

Violet finished packing, attempting to control her usual excess. She tucked into place her minimal investigative gear, which included a small high-intensity flashlight, Victor's lock-picking ensemble, a Minox camera, a small roll of bills, and an unloaded, "ladies design" chrome-plated pistol, which looked as harmless as a cigarette lighter.

Violet was rattling with the anticipation of finding Kate. Her more external mood was bouncing around the edges of hysteria, but somewhere near the core was a straight line to Kate that she was reeling in.

When Romaine returned to the bedroom, Violet was snapping her suitcase shut. Romaine stopped in the middle of the room, striking a runway pose.

"So, have I got the part right? *Recherché* shrink to the rich?"

Romaine was wearing a triangular hat, a two-piece Claude Montana suit, pumps, clutch, and lipstick all in the same shade of fire-engine red. Against her dark brown skin the effect was stunning. Violet and Romaine shared the same basic attitude toward fashion, which was kind of a war-whoop: part backlash, after years of politically correct unshaven legs and sexless uniforms, now simply a matter of choice rather than statement, and a renegade sense of the exuberant that answered to no one. Or as Romaine described it, "You'll get hit on no matter what you wear, you might as well have fun with it."

Violet grinned at the outfit in approval. "You look good enough to eat, as they say."

"Oh, is that what they say," Romaine dead-panned.

"Yes, and I wish we were running away from home or going on our honeymoon instead of this little subterfuge."

"Sure you do, you little traitor. Let's go."

They were silent for a long time, as Romaine steered them out of the city and onto the thruway. Violet, listening to a Miles Davis tape cranked up loud, window down in spite of the cold, head cocked toward the sun, reveled in the movement, the rush of visual change from the city.

She closed her eyes, envisioning a scene to replace the city's pall of winter greys. They wound up through the landscape on Route 8, the road a single wavering grey line through bright green, crayon green, lime green, the phosphorous green of late spring. The hills were punctuated by cows, mottled statues that never looked quite real. Violet opened her eyes. The wishful thinking evaporated: the trees were silver grey, the snow on the hills was melted in patches, the cows looked impatient. After all, it was February.

• • •

They stopped for lunch at a tavern. Fortified by several Genessee ales, Violet and Romaine discussed what approach they would take with the admitting doctor, the odds of finding Kate, and the option of driving to Montreal instead.

"What are you going to do when you see her, just ask questions, kidnap her, what?"

"I really don't know. I've simply got to make contact with her, that's all there is to it. I'll figure something out then."

They sat silently, their silence acknowledging a madcap scheme made real. They were both becoming tense with a more formal anticipation of what was to come.

It was clear to Violet that Romaine wanted very much to voice a final objection to the upcoming escapade, and was wondering if their plan would help Violet or endanger her, but Violet knew that in observing her determined air, Romaine realized that she had become resigned to Violet's resignation.

Forty minutes later they arrived at the gates of Cobb Hill. Violet, with the last vestige of panicked stage fright showing, shouted, "HEATHCLIFF!" out of the window while Romaine tried to shut her up before someone heard.

The estate rested on the crest of the so-named hill; except for an electrified fence that contained the buildings in a large circumference, the grounds looked like an old country manor, sedate and innocuous. The main building was a huge white Greek revival affair, with several buildings stretching out behind it that were clearly more recently built. Romaine gave their fake names at the gatehouse, and they drove up to the main house.

"Violet, I know the undercover concept tickles you to death, but if it's going to work you have to play it with a little restraint, okay?"

"You mean like that outfit you're wearing?"

"No. I mean take it seriously."

They entered into a majestic front hall, so classically appointed there were no indications of a psychiatric facility, or hospital of any kind. Beneath them were black-and-white marble tiles stretching out like a wide, cold carpet. To the right, Corinthian columns framed the entrance to a room off the hall. Ahead was a sweep of black marble stairs and a sumptuous Art Nouveau railing curving up beside it.

In the center of the hall was a long, heavy wooden table, topped with a huge cut crystal vase of dahlias. Next to the vase was a long silver tray filled with mail.

Music drifted around them, an opera that would have sounded strident at full volume, but was turned down so low that the emphatic voices were reduced; they sounded like cries for help behind thick stone walls.

The room was so atmospheric—eclectic antebellum with no faux or trompe in sight—that it hushed Violet and Romaine into a moment of observation.

Standing next to the table was a woman sorting through the mail, her wine-colored fingernails flashing against the white rectangles. She was wearing a dark red skirt and blazer, and a black silk blouse; her low-heeled shoes were a jarring shade off from the other winey reds. Violet studied her face: large, deeply set purple-brown eyes, a wide, flattish nose, thick and sensuous lips shining in still another tone of dark red, and high, wide cheekbones that gently pulled the contours of her face out and rounded them. It was a strong face, thought Violet, the components beautiful in an Indian way, an Aztec way. But as a whole her face was uncomfortably taut, oppressed by some unseen force. This appearance was compounded by the presence of fear, clear bright sparks of it in her eyes, and was further emphasized by the frantic movements of the brown hands leaping through the pile of mail.

The woman was tipped forward at the waist in a tense angle, her entire countenance so haunted and painful that Violet hoped the dreaded piece of mail would not be found. The moment was gathering itself into some significance that Romaine and Violet did not understand but were transfixed by. At that point the music swelled in an exaggerated minor chord, the chorus followed, muted by the low volume into a plaintive hum. The small cluster of sounds were enough to push the woman next to the table into a more present state of awareness. She turned her head and saw Violet and Romaine. For a split second, her eyes having collided with Violet's, the woman look trapped and exposed. During the next moment, in what Violet throught was an extraordinary act of will, the woman drew in a slight breath, casually placed the mail back on the tray, and straightened into a standing position. The eyes with slightly heavy lids blinked once at Violet, then changed into a rehearsed and measured opacity, smooth professional cataracts dropping into place.

"I'm sorry, I didn't hear you come in," she said in even tones, with a Spanish accent so slight its effect was merely to soften the edges of her words. In the given atmosphere the innocuous sentence startled Romaine and Violet, and their shoulders jostled together in surprise.

Romaine began to reply, when a door opened on the left side of the hall, and a man and woman emerged in mid-conversation. It stopped as the man saw Romaine and Violet.

"Ah," he said, "so you have arrived after all. I'm Dr. Shelby." As he walked toward Romaine and Violet, Romaine stepped forward and extended her hand to the doctor. "Hello, I'm Dr. Anthony, and this is Sheila Haverhill." Dr. Shelby shook her hand firmly, then turned his attention to Violet, who smiled nervously, shook his hand, and openly looked at him in an appraising glance.

He was of medium height, only slightly taller than Violet. His coloring was very pale, his skin lightly freckled, his eyes light blue. His face was impassive and his voice deep; this in contrast to his generally boyish looks, which were helped along by bright red hair.

"Won't you join me in my office?" he said in response to Violet's close observation. He turned to lead the way, then stopped. "I see you have already met Nurse Vincent."

"Actually no, I'm afraid not," said Romaine.

"I see," said Dr. Shelby, sending a look of disapproval in the direction of the nurse, who had remained standing next to the table. "Well, ladies, this is Theresa Vincent. She is our head psychiatric nurse, and is in charge of the section of the hospital Sheila will be a part of, if things work out that way." Nurse Vincent nodded at the two women.

"Nurse Vincent, we'll go to my office now and get started. I'll call for you in a few minutes." The doctor turned away from her abruptly, and Romaine and Violet followed him through an outer office and into his own. He closed the door behind them.

He gestured toward two chairs placed in front of a desk.

"Please sit down and make yourselves comfortable," he said, moving behind his desk and seating himself. As Violet took her seat she looked around at the layout of the room, observing the arrangements of file cabinets, the direction the windows faced. But her attention was drawn back almost immediately to the doctor, who was addressing her.

"It's a pleasure to meet you, Sheila. Are you of the Shaker Heights Haverhills, by any chance?"

Violet snorted. "Are you kidding? Actually it's the Fargo Haverhills, formerly the New Orleans Haverhills, originally the Tempest-on-the-Thames Haverhills. How's the food here?"

Dr. Shelby ignored this, continuing to address his remarks to Violet. "Before we get started, I want to point out that this is a rather unusual circumstance. Normally, procedure for entering Cobb Hill includes several lengthy consultative sessions with both the patient and the attending psychologist, and a more formal assessment of the patient's condition and needs, in order to design an effective course of treatment.

"However, Dr. Anthony has convinced me that you would benefit most by some immediate attention, some rest, and a short stay here. Sheila, would you please tell me how you are feeling?"

Violet glared at him.

"I'm on edge, I'm a woman on edge. I can't eat, I can't sleep, and when my boyfriend touches me I scream. I'm losing in the stockmarket, my hair has stopped growing, and I can't remember anyone's birthday. I must say you have the strangest shade of hair I've ever seen. Remind me to give you the name of my stylist. At least you could get a more professional dye job. How's the food here?" Violet surprised herself with the shrill speech, whose tone played very close to how she actually felt. She picked up a magazine and started thumbing through it.

Romaine shook her head. "As you can see, Doctor, Sheila is rather wound up, even slightly hysterical, and her lifestyle only encourages this. We've agreed that Sheila needs an extended rest, removed from her frantic surroundings, and the opportunity to focus on her problems with counseling and therapy."

Violet rolled her eyes and dropped the magazine in her lap.

"Yes, Dr. Shelby, the exigencies of urban stress place me in your hands. It's not easy being rich and beautiful and hounded. I need a rest. I'm a fugitive from modern life, a cat on a hot tin roof, Porgy without Bess, the dark at the top of the stairs. How's the food here?" Romaine pulled on one of her earlobes, an old sign between them that Violet was about to go too far. Violet read the signal, crossed her legs, and visibly calmed herself.

"I'm sorry, Dr. Shelby," she said demurely, "I guess it's the relief of admitting I'm feeling out of control. Is that better, Dr. A? I wouldn't want to embarrass you."

"Yes, thank you, Sheila," said Romaine, attempting a covert glare. Dr. Shelby looked somewhat dumbfounded by Violet's performance. "Sheila, I'd like to take a few moments to describe the basic structure of Cobb Hill. Do you mind if I smoke?"

"Smoke? I'd love to," said Violet. "Will I be allowed to smoke here?" Dr. Shelby produced two cigarettes, handed one to Violet, and lit each.

"Yes, Sheila," replied the doctor patiently, and continued in a patronizing tone. "Now, as I was about to say, Cobb Hill is a private hospital, a facility for women only, which was stipulated in the rather strict outlay of the original endowment. The founder of the hospital had a manic-depressive wife who, after many unsuccessful attempts, finally took her own life. In response to his grief, he started a small research group whose focus was on treatments for depression. This house was his personal residence.

"Over the years the hospital has changed hands many times. In its present incarnation, it is an unusual institution and one we think eminently worthwhile. The charter continues to stipulate treatment for women only, and still centers its research attention on depression.

"The hospital is divided into two sections. The first, and the part of the facility you will be involved in if you wish, includes up to thirty patients who are much like you, Sheila— no severe clinical problems, women who seek a retreat or sanctuary within the context of therapy. Group therapy is optional but highly attended, and each woman spends an hour a day with myself or one of the other doctors. The women reside in this building, in suites on the second and third floors. This building also includes a small wing devoted to medical and therapeutical rooms, a dining room, and on the lower level is a swimming pool and exercise room.

"A corridor leads from the pool to the newer buildings behind us, which is where the research section of the hospital is located. The women who reside there are a voluntary control group of chronically depressed patients who are being treated experimentally. They come to us as a last resort. These patients allow us to run many monitoring tests, and experiment with diet, therapy, and medication.

"Thus far we have gathered a lot of data on the treatment of depression through this research department, out of which we fully expect to produce some landmark breakthroughs in treatment." Dr. Shelby leaned back in his chair slightly, folding his hands together on top of the desk.

"Do you have any questions?" He addressed himself to both Romaine and Violet.

"Well," said Violet brightly, "that was a wonderful speech. It would make a lovely brochure. TV?"

"Yes, each room has a television, and we also screen movies quite often."

"And I won't have to hang around with the real loonies?"

"No, Sheila, the more seriously troubled patients are quite separate."

"And the food, Dr. Shelby?"

"We have a sophisticated chef who appreciates the tastes of the guests here. And if you don't agree, you may order whatever you wish."

Violet sighed contentedly. "Well, thank God for that."

"Now," said Dr. Shelby dismissively, "I'll go speak to Nurse Vincent about your accommodations and have your bags brought in. I suggest you spend a relaxing afternoon and evening getting oriented here, and in the morning we will discuss an approach to making your stay here worthwhile. Upon deciding to stay, there are some simple forms to fill out, and each entering patient receives a complete physical examination . . . Dr. Anthony, I assume you would like a few minutes with Sheila before you go."

Romaine nodded. "Yes. And thank you for suspending your usual format for us."

"Not at all," he replied. "Actually, before I leave you, Dr. Anthony, do you have the material I asked you to bring?"

Romaine pulled a manila envelope out of her purse. "I believe I have what you requested. My summarized comments on Sheila's progress in therapy, a statement concerning her present condition, and a list of medications used in her treatment within the last year. I also have a cashier's check for the amount of the first week of Sheila's stay here, with the understanding that if you and Sheila decide she will remain for a month or more, she will give you the balance of a month's fees. Is that correct?"

"Yes, thank you, you've been most thorough," he replied, taking the envelope from her and leaving the room, closing the door behind him.

It was barely closed when Romaine spoke.

"Jesus, Violet, what are you up to? You're supposed to attract as little attention as possible, instead you come on like Judy Holliday playing a refugee from Bayside, Queens," she hissed.

Violet unsuccessfully tried to suppress a burst of laughter. "I'm sorry, I really am. I'm nervous, I'm scared to death. It will take all of one day to figure out if Kate is on this side. What if she's in research?"

"I know, it's a big risk. Should we leave?"

"God no. I have to follow this through. And by the way, you read the fake reports to me, but what is this list of medication stuff?"

Romaine smiled. "Not to worry. It's a short list, in fact it's comprised of Valium and calcium carbonate in therapeutic amounts. Okay?"

Violet nodded in awe. "You've really covered it all. I think we're going to pull this off."

Romaine looked at her sternly. "It gets more difficult from here. You'll be on your own. But, I know better than to try to talk you out of it, so for the moment I'll stick to the plan. The car will be at the train station, which is two miles down the road. For God's sake, remember to turn right past the gate if you have to do it this way. The keys and money will be under the seat. I'll take the train back to town and hold my breath until you call. Please—be careful." Romaine hugged Violet hard, and opened the door.

They walked into the outer office, where Dr. Shelby was talking quietly with Nurse Vincent. Violet was impressed once again with her haunted look. Violet smiled shyly at her, but the nurse regarded Violet with the same cool mask she had affected earlier, her bruised-brown eyes yielding nothing. Violet wondered if this was a reaction to their dramatic first meeting.

Dr. Shelby placed a hand on Violet's arm, which broke her gaze of contemplation. "Sheila, Nurse Vincent will show you to your room now and help you get settled in. And please ask her assistance for anything you need."

Nurse Vincent turned and started out of the office. Violet followed her obediently, with a final panicked look of longing toward Romaine. She felt infantilized; suddenly it was the first day at a strange school.

As they ascended the stairs, Violet felt stirrings of frustration. It was important to make contacts and friends as soon as possible, but Nurse Vincent was clearly not a candidate.

The second floor was a huge wide hall flanked with massive doors, side tables, and weak pastoral paintings. Violet denounced all paintings or art objects that she didn't totally adore as Motel Art. These qualified. The nurse led Violet down near the end of the hall and unlocked a door; Violet followed her inside.

"Oh, how lovely, it looks like a showroom at Bloomingdale's," she said brightly to the nurse. "Or is this the Laura Ashley memorial suite?"

"Is there something here you don't like?" said Nurse Vincent defensively.

"Not at all, I think it's divine."

The room was filled with pattern upon pattern, from the spread on the fourposter bed, to the curtains, wallpaper, and upholstery, each of them different though all decidedly floral. It occurred to Violet that the sum total was enough to invoke a fit of schizophrenia in the most stable of patients. Nurse Vincent showed her the closets and bath, announced that dinner was in half an hour, and left. Violet unpacked, washed, and reapplied her makeup.

As Violet left her room she heard soft musical chimes that sounded like a phrase from *Kismet*. She decided that this meant dinner and after looking around the second floor for a few moments she wandered downstairs in search of the dining room. Down a long hall at a right angle to the staircase Violet heard a familiar refrain from *South Pacific* softly emerging from a room at the end of the hall. Violet followed the music into a large, softly lit dining room. Portraits hung symmetrically on walls framed by elaborate molding; the pale blue tablecloths, and the chandelier and candles all reminded Violet of one of Paul's favorite pretentious restaurants. She felt a wave of affection for him, coupled with a pang of guilt for lying.

Violet counted eleven women scattered at four of the many tables. Nurse Vincent walked up to her.

"If you'll follow me, I'll show you to your table," she said, and led Violet to the nearest one, at which two women were already seated, and had been served their dinner.

"Ladies, this is Sheila, who just arrived today. We use only first names here, Sheila, but any other personal information our patients exchange is up to you . . . Barbara, and Jacqueline," said the nurse, nodding toward each of the two seated women.

Violet gave them her most polite smile and took a deep breath. She was nervously excited, intrigued; she hoped she would have better luck with her dining companions than she had had so far with Nurse Vincent.

"Hello, it's nice to meet you both. Is the food as good as Dr. Shelby claims?" She sat down, the two women smiling politely.

"Yes, as a matter of fact, it is," said Barbara in a cheerful voice. She had long, burnt-auburn hair, and eyes that were close-set and luminous green; she was wearing a multicolored caftan in muted tones and, resting in the middle of her cleavage, a very large tourmaline crystal. She appeared to be in her late forties. She smiled broadly.

Jacqueline had bright blonde hair not quite successfully swept up into a chignon, high Hepburn cheeks that were lightly rouged, deep brown, mournful eyes, and she wore a black Trigère dress with the requisite string of pearls.

Violet was dying to see their shoes.

Barbara continued. "The chef here does some amazing things—you wouldn't believe what he does with tofu. They have a complete vegetarian menu, the only place I've done time in that does."

Violet relaxed and poured herself some white wine from the carafe next to her. As she lifted the glass to try some Barbara's face grimaced in a disdainful expression. "Ugh, watch out, that's some of the worst nonalcoholic so-called wine I have ever had the misfortune to drink. I don't know why they won't give us the real thing. *I'm* not on medication."

Violet took a sip, wrinkled her nose, and nodded in agreement. She looked around at the other women in the room, then addressed her dining companions.

"I have no idea how much anyone here keeps to themselves, and I certainly don't want to step on any toes, but what are you in for?" Violet looked directly at Jacqueline as she spoke, who looked as though she was going to choke on her trout almandine. Jacqueline gave Violet a tight hyphen of a smile, took a deep breath, and spoke as if in a slight trance, or reciting an often repeated and dull schoolroom lesson.

Violet was tense with curiosity, leaning forward in her chair in alert anticipation of learning whatever she could from the two women.

"I live in Greenwich with my husband, Trip, and two perfect sons, three Great Danes, and a Shih Tzu, in a large stone mansion with twenty-four rooms, eight with fireplaces. We have a view of the Sound and a large imported household staff. My husband is the head of a multinational corporation of which I know nothing except that one of their subsidiaries manufactures croutons. We use them ourselves. One of my sons is at Yale, the other at Princeton. I design immense dinner parties for our business friends, I am on the boards of countless charities, I attend the largest Episcopal church, I take French, painting, gardening, I summer on Nantucket and winter on St. Bart's, my breasts have been lifted, no one in my house speaks English, and the Valium doesn't work anymore." Her eyes were glazed, with tears or medication Violet could not discern, and the woman looked quite emptily at her.

Violet was shocked at the speech. This was way out of

her league, and, characteristically, her heart went out to Jacqueline. She could think of no appropriate reply and glanced at Barbara, who looked distinctly unimpressed.

"And you, Barbara, how did you end up in here?"

She shook her head. "It's just a misunderstanding. I'm a channeler. Do you know what that is? I connect to people's past lives. You see, there's this large pool of light, and in the middle of it, well, it's like Grand Central Station, all the people who ever lived hang out there. I can pick out which ones you used to be. A lot of people can do it.

"The problem is I channel through my G-spot. You know there really is one, it's just a myth that there isn't. So anyway, I make my connection to the other place while I'm having an orgasm. Bob, that's my husband, seems to have a problem with this. I mean, it does call for intimate contact with the client, but I consider it a public service. So he strongly suggested I check in here, to talk to the doctors and make sure I'm not a nympho. Isn't that ridiculous? Bob just isn't evolved, that's all, he doesn't get visualization, and he totally rejects the idea that you can *think peace*. I left him a lot of books to read on the subject while I'm gone. I told him he should take a course at New Light Waves. Both of you should, too." She looked at the two of them in a guileless challenge.

Violet needed a drink. She shrugged and smiled at Barbara, then looked across at Jacqueline, who was grinning at her conspiratorily. Violet lit a Gauloise and leaned back in her chair.

"I know I'm being outrageously direct, but my arrival here was so sudden I'm rather disoriented. Would you mind if I ask you a couple of questions, so I can get more of a feeling for Cobb Hill?"

Both women nodded their heads.

"How much contact do you have with the other patients?"

"Thank God, we hardly see them at all," replied Barbara. "You might run into them down at the pool. Of course, I wouldn't consider sticking one toe in that primeval fish tank. God knows what one could contract in there."

"So you never talk to the patients outside of this group?"

"God no, whatever for? They quite discourage it anyway."

Violet frowned. "Would you mind telling me the names of the other women here?"

"Not at all," said Jacqueline. "The four at the table in the back are Maggie, Joan, Elizabeth, and Tricia. The three at the table in the middle are Jennifer, Pony, and Felicia. The two closest to us are Kathryn and Pamela."

Violet snapped to attention, but kept her tone casual.

"Kathryn looks slightly familiar. Do they call her Kate?"

Barbara laughed sarcastically. "No, certainly not. Besides, her name isn't Kathryn, it's Pippi, but she has some fixation with a historical character. Do you suppose it's Catherine the Great or St. Catherine of Siena?" Barbara and Jacqueline laughed, but Violet's heart was sinking. She was afraid of this, that Kate would not be in the most accessible group. After further small talk and more chimes, the women left the dining hall and proceeded to an equally large living room with an enormous TV screen at one end. After some heated discussion the women chose a videotape of *Funny Girl*, and Violet was beginning to feel that she was in a home for unbalanced musical-comedy addicts. She excused herself promptly, after telling the mournful-looking Jacqueline to stop by her room anytime.

Reensconced in her room, Violet was rapidly becoming depressed, convinced if she stayed there one minute more than necessary she would become a depressive herself. Torn between taking the longer and more conservative route, or creating a more dramatic course of action, she was trying to determine options when she heard a soft knock on the door.

"Come on in," Violet called out.

It was Jacqueline, looking rather timid. Violet, needing the time to think, felt somewhat irritated at her arrival; she forced herself to switch gears.

"I hope you don't mind, you did offer, and I couldn't face that group of mannequins tonight."

"I'm glad you took me seriously, I did mean it. Sit down." Violet lit a Dunhill and sat down. It was Jacqueline who spoke first.

"You don't belong here, do you? You're not one of us . . ."

Violet was startled. "What do you mean?"

"Look, Sheila, I'm depressed, not stupid. You are as far

away from these holograms as you can get." Jacqueline sighed and relaxed into the chair, closing her eyes. Violet looked at her intently, impressed by her demeanor.

"It seems to me so are you. Why do you keep playing the game?"

"Because I don't know any other. At least I speak this language, I know the rules of my suburban life by heart. Sometimes I just get sick of playing by them, the gauze unwinds a bit, and I end up here or someplace like it. This is just another part of the dog run, just a little ways off from the kennel. A little rest and a few tranquilizers, a reminder that I have no place to go but back, and I return home and plan another party."

"Why do you say you have no place to go? Why don't you just break away, quit, vamoose?"

"It's not that easy. I don't mean to be flip about it. Actually I have a recurring and debilitating cycle of depression that at its lowest point causes extraordinary despair. Once inside you think why not jump, or swallow the pills, or drink yourself to death. You can't discern that this phase of darkness has an opening or an end. It's a very scary feeling, and I'm on intimate terms with it. They haven't come up with a combination of medications that work for more than a few months at a time." She looked at Violet wistfully.

"The worst of it is I see that darkness as safe, as release, as a form of peace, which isn't exactly the best form of determent." She laughed ruefully. "Enough. Besides your not being one of the regulars, I meant that I don't think you're here for treatment. I've been to a lot of these places, some of them country clubs like this one, some more clinical. There is a lot of questionable stuff going on, ripe for exposure from some determined undercover journalist. Like you. Am I right?"

Violet was unnerved. "Actually, I am here under false pretenses, but if I couldn't convince you, I won't last long. Am I really that transparent?"

"Probably not. I've spent so much time hospitalized, there is very little to do but study people. It's a very exposing and vulnerable situation for a person to be in. So don't worry. Why are you here?"

Violet decided to trust her. "I'm looking for someone. And my name is Violet."

"Call me Jackie, okay?"

"Okay." Violet smiled. "Actually, references to less than perfect practices could be very pertinent to my situation."

"Now you sound like a detective," Jackie said teasingly.

"Well, I guess in this case I am. Can you tell me what goes on, or would you rather not discuss it?"

"I'd probably tell you anything. Besides, you are the first bona fide human I've spoken to in so long I would like to prolong the experience."

"I'm flattered."

"And I'm grateful." Lighting up and drawing deeply on one of Violet's cigarettes, Jackie blew smoke rings and fingered a diamond solitaire large enough to choke a thoroughbred. Violet opened a window in the stuffy room. A cool breeze wavered through the various hanging shapes of densely printed cloth, the curtains, the dust-ruffle and drapery around the fourposter bed, the bottoms of the overstuffed chairs; the shifting patterns formed a strange backdrop behind the two women.

Jackie frowned. "Over the years I've become a student of these places, and I've seen both ends of the spectrum.

"In an exclusive environment like this one, if you mix in millions of dollars and add a relative or spouse who is causing trouble or is in the way, you can see the temptation for manipulation. These are very particular circumstances, it's not an epidemic—but I have seen it more than once."

"And the other end of the spectrum?"

"Oh Lord. When Trip and I were first married the company was headquartered in Pennsylvania. At one point I was hospitalized in Philadelphia, and of course while I was there a major scandal erupted—I'm sure you read about it. It started with a questioning of the sterilization of institutionalized women. As it turned out, they were not being sterilized because they were too disturbed to have children, which is a questionable concept as it is, but because they were systematically sexually abused by hospital staff—and an institutionalized woman with no contact with the outside world, who turns up pregnant, is an embarrassment to the institution, to say the least. Of course Trip yanked me out of there.

"Then there's the problem of chronic overmedication, and the convenient diagnosis of patients to ensure funds. The state hospitals are riddled with these problems."

"You seem to have absorbed a lot of information. You're the one who should be writing an exposé," Violet mused.

Jackie smiled. "Oh, Violet, please, there are many legitimate people looking into these things. I've been in eight of these places in fifteen years, my credibility is rather suspect."

"It sounds as though you have rather free access to observe."

Jackie nodded. "Yes, but in an odd way. A lot of the staff acts as though you can't hear or understand, as if the fact that you are supposedly disturbed, or on medication, reduces your intelligence."

"What do you think of Dr. Shelby?"

Jackie shrugged. "I don't know him at all, though he has run several of the group therapy sessions. He's a fairly recent arrival. I understand he's here to oversee some new therapy method. Dr. Connors is my personal doctor. He's been here for ages and I trust him completely. He's come the closest so far to making me feel human for any length of time."

They were silent for a moment. Violet was thinking about what else to ask Jackie; she wasn't sure the stories applied to her own search at all. She wondered how candid she should be.

"Considering what you have mentioned so far," Violet began, "do you think it's possible that someone could be held here against their will?"

Jackie laughed. "Here? At the Club Med of Psychiatry? I doubt it." She spoke more seriously. "Although it's true we have no contact with the research half of the hospital. Why, do you think the person you're looking for is some kind of prisoner here?"

"Not necessarily. I don't mean to be mysterious about it, I just don't have much to go on myself."

Jackie leaned forward in her chair. "And I don't mean to pry. But, Violet, if you have any evidence, or even real suspicions, please be careful. I don't know how far your work takes you from menopausal husbands cheating on their wives, but this could be dangerous." The dramatic words sounded ironic in the flowered surroundings. It was such a neutral space, a Caribbean hotel room.

"Jackie, I'm a street kid. I've lived with danger all my life, I take it for granted . . ."

"You also raise the art of the hackneyed phrase to new heights," replied Jackie. They both laughed.

"And you are wasted on your suburban continent," Violet suggested.

"Please don't. You have your territory and I have mine, let's leave it at that," said Jackie, sinking back farther into her chair, withdrawing.

Violet realized she should go no further. "For the time being perhaps," she said quietly. She stood up and slowly stretched.

"I would love to spend the rest of the night talking to you, but you've given me an idea of how to approach my problem. I have to get going on it." Jackie nodded and rose, walking to the door with noticeable reluctance.

"Well, I hope I've helped. It's been a long time since I counted for something, somewhere." Violet was touched by the odd meeting; impulsively she embraced Jackie lightly.

"Thank you."

"No, it's me thanking you that you should remember. Good night, and for God's sake be careful."

"Same to you. But this isn't the last we'll see of each other."

"I hope not . . . I see, you'll be back to rescue me, right? How cinematic." Violet laughed, embarrassed. Jackie looked at her solemnly for a moment, questioningly, then turned and left. Violet closed the door, feeling stunned and outwitted by the day's events.

Restless a moment later, Violet walked over to the large bay windows and pushed one of the dizzying curtains aside to check on this day's version of night, this night's version of darkness, her sky diary, the only litany she knew. Violet felt let loose in it, the big wading pool of possibilities. Tonight the dark was punched open by hundreds of stars, tiny fists of light. A party of strangers. Violet wondered if Jacqueline was looking out at the same sky.

15

Violet's talk with Jacqueline had had a cathartic effect. It seemed clear from what she had said that Violet was not going to bump into the research patients easily, and the prospect of waiting to discover a pretext to be admitted next door seemed intolerable. Violet decided to start with the files she had noticed in Shelby's office. She had no idea how far she would get with only a first name to work with, but it was better than the pretense of sleep.

Violet dressed quickly in a sweater, pants with big pockets, and sneakers. Rummaging down to the bottom of her suitcase, Violet extracted the flashlight, the Minox camera, and Victor's lock-picking set, and stuffed them deep into her pockets.

(Victor had taught her how to pick locks as a child—something to do in the apartment on a rainy day. He regretted this later when at the age of ten Violet was caught trying to break into the Bank of America.)

She turned off the lights and quietly opened the door, scanning the hall for sight of patient or nurse. She affected the casual walk of an evening stroll and descended the stairs.

The empty hall was eerie and coldly silent. Violet noticed that the silver tray was now empty of its mail. She thought about the sphinxlike Nurse Vincent, wondering what was troubling her. Reluctantly Violet pushed the distracting images from her mind, and proceeded to the door of Dr. Shelby's office.

The outer door was unlocked, but the inner office required a plastic card to open.

Although she didn't feel there was any particular danger, Violet was edgy. She tried to remember which direction the office windows faced in regard to the front gate and attending guard, concerned that lights turned on at this hour would cause notice. She pulled the blinds shut to minimize this possibility, then turned on the desk lamp.

The walls on either side of the large room were lined with file cabinets. Violet rued the fact that their filing system was not neatly crunched into floppy disks; it would have made her job a lot easier.

Violet went to the left bank of files and carefully scanned the labels. They were financial records and related business materials. Concerned that she spend as little time there as possible, Violet moved quickly to the other side of the room.

These were clearly the patient files. Violet looked over them carefully, finally locating the research section, by far the largest group of cabinets. She studied them further, looking for something to start with besides A.

On the right-hand column of units was a drawer marked TRANSIENTS. The novelty of the label drew her attention. She removed a very thin file from the case of tools, and played with the lock. File cabinets were notoriously easy to pick, and a few seconds later Violet pulled the drawer open.

In it were close to twenty files, labeled only with initials. Violet flipped through several and opened one randomly. The first sheet inside read:

R.M.J. P.A.C. NJ.
Imp. 10/15
Exam 10/15-7/10 wkly.
Due 7/10

Quickly she looked through several more, her heart pounding. The initials were identical in style to Victor's sheet of paper. She looked at them with a knot of resistance starting up in her stomach; she wanted Kate, not the chance to solve his last case. But the presence of this material, and the connection it implied, seemed a confirmation of the steps she had taken so far.

She snapped the file shut, opened the next, and was scanning it hastily when she felt a heavy touch on her shoulder, then large hands gripping her throat in mid-breath.

The shock of fear was tremendous; it hit her broadside. A voice thick with anger materialized, cursing; menace was apparent as the hands attached to the throat threw Violet to the floor. The man gave a small grunt, and kicked her sharply in the ribs. Something cracked. In that split second Violet was acutely aware of the surroundings, pain suspending the moment into a vivid passage.

The wind outside increased. The lamp on the desk was buzzing, its aura of light too shallow to reach the man's face. The carpet scratched into the back of Violet's neck. The room started to recede. Time wavered. The man placed his foot across her throat.

"Move and I'll crush it. What are you doing here and what are you looking for?"

"Let me up and I'll tell you," Violet gasped, breath scraping against the side of her compressed throat. The man withdrew his foot and grabbed her shoulders, dragging her into a chair. The bruised rib screamed. Immediately Violet's hand, four-finger stiff, shot out into his stomach. Her right arm scissored around his leg at the knee. Collapsing like a jackknife, the man hit the floor. Violet sprang out of the chair to run; the man grabbed her calf and jerked her leg backwards. Violet twisted and plunged into a short arc to the floor, hitting her head in a smashing thump.

At this moment another man flew into the room, grabbing her assailant's arm. Through the gauze of pain Violet attempted to focus. There was Shelby, furious, pointing down at Violet, who was lying on her side, face pressed into the carpet, taking shallow breaths and remaining very still. Close to unconscious and racked with pain, Violet shut her eyes.

Shelby was yelling at the guard. "What the hell is going on? This is a patient here, you're supposed to guard the grounds not assault people, what is this green beret stuff?"

The man who answered towered over him. "I didn't know that. I saw the light in the office go on and I came to check it out. This chick was going through your files, and look at that." He pointed at Violet's lock-picking tools on the floor.

Shelby was startled and concerned. "Get out, you fool," he said. "I'll talk to you later."

Violet's left side was hammering, she felt nauseated, and she tried to relax her breathing to evoke unconsciousness.

She could hear Shelby scowl and pick up the phone, punching three numbers into it.

"Vincenté, it's me," he said tersely. "Ben just found Haverhill going through our files. He's knocked her out cold and God knows what else, get down here, okay?"

For the next few moments there were no sounds in the room except for breathing—Shelby and his deep drags on a cigarette, Violet and her rasping. She held her still-life pose, it seemed the safest thing to do.

She was wondering at Shelby's different pronunciation of the nurse's name when the door banged open and Violet heard a woman's voice, shrill with panic, that she recognized as Nurse Vincent's.

"Nathan, what is it?" she demanded. Violet felt a hand on her shoulder. "She's out like a light. What did he do to her? Thank God, she's not dead."

Violet heard the creak of someone sitting down heavily on an office chair; she assumed it was Shelby. "All I know is that she was in our group file. I don't know why."

"Nathan, what does this mean?" was the reply. "We're so close to finishing the contract—"

"Be quiet," he said gruffly. "She could wake up any minute now. We'll talk later."

The room was silent for a short time, so quiet Violet could hear the varying wind outside, in the midst of it the sound of honking geese, traveling somewhere. Violet wished she were going with them.

Nurse Vincent spoke again. "What are we going to do with her?"

"Vincenté, shut up. For the moment we have to get her out of this office. Go find a wheelchair."

Violet heard Nurse Vincent walk out of the room, and return shortly accompanied by the sound of squeaky wheels.

"Help me get her into this," Violet heard Shelby say. She

felt herself being picked up roughly, and dragged into the wheelchair at such an awkward angle that her bruised rib banged hard against the metal arm of the chair. The renewed contact with an already excruciating injury was too much, and she fainted.

A short time later Violet woke up slightly, pain diffusing her reason. She struggled to understand her surroundings. She half-lay in a contorted sprawl on the wheelchair, her senses a glut of overlapping information.

Her head was tipped to the right. Cement block walls painted bright blue moved by her, a moat of sky that contradicted the dank smell of hemp and the watery echo of underground sounds. Heels clacked and scraped against gritty pavement. An object caught in the spokes of one of the wheels of the chair, clicking like a marble in a roulette wheel, intensified Violet's feeling of spinning. Strange music floated around her, a deep bass vibrating behind, shrill soprano sounds calling from up front.

Violet drew her head over to look forward, the movement causing such intense nausea that she let it flop back down to the right. Caught in the fuzzy second was Violet's vision of a crowlike figure flapping up ahead.

The chair hit a bump. The jolt of pain nudged Violet closer to a level of cognition. The music separated into voices, a dialogue of which Violet heard only scattered parts.

"His sponsorship makes my position more precarious than . . ." was one intelligible phrase, emitting from the fluttering soprano up front.

"Only three installations are left . . . be over, stop babbling Vincenté," rasped the bass voice behind Violet's head.

Violet was floundering in confusion.

Slowly, and only briefly, the content of her different layers of perception—one level gothic and frightening, another, information she could not grasp, the third her vociferous pain—now merged into one short space of recognition.

They were passing a series of huge windows. Movement blurred them into a long, slow-motion subway.

On the other side of the windows were the glowing green tablet of water, the grey-tiled walls, the rows of white benches; the scene pulsed through each passing window.

Violet realized she was in the tunnel to the research ward, her future uncertain, her brain truncated by dizziness and the seductive tug of the unconscious, to which she ultimately gave in.

Her few shreds of thought before succumbing were soaked with fear, the acknowledgment that her cheap impersonation of a detective was over.

16

Hours later Violet emerged, clearer this time. Her body felt wooden and foreign, unconnected to her rattled brain. She became cautiously aware, and slowly the white subsided into walls, shapes of figures, beds, and she knew she was lying, not floating, on one of them. In agonizing steps, the mass of fear and pain was replaced by bits of memory, until Violet knew all too well where she was, and why.

She gingerly reached for her head with stiff fingers, lightly touching the bruised bump, then felt her rib, discovering it was less painful than before. Aware of a more localized ache, she noticed the inside of her left forearm, which bore an injection mark. She glanced down. She was still wearing her clothes from the night before.

Conscious enough to be extremely uncomfortable, Violet was irked into looking around the room, aware of the combination of sounds for the first time: muffled voices and sharp ones, the dull slap of slippers versus the hard click of heels on the floor, and the sickly infusion of some dreary music. The room was large and rectangular, with beds separated by small tables lining each wall. Violet was beyond counting them. Everything from the bedsteads, tables, bars on the windows, checked curtains to the very sheets she was lying on were all various shades of yellow. Violet tried to remember if yellow had some kind of psychological influence, but it was beyond her.

She glanced at the few women in the room—were any of them Kate? She wanted to canvass the room at large. Some of them were talking to nurses, whose brisk impatient gestures stood out in sharp contrast to the rather shapeless women. It was an otherworldly effect. Violet studied the patients; they seemed vague, submerged; they had a generally unfocused look. She became immediately concerned with the prospect of being reduced to the level of those around her. Maintaining a clear head was essential for escape; she had to avoid medication at all cost.

Violet closed her eyes to feign sleep and further consider her circumstances before attracting any attention. She wondered when Shelby or Vincent would show up.

The question was answered almost immediately as steps approached the bed, and a hand lightly gripped her shoulder. Violet decided the appearance of grogginess, as long as it would appear logical to sustain, would put off any more injections. Thus she yawned, and sleepily, with a meek and casual air, fluttered open her eyes.

"Sheila," he said, shaking her lightly, "do you know who I am?"

"Dr. Shelby," she replied in a tired voice.

"Do you remember the events of last night and why you were brought here?"

"Vaguely. I don't feel very well," she said weakly. At that moment a very tall nurse walked toward the bed, one hand raised and holding a hypodermic. She had a long oval face and a large stocky build. Shelby waved her away. "She's half under, and I want to ask her some questions. Besides, I want to put her on regular oral medication, same dosage and time as the others. She may be here a while."

The nurse shrugged her assent but left looking disappointed. Shelby continued, looking at her intently.

"Why were you looking through those files?"

Violet was too dazed for clever fabrication, so was relieved when Jackie's story of the night before came to mind.

"I was looking for my own file. I wanted to see if there was any mention of my family making contact with you. I'm afraid of what they might do . . ."

Shelby thought about this for a moment, then shook his head impatiently. He looked tired and strained. "I don't believe that. The files you were looking into were marked specifically, they were clearly different from general patient materials. And your tools . . . Did you understand what you were reading, Miss Haverhill, if that is who you really are?"

"No, I didn't," she tried.

Shelby stood up and spoke brusquely. "It doesn't really matter. I mean to keep you here for a few weeks, for observation, shall we say. You will not be harmed in any way as long as you do not try to leave. I am warning you, however, that I am giving strict instructions to have you detained by whatever methods are necessary. And I'm certain you would like to avoid further contact with our guard . . . When a reasonable number of days have passed I will inform Dr. Anthony that I felt it necessary that you be transferred to this ward, because you needed a more radical approach to your problems.

"I'm not some cartoon version of a mad scientist, and I am not a violent man. I am merely protecting my interests, and the interests of this institution." He glared at her more with annoyance than threat.

Violet was relieved at his departure, and gazed around her at the patients, wondering if any of them were there under fraudulent circumstances, and if she should give up the search for Kate to save her own neck.

Violet directed her scattered thoughts toward the dialogue she had overheard the night before during her ride through the tunnel. She examined the scraps of sentences, but found she remembered very little of the exchange. The possible meanings of the fragments she did recall, "sponsorship," and "three installations," were obscured by the unintelligible sounds around them. One thing that lingered in Violet's mind was Shelby's pronunciation of his associate's name, calling her Vincenté, not Vincent. Yet the appearance and accent of the woman in question hardly qualified this as a startling occurrence. To Violet it suggested that Vincenté was in the country illegally. This would certainly help explain the woman's demeanor, particularly during the scene that Violet and Romaine had witnessed upon their arrival at Cobb Hill.

Violet wondered what it was she had unwittingly interrupted or threatened in her search for Kate and whether or not it included the woman she sought. Shelby and Vincenté's reaction to Violet's discovery of the files provoked a question: Were they involved in the substance of what Victor had been investigating?

The jumbled mass of detail was too much in her fractured state; it irritated Violet into action. She started to get out of bed to go exploring, then remembered her feigned state and lay down. Patience—no matter how alien to her—and timing were everything now, or she would be reduced to one of the reedy forms around her. Or worse.

Violet had the same reaction to fear that she did to anxiety: hunger.

As if on cue, a nurse approached with a tray.

"It's lunchtime, honey," said the rotund form.

"Then, is it noon?" asked Violet meekly.

"It's twelve-thirty," said the nurse, aiding Violet to a sitting position and placing the tray on her lap. Violet looked at it. Her first reaction was to give it back.

One plate held a grey, dry-looking hunk of fish, apparently boiled, species unknown. Next to it was a pile of sticky rice of the identical color, and hardly crowding them was a single, morose-looking stalk of broccoli. Next to the cardboard container of milk was a smaller plate where several trapezoids of Jell-o quivered for attention. Violet considered falling back to sleep. Instead, remembering her perfect-patient strategy, and needing some strength for the events ahead, she ate the entire contents of the tray. The nurse was delighted; executing something close to a pirouette, she left. Violet wondered if she had made a friend, and lay down again. Still somewhat dazed, she forced herself to focus on her present concerns, which were dramatic enough to pull her back into a sitting position rather promptly. Cautiously, she swung her legs over the side of the bed, then stood up to go exploring. She walked to the doorway, starting down the hall in a slow shuffle, checking out the arrangement as unassumingly as possible.

Flanking each side of the hall were four other rooms like Violet's, with the same physical attributes, the same gauzy occupants. A large cafeteria was located at the end of the hall to the right, across from it a room of the same size. Its contents intrigued Violet into casually wandering inside to observe.

The room was filled with various pieces of high-tech equipment, some recognizable to Violet, others not. In one area was a column of sound systems, one complete vertical unit per side, with panels that separated them visually, and within each space was a lounge chair and a pair of headphones. Other equipment included what appeared to be biofeedback monitors, electric jogging boards, a rowing machine, and a large projector-screen television. A number of women were engaged in activities relating to the various machines, with nurses in attendance noting their responses.

Violet decided to remain as inconspicuous as possible until an attitude toward her became clear. Thus far she had been totally ignored. A moment later there was a loud electronic beep, and the women vaguely came to attention. Several nurses began to give out medication from a tiered cart. The amazonian nurse who Shelby had waved away earlier approached Violet, who remembered with panic that she had not given any thought as to how best to avoid receiving medication. The nurse silently offered Violet a small paper cup with several pills in it, then a paper cup of water, and stood with one hand on her hip to observe. Violet tipped her head back and tossed the pills in her mouth, at the same time slamming her foot down on the nurse's instep. The nurse yelled and grabbed at her foot, her movement upsetting the cart of medications. Violet spit her own into her hand and shoved them into her pocket. There was a general uproar. As the nurse grabbed Violet's arm and swore at her, Violet told her to bugger off; another nurse came over to intervene, and the women nearby tried to stifle their amusement. The excitement wound down a bit after another nurse quietly pointed out to the nurse still holding her instep that Violet was a special patient of Shelby's, so as long as she had taken her medication they should leave her alone. Subsequently all three began picking up the mess.

Violet decided to stay in plain sight to avoid being followed. She strolled to the back of the room where the music equipment was. Out of an enormous collection of tapes Violet found one by Charles Ives and placed it in the stereo, hoping the tenuous reference to Romaine would be good luck. She had chosen a chair that faced into the room to watch. She slipped on the headphones, pushed the play button, and sat down. The music was a haunting and seductive cap of sound; it left her stranded in visual observation.

The patients moved in and out of the room with regularity, implying an organized schedule of testing. Violet realized that if she sat there long enough the entire roster of patients, possibly including Kate, would pass by her. Violet sat thinking of how to proceed.

At that moment a nurse entered the room holding the arm of a patient whose head was down, whose walk was so slow the nurse had to half-drag her. They proceeded to the medication desk, where the patient accepted a small cup of liquid, pushed a hand through a tangle of straw-colored hair, and raised her head to drink.

The sight of the woman's face so shocked Violet that her upper body jerked forward, yanking the connecting wire of her headphones out of the receiver. With great difficulty she forced herself to remain seated, her nerves stripped.

Violet was looking into the face of her mother. So startling was the resemblance, so eerie the physical parallel, if the woman had not been only a few years older than Violet, if Violet had not been in the room when Marie died, she would have assumed this was she.

Violet drank in the familiar visage: it was a pre-Raphaelite face, with pale opalescent skin, wading-pool-huge blue-hydrangea eyes, a tall forehead, an aquiline nose, berry-colored mouth slightly turned down at the edges, all at rest on an impossibly long neck.

Violet's brain was sending telegraph signals to itself. The Empire State record, Victor's mystery woman, her name mentioned on the tape. This was Kate, and no wonder Victor was drawn to her, even obsessed with her.

The woman glanced around the room, seeming not to notice Violet's open stare at her. She left the room, again propelled forward by the attending nurse.

Violet forced herself to take a few deep breaths. She placed the headphones on the receiver, and walked as casually as she possibly could to the door. Down the hall she watched the nurse lead the woman Violet thought was Kate into a room. A moment later the nurse emerged, and went through the doors at the end of the hall. Violet followed the course they had taken and entered the room; the bright yellow everywhere was still a surprise. A lone figure was seated on a bed. Violet approached her, stood next to her, and gently placed her hand on the woman's shoulder.

"Kate?" she asked tremulously.

The woman replied without looking up. "Yes?"

"I don't know where to begin," Violet managed to say.

"Then please don't," was the reply, glassy-eyed, mildly annoyed. Violet retained her grip on the shoulder.

"Kate," she tried again. "My name is Violet Childes. I'm a friend. My father was Victor Childes. Does that name mean anything to you?"

The head tipped up immediately, her eyes chilled. She said, with bitterness, "Yes." She paused long enough to make Violet itch. "Yes," she continued thinly, a voice skating on ice. "We were to be married."

The oblique strangeness of the words calmed Violet out of shock.

"Oh," she said, and sank down on the bed next to her. This news was confusing. While it confirmed Violet's general impression of the importance of Kate to Victor, the woman's young age, her resemblance to Marie, and the strangeness of their present surroundings made the announcement unexpectedly dramatic.

But it was now clear that Kate was the missing link, the mystery woman. She looked so vulnerable and worn-out, so sylphlike, that Violet felt immediately protective of her; the woman seemed wounded and helpless.

Carefully Violet picked up and held one of her hands, trying to focus her with touch.

"Kate, do you know why you are here?"

She shrugged in reply. "It's hard to remember anymore. My baby, I think. Something to do with my baby." Tears started to roll down her cheeks. "No one will listen, then he comes and tells me things . . ."

Another shock. In this context Violet could only assume the baby was Victor's, wherever this baby was. She opened her mouth to ask about it but realized that Kate was muddled with medication and emotional withdrawal.

Remembering the scrutiny of Dr. Shelby, Violet wondered whether or not she could maintain contact with Kate, and have the chance to talk to her further. Kate's passive ambivalent state was disturbing in its own right. But it was the keen sadness that poked through the indifference that moved Violet toward a conclusion. Kate's despair spilled onto Violet; Violet felt it raining on her, she felt like crying.

The combination of Kate's condition and Violet's precarious status in the hospital became decisive. Violet was wildly unsure of how to proceed, but she knew she had to get them both out of Cobb Hill.

She squeezed Kate's hand slightly, trying to gain her shifting attention. "Kate, do you want to get out of here?" she asked.

A small glimmer of light flickered unsteadily in Kate's eyes. "They would never allow it, he would never allow it."

Violet took a chance. "Kate, who is this 'he'?" But Kate shook her head. Violet decided to discontinue any further inquiry until after they left the hospital.

"Listen to me carefully. I can get you out; I will. But you've got to help me. I know they give you regular medication, strong doses of it. I know it's hard to keep things clear. Am I right?"

"Yes." Kate was trembling.

"Now. The first thing you have to do is stop taking the medication. Start this afternoon, hold the pills in the side of your mouth and spit them out when you can. The sooner you stop taking them, the sooner things will become clear to you, the sooner I can help you. Do you understand?" Kate looked at her warily but with vague appreciation.

"They will hurt me."

"No. You've got me looking out for you now. I think you'll get away with it; I doubt they'd expect you were capable of bothering to try to deceive them. You have to trust me. I'll get you out, I'll get us both out." Violet knew that if Kate missed one or two occasions of medication it would not change much, but she needed her to be more physically able to escape with her. Violet wondered if she could in fact do this.

Violet stood up, letting go of Kate's hand with one last reassuring squeeze.

"I've got to go. I'll be back. We'll make it. And expect anything; I may come for you in the middle of the night. Do you understand?" Kate nodded with drugged astonishment, making it known she would not miss this opportunity. Violet said good-bye and walked to the door, looking back at Kate on the way out. She had an edgily hopeful cast to the same wide-eyed stare, or was it the beginning of a smile?

Violet paused in the doorway to see if she had been observed, put one hand on her hip, and examined the fingernails of the other with great absorption. As she glanced up she was met with a rather dumbfounding scene. A group of women passed Violet, patients of some kind but certainly different than any she had encountered so far. They were moving as if in slow motion; there were ten or twelve of them, wearing identical blue velour robes and slippers, and pinned to each chest was a large white tag that had letters and numbers written on it. Flanked by two nurses, they made an odd, silent procession. It took Violet a shocked moment to realize another common feature of the group: each of the women was visibly pregnant. Violet ducked back into the room to wait for them to go by, quickly making the decision to follow them.

As the last nurse passed through the swinging doors at the end of the hall, Violet emerged from the room to go after them. As she passed through the doors she observed the group disappearing into a room at the end of the hall to the left, a room with dense blue light emanating out of it, spilling into the hall, forming a shadow on the opposite wall. Suspended dust particles captured the blue light in a small fog. Violet walked quietly down the hall to the door and looked inside.

The large room was similar to the other ward rooms, but with some striking differences. Sophisticated computerlike units were attached above each bed. Each unit had two central screens, one showed an oscillating line, the other displayed written information—impossible to decipher from Violet's distance. On the right side of the units were two vertical rows, one of knobs, the other of lights flashing on and off in a patterned rhythm. Out from under each box inched a broad line of paper, covered with print, folding back and forth onto itself in a container underneath.

A line of soft blue neon light traced the upper edge of the room, it skimmed and glinted off every shape, shrouding the figures in a strange glow. The eerie nature of the lighting suspended the room in a dreamlike state. The pregnant women milled around, the nurses standing guard. Violet looked at the patients further, their movements and faces. A shocking thought was forming in her mind, and accompanying it, a tiny knot of dread in her stomach. She studied the scene for another moment, daring it to confirm her suspicions. Music was playing, soft strains of Vivaldi that sculpted the room into a fantastic tableau. Violet was mesmerized and curious, and feeling a little bit sick. There were aspects of the scene that vaguely connected to Kate. Violet realized her mention of the baby made her follow the women in the first place, but what that connection was she had no idea.

A characteristic reflex made Violet reach for the Minox camera in her pocket. It was there. She paused momentarily in surprise. The fact that Shelby had not taken it from her struck her as corroborative of his statement that he wasn't a criminal. It seemed they were all stuck in unrehearsed roles.

Violet fired off a few frames and pulled herself away, with the feeling that her knowledge of the room and its inhabitants could be highly dangerous if discovered. Priorities sent her back to her own quarters, pressed into a slow gait by the small series of shocks Kate had offered. On the way back she checked out the nurse's lounge, where the emergency exits were, all the while mulling over how the hell she was going to get herself and Kate out. She was convinced that getting caught while trying to escape, and liberating another patient on top of that, might push Shelby over the edge. Violet had no interest in doing so.

Entering her room Violet decided to lie down for a while, to forge a plan with alternatives. She needed a detective's handbook, a rerun of "Hogan's Heroes," some sleep. Suddenly, a hand encircled her arm at the elbow and gripped it tightly. Violet looked up. It was Nurse Vincent, looking irritable and nasty.

"You're coming with me." This was clearly an order.

"Whoa, wait a minute." Violet jerked her arm away.

"Come on." Nurse Vincent pulled Violet down the hall into an office, closing the door and locking it behind her. "We'll have some privacy here," she said.

She glared at Violet malevolently, and with open consternation. "Now look," she started, "Dr. Shelby is gone. You have me to deal with now. I have no idea why you are here. But there is a lot at stake, you have to stay out of it. Just stay out of our business."

This last line was a hiss. Violet stepped back, feeling claustrophobic in the intensity of Nurse Vincent's distress. As she did so the camera and flashlight in her pocket clinked together. Though it was a light sound Nurse Vincent caught it.

"Empty your pockets."

Violet complied reluctantly. Nurse Vincent grabbed the articles from her, examining the camera, seeing that several frames had been exposed. She shook her head in disgust. "I can't believe he's let you wander around loose. That's going to change tomorrow."

Violet took her seriously. Somehow Violet's presence was disturbing to Shelby and Vincent; she had become a very negative catalyst.

Vincent continued. "Jacqueline has been asking for you. I can't have a suspicious patient next door asking questions. I'm bringing her to see you in a while. You had better behave accordingly." Her eyes blinked once in a dismissive salute. She opened the door and pushed Violet through it, directing her into the room Violet had woken up in. Nurse Vincent pointed at the bed. "Get in." She pulled a hypodermic needle out of her pocket. "This will knock you out for a while. I can keep you so doped up you'll be sick with it, and, if it becomes necessary, I can kill you with it."

She grabbed Violet's arm and roughly shoved the needle in.

17

Violet's awareness returned to her in eddies, an enlarging circle of consciousness swollen with pain, an enlarging circle of knowledge with unwelcome contents. Her thoughts were racing back and forth between two poles. Should she try to escape with Kate, and risk Nurse Vincent's reaction if they were caught, or should she bide her time, and trust that her inexperienced captors would actually release her. She opened her eyes.

Jackie's face floated into focus above her. Vincenté was standing next to her, her officious, tight-lipped mask back in place. She spoke quietly, Violet quite aware of the true meaning behind each sentence.

"Jacqueline was very worried about you, though quite unnecessarily as she can now see. This is very much against policy, but she was so agitated I decided it was best to let her spend some time with you. I'll let you visit together for a few minutes, then she must leave."

She threw Violet a look of such hateful warning that Violet closed her eyes. When she opened them, Nurse Vincent was gone.

Jackie sat on the bed and held Violet's hands. "My God, what on earth have they done to you?"

Violet opened her mouth to speak then stopped, her tongue felt thick and woolly.

Slowly, she managed, "What are you doing here, why did they let you come?" Violet was soaked with sweat, tears were involuntarily leaking down her cheeks; she was so pale Jackie was thoroughly alarmed. She removed her sweater, the only thing available, and blotted Violet's tears, her face, and put her hand on Violet's forehead, smoothing her hair.

"I made such a fuss about what had happened to you, that they knew I was suspicious of your removal. Dr. Connors walked by while I was asking questions about you, and he told Nurse Vincent to let me see you briefly."

"You don't understand, you're putting yourself at risk by associating with me."

"Calm down, I can think clearly even if you can't. I've simply made an unorthodox visit to a new friend, I'll go back and report you look fine, and that will be the end of it. Now, for God's sake, tell me what happened."

Violet relaxed slightly, for the moment satisfied Jackie was in no particular danger.

"I don't think I should tell you," Violet said sternly. "If I do you might be in the same mess I am. I think you should leave before she comes back."

Jackie continued to lightly rub Violet's forehead in a calming way. She said quietly, insistently, "Did you find her?"

"Yes," said Violet in a near-whisper. It seemed safe enough to tell her that much since Jackie already knew that she was searching for someone.

"Are you taking her out of here?" Her blue eyes pushed into Violet's, demanding.

"Yes."

"How?"

Violet was impatient for her to leave. "How the hell do I know? Now go, I'm serious. I'm not dragging you into this."

"I'm already here. And I'm going to help. Remember you said last night I needed a reason? Well, at the moment you're it."

Nurse Vincent picked this moment to return.

"Well, you've seen our favorite patient, and she is just fine, so it's time to go back." She spoke brusquely.

"Please, just one minute more, I can see she's all right, but I know you won't let me come back. Please?" said Jackie demurely, coming close to batting her eyes at Nurse Vincent.

Convinced Violet was behaving herself, Vincent shrugged and left. Jackie shifted her hypnotic look back to Violet.

"So you haven't found a way out?"

Violet decided to indulge her for the moment. "No. This side of the hospital is very well secured. Satisfied? Now go."

"Well, I've got an idea."

Violet struggled to sit up, opening her mouth to protest.

"Hush, there isn't much time. I've been aware all along of how open the main building is; there is very little security, it's supposed to give us the feeling we are trusted. As if there weren't an electrified fence or guard out there. Anyway, I noticed on the way over that the doors connecting the main building are usually only locked in one direction. You can't get out, but for convenience they are unlocked from my side coming in. Don't you see? I can let you through, and from there—"

"From there what?" But Violet's mind was already figuring out what. Jackie's insistence started her thinking—was it credible at all? Would it work? Other possibilities were not exactly beating down the door.

"You're right, I hadn't gotten that far."

"No, you're right," Violet said in a rush. "If you let us through we can pop through any door—"

"But what about the guard, the fence?"

"I can get past the guard, we can get out the front gate—"

"Wait a minute—"

"No you wait, you started this. But how will you get to the connecting door unnoticed. Which one is it?"

"It's the one this side of the pool. And don't worry about me, I'm a safe nonentity, and I'm telling you, we're not monitored. Sometimes I stay up all night watching television and see no one. We're always wandering around."

Violet saw this as the best immediate opportunity, but she hesitated. "I don't know, it's very risky for you . . . "

Jackie was flushed with determination.

"I've lived with danger all my life, it's a constant companion—" Violet laughed in spite of the situation.

The small sound of crepe soles patting the linoleum

interrupted. Violet almost cried out in frustration, and she knew Vincent would be insistent this time. Jackie seemed maddeningly unconcerned.

"Oh, hi. Thank you so much for letting me visit with Sheila." She stood up. "Now remember, I'll be thinking about you at midnight, on the dot, and you think of me too. That way we can stay in touch," she said in a sugary tone. "Maybe when you're feeling better you can come back to us." She lightly squeezed Violet's hand. Vincent was rolling her eyes in disgust. She herded Jackie toward a nurse standing at the door, and returned to Violet's side. Her voice held the same mixture of frustrated anger and fear as it had in their earlier meeting.

"That was very smart, you handled it well," she said begrudgingly. "I have to go now, I have a lot to do tonight. I've left instructions to have you watched closely. Dr. Shelby returns tomorrow morning." She shook her head. "Don't try anything foolish." She stood glaring at Violet to emphasize her words. Then she was gone.

Violet wondered how she had gotten herself into this incredible situation; she wondered if she and Kate had a chance. She could not lie still. She got up and wandered down the hall, weaving into the testing room. She noticed it was seven forty-five; she had been unconscious for hours. She saw two of the six attendants watching her pointedly. She took the cue and sat down in the nearest chair, shaking, truthfully appearing weak and withdrawn. She sat through medication time unapproached. She sat thinking about what Jackie had said, over and over—would the plan work, would she stay one step ahead of Shelby? She felt confused, the confusion spelled inertia, inertia ate up time. She was soon led off with the rest and climbed into bed. Fatigue dragged her around the edge of sleep, panic would not let her enter it, time became a bed of nails, the clock moving silently, slowly. Eleven-fifty hit the dial, hit her like a fist of snow. It was time.

She listened carefully for sounds in the hall as she crept out of bed and went to the door. She glanced up and down the hall, then ran down to Kate's room, acutely aware of the sounds of the nurses and attendants, localized at the nurse's station. She prayed it would stay that way. She ducked into the room and quickly located Kate's bed, softly shaking her awake, and letting her gather herself for a moment.

"It's time . . . Can you make it?"

Though dazed and confused, and clearly very scared, there was the small definite "yes" whispered. Violet helped her out of bed.

"Just follow my lead and I'll get us out of here. Do not speak until we are outside of the gate." Holding Kate's hand she led her quickly down the long length of hall, heading for the door at the end. Fate intruded.

"Hey. Hold it right there."

Violet turned around.

"Oh shit," she said involuntarily loudly. It was the nurse Violet had kicked, coming out of the locker room. Violet lowered her voice.

"We were just taking a little walk, we couldn't sleep," she said absurdly.

"Sure, honey, and I'm Princess Di on her way to a manicure," said the nurse, who was bearing down on her, reaching into her pocket for what Violet was sure was her emergency hypodermic. Violet gathered herself in a deep breath and adrenaline took care of the rest. She shot a karate kick into the nurse's midsection. As her upper body flung itself forward in reply, Violet punched her in the mouth as hard as she could, sending her flying back into the wall with a resounding crack. She slumped down in a disheveled heap, blood seeping from her mouth.

Violet pulled keys and the hypo out of her pocket, and at the same time the door in the wall swung open. It was Jackie, and she grabbed Kate and pulled her through. Violet followed, and pulled the door shut behind them. They were a Muybridge blur running past the windows of the pool, the same emblem-shapes of glowing green and white now signs of release. The two of them half-dragged Kate down the subsequent hall beyond the pool, slowing down slightly at the entrance into the back of the main house to hear if anyone else was in evidence. It was hard to tell over their labored breathing. They came to a halt prompted by Jackie.

"Where to now?" gasped Violet, her eyes filled with gratitude. Kate was looking stunned but disinterested, Jackie cool and directed.

"My room. Come on—" and she led them upstairs to the first landing, flinging open the door to her room and shoving them inside, closing it carefully behind them. Not stopping there, she led them to a door opening on a balcony.

The way the building was set into the side of the hill it was less than a twelve-foot drop, though they were on the second floor. On the balcony Violet took a second to assess, noting which corner of the building to go around to head for the gatehouse. She turned to Jackie.

"I'll go first, then you help Kate over the railing to me, then you—"

Jackie shook her head sharply. Violet couldn't believe it.

"Of course you're coming with us, you must. If you stay—"

"I have to stay, don't you see, that's what will keep us all safe. No one will suspect me if I'm still here, totally sedated"—she held up a bottle of pills—"out of it. At least by the time they think of any connection I might have—"

Violet looked at her wildly. "No, please, come with us—"

Jackie propelled them toward the railing. "There is no time to argue. Do you want to get out of here or not?"

In answer, Violet hugged Jackie and climbed over the railing, hung by her hands, then dropped softly on the ground. She looked up. Jackie had maneuvered Kate over the railing and, holding her hands, lowered her as far as she could, finally letting go. Violet caught her and they fell backwards on the grass. Violet struggled to her feet, pulling up Kate, looking up at Jackie, trying one last time, the wind, the dark, the stars already coming between them.

"It's your chance, too, don't you see that? Come with us, I'll take care of you."

Jackie's reply, "It's my turn to do that," hung like a banner over the balcony. She ended the conversation by going inside and shutting the door. Violet took a deep breath and turned to Kate; the movement and the shock of cold seemed to have woken her up somewhat.

"Remember. Not a sound. Just follow my lead." She took Kate's hand and they turned toward the gatehouse. Violet was never more happy to slip into a night; this one fit like a black kid glove, life-saving. Both women flung themselves forward, the frozen blades of grass slipping like knives around their ankles. Overhead the sky was a choir of stars, urging them on. The lawn tipped up and they ran at an angle, straining toward the light at the gatehouse. Violet brought them to a halt at a clump of bushes very close by.

"Stay put," she warned Kate. "Don't move until I come for you." Violet crept toward the gatehouse, there was no time to lose. She was a foot from the door. There was no sound coming from inside, but the guard was clearly visible, sitting at the desk reading, his back to the door, which was open a few inches. She silently pulled it open, then pulled the hypodermic out of her pocket, praying it was strong enough, and jabbed it into his neck, pushing down the plunger to release the drug. Automatically his hand slapped in the direction of the stinging pain. Violet grabbed it with both hands and yanked as hard as she could, pulling him over backwards onto the cement floor, head hitting first. He never made a sound.

Violet shot outside to the waiting Kate, grabbing her hand and running through the gate as fast as she could while dragging Kate behind her. They stayed on the road but hugged the side of it to enable a quick dash into the woods if necessary. Fear and its remarkable properties saved them; the two women flew through the dark weightless, charmed, on skates of panic, and ten minutes later the two sprinting forms fell gasping against the side of the waiting car, easy to spot in the lights of the parking lot. Her chest heaving, heart pummeling against the expected sounds of chase or siren or notice from the town at large, Violet somehow pushed Kate into the front seat, scrambled for the keys, started the engine, and raced them on to the first of many blank back roads, her memorized route, that would take them back to safety. Kate seemed to be aware of her freedom and sank almost immediately into exhausted sleep.

Violet stopped only once, to call Romaine and tell her they were safe. Violet asked Romaine to call Don and suggest he investigate Cobb Hill immediately, giving her some basic details to repeat to him, then returned to the unattended Kate.

After the first hour of travel Violet relaxed fractionally; away from the hospital, removed from the character of Sheila she felt safe, untraceable. She was sure of Kate's safety in the fortress of Anita's.

The surrounding darkness calmed her further. The radio, picking up signals bounced over endless groupings of clouds and planks of soaked air, was pulling in a station from Chicago, playing big band jazz. It made her think of Paul, another thread, perhaps the most important one, yanking her toward the city. The road was gloriously empty, a clear tunnel home, a conveyor belt. Violet felt the worst of the anxiety slip away, the hardest part of the journey toward solving Victor's death was over, the key was sleeping peacefully beside her.

Gliding into the city on waves of relief, Violet's final calm took root on the Tappan Zee, during a pink-hued dawn that slid over the bridge in a mirrored wash, a dawn Violet was hugely grateful to see. The Hudson looked slightly less brackish that morning, the toll-taker looked slightly less grim, the streets and buildings and clattering noises of dawn seemed welcoming. Pulling up in front of Anita's, Violet felt the full force of her optimism return.

She sat for a moment looking at the sleeping Kate, wondering if she would help answer some of the nagging questions, or present new ones.

She woke her up gently. Kate was docile and cooperative, and let Violet, who had a key to get in, lead her up the back stairs to the second floor, where Anita and Christine were waiting for them. They were met with embraces.

"Thank God you're all right," said Anita with the energy of relief. "Romaine called ahead, as you told her to, from the road. Is this the mysterious Kate?" Violet managed to nod.

Anita took Kate to a bedroom in the back of the apartment. Violet sat down in a tentative heap, her present safety permission to acknowledge her injuries and exhaustion. Christine sat beside her.

"Vi, you look really shaken up. You need tending to as much as Kate. Should I call a doctor? What can I do?" Violet looked up in surprise. Christine never involved herself in Anita's escapades.

"I'm sorry about all this. I know it isn't your idea of domestic bliss."

Christine shook her head. "Honestly, Violet, this is no

time to be talking about this or explaining myself to you, but I'm not as brittle as you think. I had a crummy, chaotic, battered childhood; it took me twenty years to gather a position in which I have some control over my life. I'm addicted to order and I'm protective of it, okay? Besides, if I didn't try to rein in Anita at least slightly, can you imagine?"

"Yes, of course, this place would look like a bus station during the Christmas holidays." Violet smiled.

"Exactly. Enough of that. What can I do for you?"

"Nothing, but thank you. I do seem to be a walking inventory of wounds, don't I? I think I'll drag it home and throw it into bed. Will you two call me when Kate wakes up?" Christine nodded.

"Now go, go. And get some sleep." She put her arm around Violet and ushered her to the door.

"So, clearly you're considering following in Victor's footsteps, is that right?" she said conspiratorially.

"Jesus, are you kidding? My heart has been in my throat for days. I'm developing a nervous twitch in more than one location. When this is over I'm going to become a librarian. Just don't tell anyone, okay?" Christine promised, not believing a word of it, and pushed Violet out the door.

18

Violet was relieved to see the beat-up door to her apartment; if there had been energy for it she would have sunk to her knees and kissed it. She poured herself inside and let out a deep breath that she had been holding for what seemed like days. At times like this she thought a waiting domestic pet was in order, Boomer or Georgia or Little Ham, something wagging a hysterical welcome. Violet splashed Scotch into a glass and lit a Gauloise, wondering if when she married Paul he could be trained to have the proper attitude of effusive welcome. She sank into Victor's chair, determined to pull herself together long enough to call him and Romaine. In answer the phone rang. Violet picked it up. Barely.

"Childes, thank God. I have been ringing this line every five minutes for hours. Are you all right? Talk to me."

Violet laughed weakly and told Romaine an abbreviated version of the events at Cobb Hill, ending up with Kate's safe deposit at Anita's.

"Our former med-school student, Anita, said time and sleep were crucial and it could be a couple of days before she can maintain any kind of clear head. We just have to be patient. She demanded I leave Kate alone for at least a day . . . Listen, I have to go lie down before I fall down."

"I don't doubt it. Need a visiting nurse?"

"Thanks, but I would be unconscious by the time you arrived."

"God, I'm glad you're all right. Victor would be proud, yes?"

"Hold off, save the sweet talk until I get to the bottom of this and impale the murdering creep's heart on a Tenth Avenue lamppost."

"Right. Now go get some sleep. Call me if you need me."

Violet slept for twelve hours. The drama and violence of the past few days shoved her sleep into nightmares. She woke up at nine-thirty, feeling only slightly rested.

Anxious to get to Anita's, Violet took a long hot shower, steaming the ache and bruise out of her limbs and jarring rib, mentally drawing together the experiences and information, wondering if Kate, who had been forced unwillingly into her position as centerpiece in this scenario, would provide the hoped-for enlightenment. Violet missed Paul very much. Now that Cobb Hill was over it was hard to remember how necessary it seemed to distance him; the lie would change things between them. She called him but the answering machine claimed he was still in Chicago.

She went to the medicine cabinet, pondering her next move. She considered screaming at the top of her lungs. Instead she swallowed several aspirin and the usual complicated assortment of vitamins. She dashed on makeup and pulled on a skin-tight, grey suede mini-dress with odd-shaped panels of silver-colored silk, grey suede cowboy boots with silver tips, and enough sterling accessories to make the Hunt brothers swoon.

Violet headed for the kitchen, or more accurately, the refrigerator. While rummaging through it she dialed Anita.

"I'm back from the dead. How's our patient?"

"She's much improved. She was up for a while and we chatted. The woman has been through an extraordinary time. She's asleep again and I think you should let her rest at least until tomorrow, if not longer."

Violet groaned in frustration. "I don't know if I can stand it; we're right on the brink of solving this thing. It's all I can think about. It's my dowry, my straitjacket, and I want out."

"I know that, honey, and I hope Kate is the answer, but she is very shaken up. She needs time to collect herself, and you need the truth from her, not some half-drugged fantasy tale."

"You're right, of course, as usual. But what on earth am I going to do until then? I'm going crazy."

"Why don't you come over here? Romaine was up here for a while, now she's downstairs holding court. You can spend the night here, on watch."

"Great. Thanks, I'll do just that, I'll see you in a few minutes." Violet slammed the refrigerator door, noting only how paltry the contents were, threw on a coat, and raced to Anita's.

Approaching the nightclub Violet could hear the jubilant noise pouring out the front door, the music and laughter a reference from deceptively less complicated times. Inside was the extended family of women, dancing, courting, pressing against the frame of sound. Violet stood watching, bathed in the flashing lights, letting the scene wash over her, remembering.

She spotted Romaine almost immediately, a head taller than all the rest, in a dress made of black lace and leather, attracting much attention as usual. Romaine caught her wave, and forged a path to her. They embraced, laughing in relief.

"Thank God you're in one piece. I was afraid I would have to go up there and do my Superfly act to get you out."

"You almost did. Listen I'm too wound up for this. Let's go upstairs and I can fill you in on all the details. Besides, I want to be on hand when Kate wakes up."

"No." Romaine was holding Violet's arms. "Kate isn't going anywhere. Neither are you. Let's dance."

Romaine pulled Violet out on the dance floor, which was an explosion of motion and rhythm in response to a complicated mixture of sound, a reggae-hip-hop-salsa tape by a group of female rap singers. Once engaged in dancing Violet realized how welcome it was to let go. The beat was pronounced, the music sexually seething, and the lyrics feminist; there was a communal writhing in response. After warming up for a few moments, Romaine and Violet moved into their famous routine that was punctuated by a few maneuvers that would have gotten them arrested if performed anywhere but at Anita's. After the song was over Violet collapsed into Romaine's arms, moaning loudly that she smoked too much, begging Romaine to take her upstairs. Romaine wasn't ready.

Violet let herself be led into a slow dance to a Smokey Robinson ballad; she closed her eyes for a moment and felt herself start to relax. The light touch between them as they danced, between the silk and leather of their respective clothing, was exceedingly sensual. Their skin was warm from the previous gyrations, it radiated an aura of heated perfume. Violet let her head rest on Romaine's shoulder for a moment. Romaine, clearly in a provocative mood, licked a drop of moisture off Violet's cheek. She pulled away in a movement of phony shock, but Romaine drew her back into the embrace, saying, "Nice to be here, isn't it?" with a coy delivery, before Violet had a chance to start swearing. "And are we not the most attractive couple in the entire room?" Romaine continued.

Violet leaned back and focused a mock-withering look at Romaine. "Knock it off, Brookes—the lady is engaged to be married."

Romaine sighed. "Okay, you can't say I didn't try." They were silent for the rest of the dance, leaning into each other. Violet was trying to ignore the small fluttering of desire that was starting up in her stomach.

When the music stopped they linked arms and battled their way through the crowd to go upstairs. Anita was waiting for them, standing in front of a table filled with food.

"What's all this?" asked Violet.

Anita grinned. "Romaine told me that when you called from the road after liberating Kate from Cobb Hill, you rushed through the part about how you were both all right, and focused on how bad the food was up there. It seemed a desperate measure was called for. Just eat. I have to go down and keep an eye on the hordes, okay?"

Romaine poured herself a glass of wine and sank into the nearest chair. Violet piled an enormous amount of food on a plate, and in between mouthfuls of terrine and smoked turkey, more fully related the events at Cobb Hill.

Romaine shook her head. "God, Violet, it sounds like a very close call. I was right to be half out of my mind with worry. If you ever do something like that again—"

"Yes, it was a close call, but it's over now, and for God's sake I'm still shaking—I have no intention of repeating a stunt like that again. Besides, that particular adventure may have been the easy part."

"It's really an incredible story. I should call the *Post,* you could be the subject of one of your own headlines for a change, 'Girl Detective Saved from Jaws of Death by Connecticut Housewife.' "

"Don't you dare. But speaking of which, can you make anything out of what I told you about Shelby and Vincent, or Vincenté?"

Romaine shook her head. "No, so far it's too sketchy. But I bet you're thinking what I am, that maybe Kate can fill in the missing pieces."

Violet nodded in agreement. Finally, having finished her food for the time being, they were quiet for several minutes as Violet restlessly checked on Kate, then put on a Betty Carter tape. She poured some Remy for each of them, handed Romaine a glass, and sat down again. She pretended to relax, but she was distracted by Romaine's concentrated look.

"You don't have to say it—this scene takes me back, too." Violet stood up and wandered over to the window, watching the women on the sidewalk below, her face lit up in warm flashes from the neon sign across the street, a big orange shoe and a large red arrow. She turned and looked at Romaine silently for several moments, aware of the simmering between them. The flutter was starting again. Romaine met her gaze.

"Brookes, I haven't seen that look in your eyes for five years."

"Maybe it's been there all along and you didn't want to see it."

"I thought that part of us was over."

"Well God, let's find out. Come on, sit next to me." Violet remained standing. She knew if she took one step away from the window the inevitable would occur, and she wasn't sure if she wanted the inevitable to occur.

"No," said Violet.

A few moments later Romaine got up and walked slowly over to Violet. A song started up as she did; it was the moan of sexual longing that taunted them. Romaine picked up Violet's hand and kissed her palm deeply, then drew her tongue in a warm wet line up Violet's arm, ending in a soft bite on her shoulder.

Violet shivered. The afternoon with Cindy was filed under unfinished business, but this was something else entirely. She was poised on a very interesting precipice; she paused only for a moment, then stepped off.

Two women are a mirror of the same softnesses and strengths. Two dresses half-off, dark skin against light, the scent of cognac and tobacco slid together in a kiss that was a long glissando, a kiss that emerged out of the past tense and into the present. The kiss, prolonged by surprise that merged with desire, invoked and sustained a heat, and the two dresses disappeared, and the two bodies found themselves in bed.

Romaine drew Violet into another kiss, a languorous beginning. She pushed Violet against the pillows and bowed over her. Romaine's tongue darted once between Violet's breasts, a hot wet plume. Violet's torso arched underneath it. Romaine moved her head to the right, and started to lick slow concentric circles on her breast. The circles became smaller, faster, and finally her tongue dove onto the nipple, her lips slipped over it back and forth, and she sucked it into her mouth.

Violet thought she would faint. The sensation was so strong it shocked her into a realization. With a small cry of surprise and regret Violet pushed Romaine up off her. They were both startled. Violet placed her fingers to Romaine's lips. "No," she whispered, shaking her head slightly, "this isn't right."

Romaine caught Violet's fingers in her own and squeezed them with a wail of protest, flopping down on the bed next to Violet. "Why?" she said in a low choked voice.

Violet put her arms around Romaine and pulled her close, their triangles of hair nestling, their breasts pressed lightly together.

"Because you're my best friend and I want it to stay that way. I couldn't stand it if things got complicated again. Because we always promised each other not to get involved with casual hand-me-down sex, the way a lot of our friends do."

"Or because of Paul?"

Violet was exasperated. "Goddamn it, Romaine, why does my relationship with Paul have to qualify everything? I know it's a continual shock to you, but I happen to love him."

They moved apart slightly, the sentence hanging between them in a soft dividing curtain; on one side was Romaine and her history with Violet, on the other was Violet and her involvement with Paul. The curtain, and the space between them that was growing, frightened them both; it was significant, charged with emotion, and capable of separating them in a lasting way. Violet's heart contracted in a painful spasm. She wanted to drop the curtain; she felt challenged and poked at by Romaine drawing Paul between them. She stabbed back.

"Okay. It's your turn. Why are you a lesbian? What is so different about two women together?"

Romaine was silent for several moments, then she spoke. "Lesbians have a different language. Women together make a different sound. And I think it's music. A sonata perhaps. No, an intermezzo, an exultant phrase of notes lifted out of the male context, which is the world's context." She paused briefly. "Am I being too abstract for you, you little tease? Okay . . . Do you know what *oonagata* means?"

Violet shook her head.

"It's the Kabuki actor who specializes in female roles—but who exaggerates surface characteristics to the point of parody. An ancient classical version of a drag queen—get it?"

Violet nodded.

"My point is, women together don't intensify the female. It's not just a doubling up of the familiar, it's an expansion. Definitions are dropped, roles are optional, women together can be anything they want to each other. They widen the spectrum instead of narrowing it."

She was quiet again for a while.

"Women together are two stones rubbing against each other. They polish each other, they transform each other. And that's my last word on the subject. Haven't you ever met a lesbian before?" She laughed softly. "Why did you make me do that?"

"Because," Violet replied, shaking a finger at her, "you didn't mention a rejection of men. You didn't mention politics. You explained it as a series of positives."

Romaine grabbed the finger and bit it. "So?"

"So, when I talk about Paul it's always contrasted to our feelings about women and it shouldn't be. Politics aren't involved, I am not with Paul as a rejection of being a lesbian. Understand?"

Romaine nodded. "You're right. The politics come later. After the broken heart, the laundry, the affair with the secretary—"

Violet reached down and gently grabbed a handful of hair between Romaine's legs. "Cut it out, Brookes, or you are going to be one very sorry woman-identified—"

"Okay, okay, I give up. You were right to stop us. I just figured out the whole thing. It was . . . crisis-bonding!"

Violet laughed. "Dr. Anthony strikes again. Maybe you should switch careers. And I might add, if we were bonded any further than we already are, we'd be Siamese twins."

"I'm not so sure," said Romaine in a sly tone, and rolled on top of Violet, rubbing against her. "Please, sweetie, I need more bonding, I'm incomplete . . ." she moaned plaintively. Violet pushed her off again and whacked Romaine with a pillow. "You queer, if you don't stop it I'll tell your mother you're sleeping with a WASP."

Romaine gasped. "No. You wouldn't, you couldn't, I'd get axed from the Christmas card list, cut from the will—"

Violet put her hand over Romaine's mouth. "Then chill the South-Side loins so I can get some sleep."

They resumed their affectionate huddle, talking quietly until they fell asleep, entwined, and dreamed the same dream.

It wasn't long after that when Anita knocked softly and opened the door, a mischievous smile on her face. "I'm sorry to wake you, but breakfast is ready. And, in case you're interested, Kate is already up and eating," she said dryly. She winked and closed the door.

Violet groaned. "We'll never hear the end of this." They jumped out of bed, showering, putting on their previous evening's clothes, bumping into each other in haste, laughingly racing through an abbreviated morning hygiene, and rushed out to the dining room.

19

The sight of Kate splashed into Violet's face like a pail of cold water. Her resemblance to Marie struck Violet again. But the long line of question marks, and Violet's earlier wild notion that Kate was somehow responsible for Victor's murder still nagging, dragged her back into a corner of ambivalence. The giddiness of their escape, the serial heroics, had evaporated; in their place was suspicion of who she had rescued and why. Her heart was beating so loudly it was a wall of noise, drowning out logic. Romaine saw the change, was aware of the danger, had her own reaction.

"Jesus, Violet, why didn't you tell me?" Kate was mute, looking fuzzy around the edges, waiting. "No wonder Victor—" and stopped, also waiting.

Finally, the moment was at hand, but what was it. The curtain was up; Violet was a big mixed metaphor, hound dog with a scent, Oral Roberts asking for money. She had no idea where to start. She leaned on herself internally, hard, to keep from jumping into a barrage of questions about Victor. She lit a cigarette. She looked with tense benevolence at Kate.

"I think you know where I hope this will lead."

She gave an abbreviated account of how she discovered Kate in the first place, how the trail led to Cobb Hill; she gave an impersonation of sitting down patiently.

"Well, how did you end up there?" The room was topheavy with emotion, pressing down on its weakest link. Romaine intervened.

"Violet," she said softly, "back off." Violet did as she was told, drifting off into a corner of the room. Romaine put her hand on Kate's shoulder. "How do you feel?"

Kate looked up at her through a mournful haze, an orphan in a magazine ad.

"I feel a lot better," she said slowly. "I'm waking up out of a nightmare, a horrible dream that still isn't over. I'm not clear about a lot of things." She was trembling; tears were running down her face. "I'm just beginning to put certain pieces together for the first time. Some of it is very hard to accept."

Romaine sat down across from her. "Is there someone we should call? Family, friend?"

"No. Thank you, but Anita asked me that last night—there is no one I trust at the moment, at least not until I sort some of this out." Kate lit a cigarette and inhaled deeply, pulling fingers through her hair, trying to concentrate, trying to stop shaking.

"I'll be surprised if you can make any more sense out of this than I have," she began. "It's going to be confusing, so please bear with me. My name is Kathryn Yardley Trent. My father is John Maxwell Yardley."

"*The* John Maxwell Yardley?" Violet said loudly. Romaine was equally startled. Two puzzle pieces had just slammed into each other, but their union asked more questions than it answered.

"Yes," Kate replied. "Okay, here goes." The words tumbled out. "Two years ago he found out he was dying of cancer.

His doctor said with treatment he could live for several years, maybe more. Actually, Anita told me he was still alive; I wasn't even sure of that."

"Anyway, he went into a tailspin, more so than the average person would, if that's possible, in the sense that men with that much power resent mortality or anything else they have no control over. I asked him to hand over some of his responsibilities to someone else and take care of his health and enjoy the time he had left. Instead his response was to throw himself into a huge project, on a larger scale than he's worked on in years. His version of a last fling.

"He was accompanied in this by an assistant, who my father refused to introduce me to because he knew I would ask this man to advise Father to get out of the project. My sensation was that the assistant had a large stake in encouraging my father. I could tell when they had been together; my father would call me and talk about his grand plans of networking a certain level of political control of the country. Then he would ramble on about whose hands his estate would fall into if he wasn't very careful."

Kate went and stood at the window, separating the blinds enough to see out. "My father is a brilliant man who went out of control, though no one seems to see it. His interest in power goes beyond the stereotype. I would say he is sadistic, I would even use the word 'evil,' if it didn't sound so . . ." She shook her head. "I'm getting ahead of myself.

"My husband, Tim, worked for my father, reluctantly at first for the obvious reasons, but after a few years they both adjusted to it and Tim seemed to be quite involved and gratified. It was a demanding position that was increasing in responsibility.

"During this same period of time, Tim and I were trying to have a child. But we were having trouble conceiving one. Finally we decided to try artificial insemination. We were waiting to hear the results when my husband was sent to Kenya on a business trip. The company plane crashed. Mysteriously, I came to believe." The tears had dried, so had Kate's voice.

"It was in a region so remote it took days for a rescue team to get there. Everyone was dead. On the same day they found the plane, I had a phone call confirming I was pregnant. It was incredible, as if one life had been traded for another.

"It was all too much and I decided to move into my father's house for a while, at his suggestion. It's why I had been on hand to notice just how strange and excitable he was, and obsessive. At first he seemed delighted to have me home, but he was becoming increasingly abstract and muddled. He was rambling on about his child and heir, confusing my child with his. I really thought he was losing touch.

"In my depressed state it was a very eerie environment. I couldn't sleep and was extremely nervous, and I started seeing a psychologist in the city. Something my father doesn't approve of. One afternoon while I was waiting for an appointment with my psychologist, I read an article on Victor in the *Tribune*. It was very timely—I had continued to have suspicions about my husband's death, and my father refused to talk about it. I was fed up with his behavior. I looked up Victor's number and called him. I told him everything." She stopped.

The scene became an excerpt from the Cabinet of Doctor Caligari, lots of odd shadows, daylight trying to force its way into the heavily shaded room. It did, in coarse bursts of light that shot around objects then died away. Shadow, light. Shadow, light.

"Well?" demanded Violet, ready to pounce. Kate was washed out, beyond offense at Violet's aggression.

"I told him what I wanted. He seemed terribly interested in the whole situation, he was very supportive. We talked on the phone many times before we finally met. It was quite something when we did. He was enthralled, and I must say so was I. We started spending a lot of time together. We seemed to have a lot in common, and we were both lonely. Then something happened, and we stopped seeing each other." Kate paused, then answered Violet's questioning stare.

"Not yet," she said softly. "I went to my father and confronted him with everything. I think I was breaking down at that point, it was all too much. He said a lot of soothing things, he said a lot of what sounded like rational things about my husband, about Victor, about his project. He begged me to go to Cobb Hill, one of his hospitals, and rest.

I was defenseless, I was without resources, I was done in. So I went.

"The first two weeks were fine. It was a comfortable place to be, the grounds were beautiful. I loved the women in group, I started to feel human and sane. I was getting a perspective on things . . . Then the nightmare began. Talking about it now makes it seem so arbitrary, so nonsensical. Dr. Shelby asked to see me in his office. My father was there. He said that he had studied the evaluations of my response to treatment so far, which of course he had no right to see but clearly had access to. He told me I was a chronic manic depressive, that I must have an abortion, and extend my residency at Cobb Hill for an indeterminate length. I was four and a half months pregnant at the time.

"Of course I was stunned. I protested, needless to say. At that point my father nodded and Dr. Shelby left the room." She stopped again, her face drew into a mask, as if shielding herself from the pain. She turned and looked at Violet.

"My father told me Victor was dead, that he knew we had plotted against him, that I would stay there until his project was finished and he was ready to let me out. His anger was incredible, he was seething. My own reactions stopped. After he told me about Victor, it was one shock too many.

"Since that morning I've been under constant sedation, though they needn't have bothered. I became as indifferent as a jar of strained peas. I remember the abortion, I remember when the staff stopped paying close attention. So did I. Since then it's been a long vague blur, until Violet appeared.

"I know it sounds Gothic," she said finally, "but I've been lying in the guest room thinking about it all. I was held prisoner there, it's as simple as that. He'll take me back there, if he finds me."

Kate sank into her chair, exhausted with release.

Clouds drifted over the sun outside, dimming the light in the room as if in recognition. There was a bright ball of pain in the room that their silence kept polishing, and polishing. Romaine spoke quietly to Kate.

"It's over now, and you're safe."

"Yes," she said, equally quiet, glancing over her shoulder at Violet with an odd smile. "Thanks to Violet, of all people."

Violet stood up. She was moved by the story, angered by it, but this was pushed against the talk of marrying her father, against the record made at the top of the Empire State Building. The story wasn't quite enough. She felt territorial, predatory.

"So," said Violet, in a more hostile tone than she meant to, "what happened to stop you and Victor from seeing each other. In the hospital you mentioned you were to be married."

Kate was all stripped gears at this point; she had no energy for artifice left.

"He discovered that I was his daughter."

There. The announcement hung in the air like an off-color joke, weighted silence followed. Violet looked wild. She was reeling. She wanted a drink. She wanted her fortune told. She was losing language. This was the point where you look into your napkin or pretended you were at the laundromat reading *Interview* or weeding the garden, anywhere but here.

Romaine picked up the ball. "How on earth did you figure that out?" She was equally stunned; she was having a hard time, there was too much information for one room and three bodies to absorb. Kate complied, directing her comments to Violet.

"You know about Victor and Marie and my father during the war." This was a question as much as a statement.

"Yes," Violet managed. She watched in tense observation as Kate stood and resumed her post at the window, grasping the sill. She appeared to be seeking edges now, hard surfaces, definition. Her voice was angular. Minimalism was hacking the room into emotional phrases.

"My father told Marie that Victor had been in solitary for months. That he couldn't last much longer. He offered to get Victor out, for a price, and the price was me. He tortured her with details of Victor's imprisonment, he pointed out that she and Victor could have more children. She was sick and weakened and terrified for Victor and she said yes."

Violet was mute, her jaw wired shut. But she was thinking about Donald. Was this their missing piece? The hateful thing that drove Victor into his final push against Yardley?

Romaine looked at Violet with concern but continued to carry the ball. "I don't mean to challenge your story, but I find it very hard to believe that Marie Childes would give up her baby, even if it was to save Victor's life."

Kate nodded. "I've thought about that many times. But remember that Marie was terribly sick with malaria. I believe she thought she was about to die herself, that she gave me up as much to save me, or ensure some kind of home for me, as much as it was to help Victor."

Romaine nodded. "That makes sense. But you still haven't explained how you found all of this out."

Kate wanted it over now, the rest came out in one push.

"My father sent for Victor. He was very reluctant to go, but I think he decided it was a chance to try and trick my father into saying something that would confirm or deny or clarify what Victor had found out about my husband.

"My father told Victor that he had had me followed, that he was aware of our relationship. He told Victor that in case we were sleeping together he might want to know that I was Victor's daughter. Then he told Victor the details of the trade—myself for his release. He reveled in saying that he had stolen me from Victor just as Victor had stolen Marie from my father."

She interrupted her story. "You know, I've experienced kind of a retroactive understanding of my father. And I believe his actions, his life since the war has been in the same mode. Grade-school one-upmanship on a billionaire's level." She shook her head.

"Anyway, Victor was so upset, so angry, that he made a lot of wild claims about having found what he needed to ruin my father. He wouldn't say what it was. Then Victor left. He called me, and repeated the entire story. He said he was very shaken up; of course so was I. He said he couldn't face me for a while and I agreed . . . You know the rest."

They were quiet for a moment. The wind picked up outside; the mood in the room was getting darker still, dragging them all down. They all wanted to flee; they wished they were someplace else, anyplace else. Dear Mom, at the shore, weather great, Tommy caught his first bass, Dave has finally managed to relax, much swimming and sailing, just lying here now, waiting for the tide, waiting to be covered by the sea, wish you were here, love . . .

Violet looked at Kate, the only child testing the word "sister" to herself. It didn't register. "Kate, I'm sorry I just can't stop there. Can you handle a few more questions?"

Kate nodded. Violet took a deep breath.

"Do you think Victor was killed by your father, by Yardley, I mean, or that he ordered it?"

Kate nodded once.

"Was it because of what Victor told him, that he had found a way to hurt him?"

Again a slight nod.

"Did you know what he had found?"

"Yes. Much of my father's wrath during our meeting at Cobb Hill was due to my refusal to tell him what it was. Of course, I didn't admit to knowing anything at all. It has occurred to me since then that Victor was killed without my father finding out what he knew, otherwise why question me about it, unless it was to confirm that they had found the right material."

Kate suddenly looked very annoyed. "I don't know why I'm saying this. I don't give a damn anymore. I lost my husband, my child, and Victor all at the hands of this creature I called Daddy all those years. I wish I was still on Thorazine," she said in a small voice, a child's voice.

Kate was closing down; Violet had to catch her.

"Kate, one more thing."

"What?" she said with impatience.

"Are we talking about that weird blue room?"

Kate was startled back into being interested. "Yes, but how did you know?"

"I saw it," Violet said simply. "But it was just one of them, wasn't it?"

"Yes." Kate crossed her arms. "I really can't stand any more of this."

"Please," Violet begged, "what was the evidence?"

"It wasn't any big deal, it was an early part of Victor's substantiation of his findings. He wanted an airtight case, so he was working slowly. It was a videotape of a 'blue room,' as you call it, in Tennessee, sent to him by one of his operatives."

"Where did he keep it?"

"He edited it into one of his baseball tapes. Violet, it couldn't possibly matter now. Anita told me you sent a detective to Cobb Hill—either he found the blue room or he didn't. Remember, I'm missing. Yardley has been covering his tracks since then, perhaps dismantling or relocating the whole system."

Violet shook her head. "I disagree. He doesn't know either of us are aware of it. Why would that be his focus? Besides, if you're right, then the video still exists as a tangible—"

Kate interrupted. "Violet, you're draining the two brain cells I have left. The tape doesn't prove a thing by itself. It could be an excerpt from a music video for all the good it will do."

Violet thought all of this over, her spirit beginning to sink to Kate's level of acceptance. The continuing revelations were pressing down on her, she was trapped under a paperweight with Marie and Victor encased inside, in their smiling tropical portrait. Violet stood up as if to heave the weight of it off her shoulders.

"No. I won't give up. I think it's my turn to pay Mr. John Maxwell Yardley a call."

Romaine stood up, she finally had an entrance. "And say what? Kate and I decided you killed our father, would you mind confessing? And by the way, we've got the goods on the blue room?

"What is a blue room, anyway? God, I can't stand it, I'm trapped in the worst B-movie I've ever seen. Haven't you learned some caution from any of this?"

"Listen, Ro," Violet countered, "in the past week I've been shot at, proposed to, I impersonated a neurotic to go undercover to spring a woman I thought had some connection to my father's death who turns out to be my sister, my lover is out of town when I need him the most, the economy is collapsing, the idiot Yankees are trading Ralph Peterson, the Presidential candidates are boasting about what they can't remember, the swallows didn't show up in Capistrano—"

Romaine started to laugh, she had to; even Violet could hear Sheila Haverhill coming out of her mouth. The two women collapsed into chairs, Violet joining in Romaine's hysterical laughter until tears came. Even Kate managed a smile, and took her chances by impulsively throwing her arms around Violet in a hug. Violet hugged her back, then gasping for breath and calming down slightly, she pushed the stranger who was her sister away, looked up at her through the center of the swirl of hysteria and announced, "This is the start of a beautiful friendship. We'll sell the movie rights, we must call William Morris—"

"Stop," Romaine demanded.

The tension finally broken, the three of them sat at the table, wondering who would deal the next hand. Kate turned to Romaine. "Does she often expound like that?"

Romaine snorted. "God yes, just pick a subject, then hold on to your hat, the woman is a walking lecture circuit. But weren't you warned? Wasn't there a pamphlet next to your bed, 'Violet's List of Cardinal Sins'? Let's see. Arbitrary rudeness, mediocrity, synthetic fabrics, fashion mistakes, failing to return library books, hypocrisy—have I missed anything?"

"Symmetry."

"No, honey, that's your epitaph—'She was allergic to symmetry, and convention never caught her eye'—except once, that is," Romaine said, winking at Violet.

Violet ignored her. "Okay, let's keep going. Unexamined liberal politics—"

"Ooh, a sin we indulge in ourselves. I didn't know there was one—"

"What do you mean by calling me a liberal? I'm an A-one anarchist—"

"With enough hot air to raise the Titanic."

"You want that mouth slapped shut?"

"Is that a threat or a promise, you pedantic dyke."

"Home-wrecker."

"Fanatic."

"Bourgeois black lumulus." This finally stopped her, as Kate and Romaine said simultaneously, "Lumulus?" and the three joined again in the release of laughter, however shielding it was. Suddenly the sun slammed through the clouds and into the room, the city fugue rising to the windows in a rush, a moment spent in the good-luck heart; it levitated them.

Romaine thought of something. "Listen, it's about time

someone explained the blue room to me, or do I have to wait for the movie of your lives to be released?"

At that moment the phone rang, startling them. Anita was downstairs, so Violet answered. As she picked up the receiver she said to Kate, "Go ahead and fill her in, do you mind?" Kate shook her head. Violet said hello into the phone.

"Violet Childes, if it weren't for the fact that I loved Victor like a brother I would haul your ass down here and personally throw it in the slammer. What the hell did you think you were doing? Breaking and entering, abducting a patient who they claimed never existed—what kind of dream state are you in? Who is this woman? I called a friend of mine on the county force up there, he stormed over with the cavalry and you know what he found? Nothing. No bloody blue room, nothing out of order, no patients missing. For this I look like a jerk. Do you read me? If there is something funny going on up there they sure moved quickly to smooth it over. And now they are warned." Don was silent for a moment; when he continued speaking his voice was quiet and concerned.

"Violet. I've been thinking about all of this. I regret telling you that story. It obviously sent you in a certain direction, but, honey, it's not going to get you anywhere. I think I was wrong, I was just spouting off, I didn't want to think Victor was killed because he was working on the drug syndicate for me. But he was. I had a long talk with Paul when he came in with the cassette tape, I agree with his theory, I agree you've got to stop meddling, this is an ugly bunch Violet, they'll do anything . . . Violet, forgive the ramblings of a man who misses his best friend, and stop. Just stop."

"But, Don, you were right, you were right about everything."

"I need proof, Violet, not your crackpot stories."

Violet's mind was racing. She had Kate, but exposing her to Don might land Kate right back in her father's hands unless she had something more, something tangible.

"Donald," she replied, "when your men went through Victor's apartment, did they go through the videotapes?"

"Yes, of course they did. As a matter of fact I caught them at one point, standing around watching a Thurman

Munson tape. They were playing back all the tapes, but all Victor had were baseball tapes, so I stopped them. Why the hell are we talking about this? You're raving."

"I've got to go, Donald. I'm going to change your mind about all of this. Bye." Violet hung up to avoid another speech. She walked over to where Kate was sitting. She had pulled herself into a very still place, staring into whatever was left for her. Violet hoped she was finding some strength there.

"Kate."

"Violet . . . What's a lumulus?"

Violet smiled. "And I thought you were thinking deep thoughts."

"I was. But what is it?"

"A horseshoe crab."

"Oh. I thought it was some horrible lesbian curse. I guess I have a lot to learn." She smiled and shook her head. "So you and Romaine are lovers?"

"A long time ago. Now we just torture each other with all the secrets we know about one another." Violet thought to save the news of her marriage for a more appropriate point. "So, Kate. Now what?"

"If it's all right, do you think I might stay on here a little longer? I have no place else to go right this moment, and I'm afraid of being found by my father."

Violet nodded her head. "Of course. I agree with you about your father. As weird as the outcome was I'm glad you're out of that place. But I'm the one who dragged you into this, and Anita's with us on this one, so stay as long as you like."

"I did need to be rescued. What for, that hasn't caught up with me yet."

"How about joining me on the last leg of this Yardley thing?"

Kate cringed. "I don't even want to hear his name, not for a while, much less go after him."

There was a febrile pain and confusion skittering around the room; they were both caught up in it, they could go no further for the moment. Violet plopped down on the couch, wondering where Romaine had gone, wondering what to do next.

Kate stood up. "I have to go lie down again. Having a clear head for the first time in months is exhausting."

"Kate—"

"Not now, okay? There's plenty of time to trade childhood memories," she said with a note of sarcasm.

"But Kate—"

Kate left the room, passing Romaine who was on her way in.

"Where have you been?" Violet wanted to trade the day in and start over.

"Talking to Anita."

Violet stood up. "I want this man, Ro, I want to go see him right now and choke the truth out of him."

Romaine shook her head sharply. "Violet, stop it. If this egomaniac killed Victor and imprisoned his own daughter, he'll brush you off like a fly—maybe permanently. You either come home with me or you go to your place and rest on this, and get Don and Kate together."

Violet put her arms around Romaine, holding her close, but there was a stiffness between them, a rustle.

"Okay," Violet said softly. "I'll let it go for a few hours. And I guess I'll go home. You've had enough of this. You've been a saint, you deserve some peace and your Midwestern liaison."

Outside a cab smashed into another cab—yellow is a color you can hear—and suddenly there was a great deal of noise poking into the room, irritating them both. The day had evaporated somehow; it was suddenly nearing dusk.

"Let's just leave it for now. Let's just go."

Violet agreed silently, as they gathered their scattered things. Then she tried once more.

"I'm scared. It's not just this pumped-up drama, it's everything. It's the way I've drifted since Victor's death, the way things feel like they are escaping out of reach. I just can't focus. It's like a long, slow-motion skid. In some part of your brain you can see you are going to hit, hit hard, and you try to stop, but it's movie time, it's been recorded already—you can see the before, during, and after, but you still can't stop. I guess I'm in the middle, heels dug in but slipping. Don't give up on me now."

Romaine looked at her, considering. "Of course I won't.

I'm not going anywhere, I just need a little distance to be able to help. We'll meet tomorrow morning, we'll talk strategy."

They grasped each other's hands. The audio outside was throwing itself in; the rush-hour glut of sound, it seemed harsh and mean-spirited.

"Are we okay?"

"We're okay," Romaine replied. They left together arm in arm, pretending for the moment that it was, in fact, okay.

Violet let Romaine loose downstairs, spoke to Anita for a few minutes, then went home, wondering if she weren't pushing too much, in every arena, to the brink, at the same time. But she didn't know how to stop.

20

Entering the apartment, with her dead parents and her new sister and her confused life in tow, Violet continued to pretend that things were all right, that she had gotten somewhere.

As bold as she had been on the phone, she was not immune to Don's comments, nor to Paul's or Romaine's. The image of Max and his open throat had not strayed far, and a day did not pass that Victor swooping by in his shroud did not graze her. She wondered if her brash quest was a death wish after all. It wouldn't be much of a tribute to Victor if her efforts ended in her own death.

She thought of calling Dr. Green on talk radio. She cleaned the apartment with a fever and thoroughness that rivaled a Stepford Wife, finding eight dollars and ninety-two cents in the couch and chairs. She paid her bills. She ate a Lean Cuisine. She ached for Paul. She wished she had a houseplant to prune, just one stupid coleus. She tried to call Bernard in Bali but couldn't get through. She called Cobb Hill to check on Jackie, but was told it was too late in the day.

Finally Violet sank into Victor's red chair, thoughts racing around like misdirected mail. Kate. Max. Cobb Hill. The thugs. The tape. The blue room. Paul. Cindy. Yardley. Don. Jackie. The Empire State record. A huge junk heap, bumper cars smashing off each other in random disarray.

She lay her head back in the winged chair, wondering if finding Victor's killer would make that much difference to anyone, including herself. But this present concern was something to do, a focal point; perhaps Romaine was right—resolving Victor's death had become emblematic of purpose in her life, of control. If only she knew how to knit, to build ships in bottles, something safe and sane that begged attention and cornered stray detail. She wanted to squeeze Paul and drink beer and gossip. She considered a convent. The National Guard. Social work. Big-game hunting.

Violet pondered the amendments made to a person she thought she knew so well; she mournfully wished he had shared more with her. She felt terribly guilty that her life in the past year had taken her away from him.

Just then she became aware of a scent emanating from the corner of the chair, where the wing met the back of the chair. It was the slightly spicy smell of Victor's pipe tobacco.

It was such an intimate reference to him, it was as though he was sending a message to her from wherever he was.

It was all she needed. She leapt up from the chair, rummaged through her desk, and located the keys to Victor's apartment.

Once inside the shrine, as her friends called it, trying to irk her into clearing it out, Violet was shocked at the heady combination of scent and familiar objects. It was so strong she nearly backed out the door.

It was like holding her breath under water; quickly Violet went to the shelf of video tapes in the living room, throwing them all in a large canvas bag she had brought with her. She escaped into the kitchen to the phone, but it was almost worse there; she had to move quickly before it all rushed back.

"Zar. It's Violet. It's an emergency. May I use your video equipment?"

"Of course," was the answer. Zar hung up.

Violet lugged the bag of tapes to Zar's studio. Zar opened

the door announcing, "Law offices of Vonetta, Hope, and Lisa, we specialize in the PMS defense—oh, Violet, I thought you were someone else."

"Who? An ex–pen pal from Ossining?"

Violet explained that she had to rummage visually through all of the tapes she had brought, and because Zar had several video decks and many monitors it would make it a lot easier if she could screen more than one at a time.

Zar led her over to the media area of the studio. She extracted two VCRs from the tangle of equipment, placed one on top of the other, and connected them to consoles. "I suppose I have to wait until you locate it before you tell me what it is?"

Violet nodded. Zar went back to work. Violet pulled up a stool, pushed the first two tapes into the VCRs and sat to watch. She considered using the fast advance by remote control, but did not want to risk going by the footage of the blue room, in case it was a short piece of tape.

It was dizzying to keep an eye on both screens. Violet wished Victor's sport passion had been a different game. After two hours the bright green of the baseball diamonds and playing action was giving Violet a headache. She stopped and went to see what Zar was doing.

"What?" was Zar's reaction.

"Actually I came over to beg coffee from you, unless you've used it all to patch cracks in the walls."

"Funny, Childes, very funny." Violet sank down on a stool next to the table nearest her, which was covered with bottles; she was light-headed with fatigue. Zar returned with the coffee. She was wearing a black T-shirt; emblazoned with large red letters, it spelled out GIRL-SPA. Violet cocked her head slightly. "So. Where is this place?"

Zar smiled knowingly. "World-wide . . . Find anything yet?"

"Not yet. I'm about halfway through. Zar, I can't stand it anymore—what are you doing with this fortune in returnables?"

Without ceremony Zar stood up and wandered to the other side of the tables. She picked up one of the bottles and blew across the top. A low reedy note was sounded, reverberating slightly in the room.

"Remember doing this as a kid?"

Violet nodded and picked up the closest bottle, put her lips to it and blew, the note much higher in tone than the one Zar had made. Zar lifted a finger in the air as a signal and they both blew at once, and the two breathy notes pushed out as a part of a minor-key chord, lingering in a slight echo.

Violet looked at Zar questioningly; Zar looked somewhat impatient.

"Just to get it out of the way, this is something I'm working on for that outdoor series on the pier. It's perfect, really, because I need the space." She walked to one of the tables.

"The first half of these bottles are arranged in a chord; each row is one note. The bottles, and each one stands for a certain number, represent W.I.D.s—Women In Distress. Political prisoners, battered women—you know. Thank God I don't have to spend eight hours on the list with you.

"Anyway. The first chord is the lament, this huge musical ache. At the beginning it is mournful, a dirge, but as more notes are blown it becomes discordant to such a degree that it is almost painful to hear. It's about anger now, frustration, chaos, even violence. If it works right you'll want to put your hands over your ears.

"Then the white bottles start up, all whole notes adding up to major-key chords, and they start to overshadow the first chord, they start to pull away from it. Then, and believe me babe, this has taken me months to figure out, what the level of water in each bottle should be, comparing that with a specific note. Anyway, certain rows of notes from the first chord stop and the remaining ones continue, and the rest of the white bottles are blown in unison, and altogether they're an ascendance, a huge bloom of transcendence and overcoming, the sound of titanium white, the sound of pure hope. It's totally unlike me, so don't spread it around. All the bottle-blowers are dressed alternately in black and white; it's a big girl-piano, Femmes from the Continents; I'm fucking swooning just thinking about it. You must come to the pier and bring a lot of dykes with you. And Paul, too."

Violet felt slightly overwhelmed but thought it was wonderful and said so.

"Then you'll be there? Or better still, be one of the blowers, okay?"

"I would love to."

"Good. Will you beat it now? I'm working on the broadcast."

Violet went back to the tapes. The pile in the bag was getting smaller. She started the next two tapes. One of them was clearly the tribute to Thurman Munson that Donald had mentioned; there was chubby Thurman waving his wide catcher's mitt at the crowd. Violet thought this one would be safe to skip, since the investigating cops had screened it. Then she remembered that this tape was where Donald stopped the whole procedure, so she let it run. She had a feeling about this one.

Thurman at bat was no Hank Aaron. Violet had the sound off to keep from bothering Zar, but she could hear "Swing and a miss strike one," as easily as if it were on. She could smell the popcorn and the slightly sweaty Victor; she remembered the bitter-tasting sips of his beer.

The pitcher threw a couple of wide ones past Thurman, as if to keep him in the batter's box a little longer, since the crowd liked him so much. Then Thurman swung and missed by a mile. He was down by two, his jaws working the four packs of gum ferociously. Violet could hear her father muttering, "Come on, Thurman, forget the heroics, just bunt." At this point Violet watched Thurman choke the bat and lean into the batter's box as if to comply; his body held in a taut pose. The pitcher wound up and threw.

And there it was. The change of scene happened so quickly that the jump-cut from bright green to saturated blue was a shock. The room was similar to the one she had seen at Cobb Hill, though larger, with more patients. The camera was in a fixed position, probably looking in through the door, but it kept up a repeated pan, and zoomed in several times to catch certain details, one of them making Violet as queasy this time around as it had the last. The scene ran only a minute and a half, but was so mesmerizing it seemed longer. Violet jumped up and rewound the tape to the beginning of the scene, to find the number on the counter. She yelled for Zar, who walked over to her casually, her gait implying disbelief that Violet was going to impress her with baseball.

Violet pushed her into a chair. She explained the connections between Cobb Hill and Kate, Victor and Yardley and the blue room. She pushed the PLAY button and they watched the scene again.

When it was over Violet wound it back once more.

"Can we make several copies of this?"

Zar's reaction was to throw her cup of coffee as hard and as far as she could. When it finally reached a wall the sound was an explosion.

"Yes, we can make copies of it. And one of them goes on the broadcast. The dickhead has celebrated his misogyny for too long. Victor was looking for a chink in his armor. A toehold. This is a start. Now go over all of this again, I need it for copy."

"No," was Violet's quick reply. "It's too soon. The whole point is to make it stick. I've got to get a copy of this to Don, along with Kate and her story."

"Come on, Violet. They'll just cover it up. You know how immense this man's power is. No one will ever hear about this unless we go over their heads. Take it directly to the public."

"No. Please. Only as a last resort. Let me start with getting it into the right hands, and Kate's story, too, and get the process going."

"The right hands?" Zar said with sarcasm. "Okay, okay, I'm sorry. It's your trip."

They made three copies of the blue room scene, one for Violet, one for Don, and one that Zar talked Violet into giving to her, promising not to use it. When they finished it was three in the morning. Violet was so tired she couldn't move.

Zar led her into the sleeping alcove and tucked her into the huge bed, pulling the curtains around it. Violet fell asleep immediately. She dreamed of Thurman, who became the first player in baseball history to bunt a home run.

When she woke up it was nine. Violet sat up and rubbed her face and called out to Zar, but there was no answer; the studio was silent. She pulled the curtains aside and was greeted with the sight of a huge corrugated cardboard heart, as tall as Violet and three times as wide. It was painted red, in the middle was a packet of flower seeds stapled to the cardboard—violets.

She was mystified for a moment. Out of habit Violet looked at the date on her watch. The fourteenth. Six months to the day since Victor had been murdered. Valentine's Day.

Violet put her shoes on and placed her copies of the tape in the canvas bag, leaving the rest of the baseball tapes to pick up later. She found some sections of the *Times* and a matte knife, and cut the shape of half a heart through all the pages. Once flipped open the pages made full, wide hearts with a crease down the middle. Violet put them all over the room—there were over twenty—saving one to spray gold, scrawling "thank you" on it accompanied by many X's in black crayon, and left it in a prominent place.

On the way home Violet felt suddenly organized and determined in a way she hadn't in a long time. She would call Don and Kate, show them the tape, they could all get things rolling.

As she entered the apartment the phone was ringing.

21

Valentine's Day. When hearts shed their little cloaks on demand, plighting troth, sending FTD, hearts pounding around town in the guise of chocolate and long-stem roses, balloons and Taittinger. Tables for two. Sweetie-pies dancing like Siamese twins. Close and slow. Like white on rice. V-day prescribed; love takes its tangles, its randy mid-adventures, its small and large betrayals, its hot and cold taps and chucks them, smooths them out, trips a switch into the warm, sleek cheek of the stylized heart. B mine, baby, B mine. Irony flees. At least that's the myth.

The nightclub was empty. The big picture window up front was veiled with snow slow dancing, flakes pressing their sides to the glass momentarily before flying off. The snow's curtain of gauze made the bar darker than usual, but in a pleasing way. It was nine A.M., and Christine was doing her reluctant holiday routine, helping out in the club during special occasions. Her compensation was trading the daily power outfit for a white tuxedo shirt, red silk bow tie, black stretch pants, and crimson high-tops. Anita was in the kitchen supervising food preparations for the day, while Christine put finishing touches on the decor. Christine grinned to herself. Hallmark did not have a category for the clientele at Anita's; she doubted it ever would. Today the club looked like many other singles bars in town. A mass of corny decorations to signify the day—lines of crepe snaked everywhere; there were accordian hearts and penny valentines; cake-frosting pink and blood red were abundant. The tackier the better as far as Anita was concerned. Along with the more traditional decorations, certain club regulars who were artists had contributed works based on a heart motif. One was a broken heart traced in neon. Another appeared to be a satin heart shot at close range. One was made of shards of broken glass. One was fur. The result was a riotous visual collage.

Christine put a Schumann record on the sound system. She loved the effect of classical music booming out in the same aural space usually assigned to dance music. She gathered up tape and scissors and tag ends of crepe and went to put them away at the end of the bar. The front door opened and closed behind her, which she wouldn't have noticed except for the blast of cold air that swept up her spine and encircled her bare neck. Christine turned around to tell whoever it was that they weren't open yet.

A man had entered the bar, knocking the snow off his boots inside the door. He was tall, very tall, wearing a mackintosh and gloves. And a ski mask. A gun appeared out of the folds of his coat.

"Anita," was cried out in some deep part of her, squeezing its way up from the heart into a syllable of shock.

Is it true you can tell when your time is up, when your number's called, when you know it's over, and you remember the day on the beach when your kite flew away and you were six years old, so it was tragic, and how, after forty-six years of painstaking life, could it be yanked away in a few crummy seconds?

The first shot sped out of the silencer in a slick line, swift as a blink, and popped through her forehead into her brain. The impact snapped her head and body into a back-dive arch, arms flying up in agreement. She lay dead immediately, blood red running in a wet aureole on/over/around her head and shoulders in jagged shape, an Aztec mantle. The man stepped over to the body. The mask contorted itself because the man underneath was smiling. "No holiday should go unnoticed," he mumbled to no one, and pumped out another sleek silent bullet into the vicinity of her heart. A moist red appeared, that felt its way through the white tuxedo shirt in waves, like a seismograph reading, farther and farther. The man quickly grabbed a penny valentine out of a bowl on the bar, scribbled something on it, tossed it onto the body, and left.

As the door opened and shut the wind rushed in, boosting the paper valentines out of the bowl into the air, where they fluttered like reluctant birds, and floated down in a similar way to the snow outdoors, darting around, some of them landing on the body, the rest in a scattered crossword on the floor.

The loud sweet sounds of Schumann, still lilting around the room, had forced the murder into pantomime. Now suddenly the mass of hanging decorations looked like entrails, the festive colors turned lurid. The chorus of hearts observed: the square window of white casting a soft glow on the body, blood still scooting out, inching onto the black-and-white floor. The snow continued to fall at its steady pace, unmindful of what it had witnessed, its quick rush against air a prolonged hiss.

22

The scream let loose like demented sky-writing; it was suspended long enough to read the transition from shock to recognition to extreme pain, and wind its way down through a wail, and finally subside into a protracted moan, a guttural animal moan, wrenched from the bowels as much as the vocal cords. Only the author of the scream understands this language.

It came from Anita, who dropped to the floor next to Christine—to her it was still Christine—and pulled the body to her, and cradled its head on her chest, soaking up blood on her dress, her face, her hands, her hair. In some part of her mind the why why why staccato was starting up; the rest of her was numb.

The hideous protocol followed. There was movement out of the kitchen, and somebody called the police. Somebody dialed for an ambulance. Somebody had the grace to yank the Schumann off the turntable. Somebody put their arms around Anita and observed the scribbled valentine and pocketed it. Somebody closed the blinds, and several had to pry Anita off the body as they came and wrapped it up and zippered it, and Anita followed it out the door, her covering of blood her only coat.

The cop in charge, a Detective Reynolds with a clip-on tie and dirty white bucks, sighed and clucked and said we see this all the time, this is how you end up by leading the ho-mo-sex-you-all lifestyle, we got a hundred unsolved of these, this is just one more. There was a flurry around the Detective Sergeant Officer Reynolds whoever he was, who left escorted by two patrolmen before he was seriously damaged. Somebody started to clean up. Somebody gathered the paper valentines from the floor and threw them out the door in a disgusted fling, to mingle with the petals of snow. Red-white, red-white. The participants knew an anguish that day they would never forget. Somebody went to the hospital to be with Anita. Somebody called Violet.

The apartment above the club had never known such pain. When Violet arrived it was a dirge in motion. Violet went to Anita and took her away and washed the blood off her and changed her into clean clothes and held her, but Anita was inconsolable, Anita was too far-off. A doctor gave her a shot and Violet gently put her to bed. Romaine was talking to still more policemen. A woman from the kitchen drew Violet aside and pressed the bloody written valentine into Violet's hand. The tiny scrawled note rocked her so hard it might as well have been a billboard. It read: "Will you stop NOW, Violet?" She wanted to run and smash herself through the window; she might as well have killed Christine herself, part of her brain was chanting, "Stop what? Stop what?" unable to connect anything she had done to this level of violence. She gave the valentine to Romaine who was equally shocked, who gave it to the policeman who grumbled that it had too many prints on it, and Violet rushed at the man meaning to kill him, and then the doctor gave her a shot, too, and then there was only blankness.

"Violet," said Anita, many hours later, both of them groggy, "I want to talk to you now, because we will never discuss this again." Violet was sitting in a chair, arms hugging herself, rocking back and forth, crying uncontrollably. Anita was propped up in bed, in the big brass bed she had shared with Christine, looking at Violet with stark sorrow.

"Vi, you lost your mother and then you lost Victor, and you know what it feels like; there is not much more to say than that. I do not want to discuss any bullshit about you causing Christine's death. Now listen to me. That horrible note means you must be very close to solving this, or else why the drastic measure? You must continue. But none of this vain stuff about doing it alone, not anymore. Gather as much help as you can, and find the person who killed Victor, because now they have killed Christine as well." Anita was smoothing the white quilt on top of her as if to soothe herself. Violet's body was jerking with spasms of sobs.

Anita continued. "The one thing I will say about all this is the strange sensation that the worst thing that could happen in my life has happened. It's important to me that you know that there is a meager and abject peace in that sensation.

"Tell Kate she can stay as long as she likes. I want to be alone now. Please go out and tell them to open the club, I want the club open tonight."

Violet looked at her in dismay but said nothing. She could not speak. She got up to walk to the bed, the waves of grief and guilt pouring out of her in a sad, rainy scent. She wanted to go to her and hold her and cry with her, but Anita's whole posture said no, she was out on a limb, in some dark place, with Christine. Violet left the room.

Out in the main rooms of the apartment there was a lot of impotent milling around as there is after tragedy; shock and grief hacking gestures into marionette moves. Violet told the appropriate women Anita's request to open the club. They were startled but relieved to have something to do and went downstairs to do it. A valentine party turned into a wake. Romaine drew Violet into the guest bedroom and shut the door and held her, and they both wept; they lay down together and held hands, staring at the ceiling as if the big square would make sense out of the misery. Violet sadly recounted her conversation with Anita, and Romaine agreed. She left the room to find Don. Kate was downstairs helping out. Anita was sleeping. Christine was dead. Violet washed her face and dialed Paul. Sharon, Paul's secretary, answered.

"Sharon, it's me. Is he there?"

"He's back in town, but he's not here. He left a message for you."

"Where the hell is he? Doesn't he know what happened?" she said plaintively.

"Yes, he does. He said it was awful and I agree; he was very upset about it. He simply could not get out of this business meeting. He said to meet him at this address."

She recited the number and street on the Upper East Side. Violet groaned. What was he doing dragging her out at a time like this; was it an attempt at distraction?

Sharon continued. "He apologized profusely; he said there was no other way, and he had some news that would cheer you up. That's all I've got—and Violet, I'm very sorry."

"Thank you, Sharon." Violet hung up feeling miserable and hurt. What business could be so important that it made being with her impossible? She felt panicked; Paul's absence felt very wrong. Maybe he found out about Cobb Hill, maybe he was furious with her. With a great deal of effort she pulled herself together.

It was nearing seven. Violet dragged herself out to the living room and told Romaine where she was going and to pass that along to Don. She glanced at Anita's door but did not go in. Shoulders sagging, she felt like a child banished from school.

The walk home in the relentless snow had a bracing effect. Working its way up from a hiding place under her pain, the anger was beating its way back to the surface, heating her up. On reflection it seemed impossible that she could feel it increase, but Christine's death had fueled it into a bright spuming flame. Violet's entire being was caught up in anticipation of looking into the killer's face, certain that the intensity of the hate itself could strike out at him, could mutilate him, the thing that had altered her life and forced the passage of her faith into a fissured and less certain territory.

Violet felt sick and bitter. It was a difficult task to drag herself through the motions of getting ready to meet Paul. In a churlish, somewhat crazed move she threw on an ensemble antithetical to her dense black mood; a white silk gown, sheer white stockings with martini glasses woven into them, white silk pumps, white moon-glass earrings, and a white felt hat with veil to cover her soaked eyes.

"The Bride Dressed to Kill," she said to the mirror. She decided she was cracking up. She had the prickly feeling that she was very close to solving the mystery but lacked a vital piece. The answer, the prey, the hirsute truth of the matter, the man himself, was somewhere up ahead, lying in wait, ready for her, and she was ready for him. She took a cab uptown.

23

The penthouse was already crowded when she arrived. On another night the incredible view of the city would have saved the evening for her. Tonight she didn't notice. The surroundings were benign, but Violet's perceptions were colored by her mood. Tonight the elegance was a failed attempt; the apartment seemed stuffed with totems of opulence. Violet was ready to bolt. Suddenly she had no idea why she had come.

She headed to the bar for a double Scotch of impeccable age and breeding, overhearing bits of conversations, all of them about the "sordid lesbian murder." A Bobby Short record was playing. A group of unemployed actors dressed as bellhops served the latest in catered tidbits to the crowd, which Violet ignored. She was halfway through her drink when Paul walked up to her. He threw his arms around her and pulled her close, something he had never done in public before.

"Paul, why are we here? For God's sake, take me home." She was bursting to tell him everything that had happened. His embrace was comforting, yet Violet could sense that he was excited about something. It was disturbing under the circumstances. Paul held her face in his hands, looking at her solemnly.

"Violet a lot has happened in the last few days."

"You're telling me."

"There is someone here I had to speak to, someone I want you to meet, there is so much to tell you and God, Vi, I'm sorry about Christine. And I love you. Just hang in there for a minute, and we'll leave."

"All right," she said faintly, unable to utter anything else. Paul let go of her.

"Just stand right there, I'll be right back." He disappeared into the crowd but returned almost immediately. Accompanying him was a tall, striking white-haired man, with a strong lean face, blue eyes, heavily tanned, all shown off by a white linen suit. He looked very familiar.

"Honey, this is John Maxwell Yardley. John, may I present Violet Childes."

If air or time or blood could freeze, could stop dead, they would have in that instant. Violet had such a severe physical reaction to this shock, that if her highball glass hadn't been so thick it would have shattered under her grip. She came very close to fainting. He was a perfect incarnation of the aging Adonis press photo tucked in her file. The veneer was smooth, a shield of suave containment.

Instead of collapsing, somehow she stretched her mouth into a thin smile, and extended her hand. What else could she do?

She spoke in a flat, barely controlled tone. "I'm honored to meet you, Mr. Yardley. You are *the* John Maxwell Yardley, are you not, hunter of heads, maker of fortunes, blessed among men, journeyman of power? I'm charmed." Yardley shook her hand, observing her coolly. There was one slight flicker of the metallic blue eyes, the hand withdrawn a fraction of a second too soon.

Paul glared at her openly, attempting a laugh.

"Violet has a very droll sense of humor, John, don't let it put you off. Vi, John is the reason I went to Chicago. Wait until I tell you about the deal we've put together with the *Herald-Sun*. Baltimore and Washington are next, right John? Honey, we'll have to get married this week. We have to move to Chicago for a while to get this project off the ground, and—"

"What?" Violet could not suppress this reply. Her mind—

was reeling, racing to keep up with the situation. The information pressed on her in the last few seconds was riddled with confusion and questions. How could Paul have gotten so deeply involved with this man without telling her? Paul's announcement implied that the two had been working together very closely and for quite some time. Had it been Yardley all along, not McKinley the publishing baron, as he had led her to believe? The question seemed foolish at this point.

Clearly it was crucial that she get Paul away from there and tell him about Kate, Cobb Hill, and everything else she had learned about Yardley. She felt ill at the thought that Paul was so involved with the man she was convinced was responsible for Victor's death. She was appalled at Paul's unabashed looks of admiration in Yardley's direction. She had never seen Paul so animated about a project; her heart sank at the thought of ruining his enthusiastic plans. He was in for a huge letdown.

"I know it's a lot to absorb all at once, Vi. We'll sort it all out in a little while."

Yardley was smiling, but his eyes overrode this in a cold stare, bullets of blue with watery edges.

"Violet, you are far more beautiful than Paul was capable of describing you. I'm delighted to meet his fiancée. Forgive the cliché, but I've heard an awful lot about you. I know we'll be good friends and I can certainly use your help. On occasion Paul can be so stubborn he makes me look like a pushover. You're the daughter of Victor Childes, am I right? I knew your father slightly, we met in Borneo many years ago," he said casually.

The reference to Victor and Borneo pushed her very close to the edge. The room full of people and noise started to recede. Violet's emotions barreled forward toward one man in empty space. Violet used a level of self-control she didn't know she had. Her limbs went numb, her scalp itched, she bit her tongue. Suddenly the hostess approached and led Paul away to a phone call.

"Be right back, honey," he said, noticeably concerned at leaving the two of them alone.

Yardley observed Violet with a slightly cocked head, mouth drawn down with cool concern. He raised a hand to her shoulder, fingers touching it lightly.

"Are you all right, Violet? You look rather pale. Perhaps you had better sit down."

The touch set her off. Violet was riveted to the spot by a combined and spiraling pressure of opposites, whether to succumb to nature and punch out the man in front of her, or listen to the echo of concerns placed before her in recent days to use restraint, with the promise that the boom would fall harder and more severely if she backed off. Since she was convinced she was looking into the face of the man who murdered her father, this was an affront to every cell she owned. A foreign logic won, then slipped.

"You virulent bastard, you are a stone's throw away from getting what's coming to you. Will you be so kind, Mr. Yardley, as to inform Paul that I am going home, because if I don't it's a sure bet that I will vomit all over your endangered-species shoes."

Yardley appeared unmoved except for a slight twitch at the corner of his slim mouth. He nodded briefly, the twitch replaced by a sardonic hint of smile. His voice was smooth, the intent soothing; to Violet it sounded like clotted cough syrup.

"You can be sure I'll relate the message."

Violet could not stand his smirk.

"One last thing, Yardley," she said slowly, "your daughter Kate sends her best regards."

The words had their intended effect. The sly smile rushed off his face, his body jerked once like a snapped fishing line, the polished civility contorted into an angry grimace edged with confusion. Violet let it simmer for a moment, then she turned, and left him standing there, aware that in taunting him with Kate, she had just pulled the pin on a hand grenade.

Two steps away she literally ran into Paul. He grabbed her arms. "Whoa, where are you going? And why are you being so rude to John?"

Violet felt a hand lightly placed on her back, and Yardley moved into view.

"It's all right, Paul, no offense taken. Violet is upset about her friend. I'll tell you what. My building is just around the corner. Let's go to my office and get comfortable, just the three of us. Violet can relax, and Paul and I will explain the project, and with any luck we'll have a new convert."

Paul looked at Violet as though she had just been granted an audience with the Pope. She had never felt more trapped in her life.

"Fine," she managed.

Out on Park Avenue Violet allowed herself to be buoyed forward between the two men. She had no idea what Yardley was up to, or how much he would say in front of Paul, but it was clear Yardley did not want her out of his sight. The sidewalk seemed all uphill. She felt murderous and crazed, the strain of it forced her emotions walleyed.

They rounded a corner and there was the Yardley building looming up in front of them, a huge, wingless priapic bird.

Yardley ushered them inside and over to the bank of elevators. His own was at the end of the line. He signaled something to a security guard, unlocked the elevator, and they all rode up in total silence, Paul throwing Violet warning glances.

The doors opened on a huge room, with ceiling-to-floor walls of glass facing Park Avenue; at night this made the room appear to open out into black space, until you walked close enough to see the cascade of city lights. In front of the windows was an enormous glass table propped on a base of four-foot sections of columns with scrolled tops. The light was soft, tastefully beamed out of fluted half cones on mauve walls in front of which stood a series of mahogany cabinets.

Opposite the windows was a wall of video monitors and communications equipment. Many of the monitors were on, none accompanied by sound. In front of them was a long table surrounded by chairs that faced the screens. A man in his early twenties with bright blond hair, crisply dressed in a Giorgio Armani suit, was working at the desk on a control panel that affected what was appearing on the screens. Yardley addressed him.

"Hi, Chuck, I see you're working late as usual, trying to steal my job. Would you please cue up on the presentation Paul and I are working on and get us some drinks? Brandy would be fine. After that you may go."

Chuck nodded with a flourish and did what he was told, then left the room.

"Violet, Paul, please sit down." They did. Yardley placed the drinks in front of Paul and Violet and sat down himself. He gestured toward the screens.

"Violet, at the moment the top row are the major networds—we make a point of closely monitoring how Well-Dyne is doing in the media." He winked at Paul. "The bottom row are in-house monitors, and the middle is usually for presentations. In a moment I'll cancel them all and punch up some material that will help explain to you what Paul and I are up to."

"May I have a cigarette, please?" asked Violet. She was paying no attention to Yardley's words; his voice was just a drone. Violet looked at the video units. On the top row the screens were filled with prime-time shows; their domestic aspect was an odd contrast to their more formal and dramatic surroundings.

Yardley rummaged through one of the nearby cabinets and returned with a package of Dunhills and a huge crystal ashtray. He gave Violet a cigarette and lit it for her then resumed his seat. Violet smoked in nervous jags. Paul looked at Violet as though she were a stranger.

Yardley was speaking again, but Violet still couldn't make out his words; they were a white buzz. She drained her glass, stubbed out her cigarette, and stood up. She had to get out.

"Paul," she said desperately, "I'm feeling very ill, could we please do this another time?"

Paul looked at her as though the family dog had lifted his leg on a visiting prime minister.

Yardley rose quickly to his feet. "Paul, I think Violet is a little overwhelmed, and I don't blame her a bit. We need her on our team, Paul; I can't have you backing out of this project because your wife disapproves. We need some heavy P.R. work done and I'm just the one to do it." He emitted a sound that Violet translated as an attempt at a chuckle. "I tell you what, Paul, why don't you go next door and look over the Baltimore proposal again. Let me explain things to her in my own way—we'll have her on our side in no time. Violet is clearly an asset we cannot afford to lose."

Paul looked so relieved and flattered that Violet wanted to punch him. She started to protest but stopped herself.

Paul stood and kissed Violet on the cheek. "I couldn't agree with you more. Great idea, wonderful, John. She's immune to flirtation, so don't waste your time. Call me when you're through." And he was gone.

Violet tapped her head slightly; her hearing seemed to be off; the two men seemed to breed such a stiffness in each other it was like watching two cardboard shirt inserts impersonate men. She wondered if she had finally gone off the deep end.

Yardley strolled over to the door, locked it, and calmly walked back to the cabinet he had removed the cigarettes from, producing a glittering chrome revolver. He held it for a moment, fingering the trigger, then laconically placed it on the table near the control unit for the videos. He sat down.

With Paul gone his demeanor quickly changed, from taut control to something more overtly hostile and coated with anger.

"Where is Kate . . . ?" This was almost a hiss.

Violet breathed in his odd perfume, so strung out, so loaded with emotion that she was rendered almost listless.

"She's someplace safe. Why should I tell you? So you can finish her off? The way you murdered my father—or had it ordered—which as far as I'm concerned is the same thing. Why don't you just shoot me, too?"

His gaze was haughty. "I don't kill people, Violet. It's one of the fine advantages of money. It keeps your hands clean. Just tell me where Kate is and we'll forget the whole thing. Nothing will be mentioned to Paul." He shook his head. "What a strange turn of events—you our unexpected visitor at Cobb Hill. Do you realize you are placing Paul's position in jeopardy? Take me to Kate," he demanded.

"Answer some questions first and I'll tell you."

"Such as?" Yardley looked bored, feigned or not Violet could not tell. He was beginning to remind her of a chameleon changing hues. He pulled the control panel to him and randomly tapped buttons that made the top screens change image as well as flip on and off. The visual flutter was a distraction, as Violet knew it was meant to be.

"How about starting with Kate? Why do you want her? Why did you keep her a prisoner? Why did you force her to abort her baby? What about the blue room, and why did you kill Victor to protect it?"

He looked at her with icy amusement. "You *are* greedy, aren't you?" His fingers continued to play the control panel like a keyboard, lightly touching the buttons. "I call it the Cobalt Room . . ." he said in a dreamy voice. "What an odd thing for Victor to have fastened on. I think of it as a community service."

"A community service to whom?" she snapped. "What possible significance could it have that would override lives like Victor's?"

"So obstinate, so like your father." His tone was maddeningly casual.

The briefest of acknowledgments had just been made. Violet caught his covertly eager look; she read it as his continuing abstract rivalry with Victor, with her as his stand-in. She did not want to play.

"You and Victor had a weird symbiotic hatred for each other. It has nothing to do with me. You want Kate and you need Paul. You've got the fucking gun. Indulge me."

His eyebrows slid together in a frown as a flash of disappointment crossed his face. He folded his arms.

"For a moment, perhaps." His stare was softened slightly by memory. "Marie was the only woman I have ever loved. Your father stole her away from me. Once it became clear I had no chance of getting her back, I resolved myself to being without a wife . . . But I took Kate. That was something. She was part of Marie, the only part that I could keep. But I wanted a son. An heir. Someone to take over the magnificence of Well-Dyne.

"So I went shopping. As you know we've made a lot of progress in the area of reproduction. Actually, as I began my research into what would be the best option for myself, I became fascinated both with the procedures and their implications. For instance I began by looking into different versions of surrogacy, each of which was complicated and legally vulnerable. Then I found a doctor who had perfected a process that would ensure the delivery of a male child. All the elements were there, but each situation was somehow lacking. My interest was in total control of the circumstances under which the child was born. Over the years I worked with many professionals to achieve that total control—"

"You mean coerced, don't you? You mean blackmailed, like Shelby and Vincent?"

He ignored her, annoyed by the interruption. His look was dismissive.

"Over time we designed the Cobalt Room. It was the last step, it solved the final nagging problem—complete control over the vessel that carried the child. What a nuisance it had been the old way; never knowing if the women were sticking to their health requirements, lawsuits after birth when women changed their minds.

"Of course I protected it fiercely. I wanted the first group of children born healthy and sound. It will prove my efforts worthwhile. I will go public with it at the appropriate time. It will standardize a creative approach to a particular reproductive problem. It's as simple as that. I have twelve hospitals that include my service, and men such as myself, over a hundred of them, will soon have sons." He sounded so proud of this; Violet was sure it was why he was willing to talk about it.

"You'll go public with this? Isn't it more likely that these hand-chosen men will be permanently under your thumb for being involved?"

Yardley looked at her with surprised respect. "That's very astute, Violet. We could use that. Why don't you drop these sentimental judgments you're making and join Paul and myself."

Violet rolled her eyes at the absurdity. She spoke slowly, with dry softness. "I saw the women in the blue room, I got a close look at them. Every single one of them had Down's syndrome—"

He interrupted her with a shrug while saying, "I'm making use of otherwise useless women. They haven't the intelligence to object, or change their minds, after the children are born. Their simplicity and highly monitored health make them perfect containers for the children. They carry to term beautifully. They are magnificent host bodies."

Violet was humming with agitation. "I am aware," she said, each word punched out in a low tone, "of the neglect and abuse of retarded people in some institutions. But to use them as lab animals, to kidnap them to use as human hothouses for your little patrician pricks is beyond comprehension. It's evil."

Yardley looked at her with benign contempt. His eyes slid over her, eels glittering at low tide. "Don't be so naïve, Violet. Your thinking is too conventional, and that pinched Victorian attitude is really outdated. The government experiments on military personnel, and certain states experiment on prisoners. Those women are treated much better as my chosen incubators than they were at their respective institutions."

"And after they give birth?"

Yardley regarded her in quizzical silence.

"Why do I get the impression that these supposedly well-treated incubators are highly disposable?" She was needling him and he pricked back.

"It's a disposable culture, Violet, the age of the limited shelf-life."

Violet looked at him with loathing. "You're incredible. You speak as though you're running a dairy farm. It's inhumane, it's so ethically bankrupt it's ludicrous—"

He stopped Violet with a short mirthless laugh. "What closet have they been keeping you in? We're practically in the nineteen nineties. Ethics go to the highest bidder. But, Violet, I'm an entrepreneur, a creator not a destroyer. After an incubator gives birth they graduate, so to speak. Carrying to term with no problems proves they are physically sound. They are moved into the next phase of the Cobalt Room, which consists of impregnation in order to create fetal tissue.

"Injected fetal cells have been proven to arrest Parkinson's disease. It's a regenerative force of limitless capabilities. I believe it's going to change the future of medicine, that's how important it is." His look was openly triumphant. "I'm contributing, I'm helping, but I'm not the Red Cross. It's philanthropy with a return. It's just common sense, it's good business. At two hundred thousand per fetus I can put a high level of funds back into research . . ."

This was too much, too ugly. But in the center of her shock Violet realized why knowledge of the two phases of the blue room had proved fatal to Victor. She felt loony with despair.

"The womb is the new real estate market?" she said crazily, shifting her eyes to stare out the great expanse of window, afraid she might catch him nodding yes.

Violet had had enough. She stood and walked over to where he was sitting. He stood up to meet her. They were close enough to kiss.

"And Kate?"

"She was involved inadvertently. I admit it was a mistake. I want to make it up to her, that's why I must find her."

Violet narrowed her eyes in disbelief.

"She was having trouble conceiving. I steered her and her husband through my own service, my involvement unknown to them. It was her husband, Tim, who insisted she have an abortion. He put in motion a simple but very effective construct of blackmail. Even after Tim died I had to follow through with his wishes."

"Why did Tim want the child aborted?"

Yardley paused for several seconds. "Because he found out the child she was carrying was mine, and this seemed to disturb him."

Violet sank into the nearest chair, her head dropping into her hands, her voice low and moaning. "I don't believe it," she said softly, "the incredible arrogance . . . the surrogates were good enough for everyone else, but you insisted on a member of your own family to be your receptacle, is that it?"

"Yes," he replied calmly, as if this made perfect sense. Violet took a deep breath. "And Paul," she said in a flat tone, exhausted.

He smiled at her; the whites of his eyes sparkled like teeth. "I think Paul has become the son I never had. He encompasses how I feel about things; we both share a vision. We agree that it's time for a third political party. Paul is doing the groundwork, quietly obtaining the ownership of newspapers all over the country. The new political party will emerge after several years of carefully disseminated policy and philosophy expressed on the editorial page and in the general tone of the papers. The platform and intent of the party will consist of those views, quietly mainstreamed through those dailies—"

Violet interrupted him. "Clever, I'm sure, but just a tad fascist, don't you think?"

"I'd describe it as postmodern," he said calmly.

Violet was chagrined. Paul was clearly deeply involved with this man, perhaps even brainwashed.

The two pairs of eyes locked in combat. Violet stood up.

"Enough," announced Yardley, "this has gone far enough."

"Why did you tell me all of this anyway? Do you think I'm just going to sit on it, and not do anything about it?"

"That's exactly what I think, because of Paul. Now," he said impatiently, "how much does Kate know about these things, and where is she?"

Violet responded with a mocking linear smile, a reed drawn across a still pond.

"Victor?" was her answer.

His eyes remained constant, flashing with distaste. The two of them became an equation. They were clearly in a stalemate, two sparring partners anticipating the next move.

Suddenly, Yardley slapped his hand down toward the gun, but instead hit several buttons on the video panel. One of them was sound, which blasted into the room with such force they were both startled into looking at its source, the top four screens of the video wall. Four images of the Cobalt Room pulsed out at Violet and Yardley.

They were equally shocked. The voice-over was Zar's, booming: ". . . a profile of a supposed philanthropist, who we have shown here tonight to document the nightmare version of the misogyny of capitalism, a man whose expression of his racism, sexism, and ageism are clearly channeled down through his network of companies, bearing out his policies—"

Yardley screamed, "You shit. It's too soon," and swept up

the gun, furious. Violet caught the gesture in mid-swing, and they came together, flailing, falling to the floor in a grapple, Zar's voice curving over them in an umbrella, ". . . used retarded women to store his little future three-piece suits—" The blue light from the screens poured over them; they were entwined like lovers, struggling, when the gun went off.

Seconds later Violet rolled away. It was Yardley who had been hit in the stomach, his eyes glazing over in pain. But the shock of proximity forced her toward a choice. She could let him bleed to death as she felt he deserved to—his blood was seeping into her dress in an obscene blot—but she also wanted a confession. She pulled away. He was reading her mind. "Help, I need help," he gasped. "I'll give you anything." He was pathetic in pain, stripped of his arrogance.

There was a furious pounding on the door, attached to it was Paul's voice. "John! Violet! What's happening in there? Open the goddamn door."

Violet ignored this. "Did you kill Victor?"

"Yes—" The answer came swiftly in a small burst of air.

Violet felt something let go, something soften up. In the spasm of relief she tore off a large measure of the bottom of her dress and pressed it to his wound, pulling his hands together on top of it, stumbling to the phone, dialing 911, then Don's precinct. She went to the door and unlocked it. Paul burst in, stopping in a still frame at the sight: his bride smeared with blood, his friend encased in a moan. The blue light from the screens flickered over his face for a second; he looked up at the screen without comprehension. As he bent toward the odd ensemble on the floor, the four screens of blue were replaced with four views of a young black woman surrounded by babies, the commentary by Zar continuing loudly. Paul knelt down next to Yardley. "Did you call someone?" he shrieked.

"Yes, I did." Violet joined Paul next to Yardley. Sirens could be heard wailing outside. Paul lunged for the phone and told the guards downstairs to let the medics in and where to direct them. He yelled to Violet, "Why did you do this? Why?"

Violet had resumed her position, her hands pressed on

top of Yardley's to stop the blood. Paul grabbed for the video controls, Zar's broadcast still going; he fumbled with them, and in the middle of "one of the highest infant mortality rates in the world," the screens went dead.

Suddenly the emergency team appeared, Yardley was whimpering; Paul was rubbing his bloody hands on his suit in dismay.

They all left the building together, Yardley on a gurney, still conscious, eyes gummy, Paul telling him everything would be all right, Don bleary-eyed and shocked, a mob of people pushing in to see. The ambulance roared off and left them standing there. Violet gave Don the minimal version and agreed to meet with him in the morning. Paul pushed Violet into a taxi; in seconds the interior exploded into dialogue, the blood on them glowing wet brown under the streetlights, in repetitive bursts.

"Why did you try to kill him?"

Violet was becoming hysterical, the blood on her dress and hands mimicking Christine, Max, Victor himself. She told Paul what she could, what she was capable of telling, about the past hour. He held his head in his hands and rocked back and forth, mumbling, "Violet, of course he admitted it, he was dying, you forced him to . . ." and stared out the window. "Violet, I'm so sorry, there is so much I want to tell you, to explain to you."

Violet was staring at him, looking for their baseline, their foundation; what she saw floundered in her image of Paul linked with Yardley.

They both looked blankly at each other. Two wood statues emerged from the taxi. Violet started to cry as if being deported; Paul picked her up and carried her inside, took her up in the elevator. She started to babble, to recount, to summarize, and the lid flew off and she was mute.

"I'm not letting you out of my sight until we talk," said Paul. He undressed Violet and put her to bed with brandy and sedative, and took some himself. They lay as one ragged unit, drugged into forgetting, merged into exhausted sleep.

24

Whether it was hours later or minutes later or light years later, Violet did not know. She emerged from the thick sedative sleep anyway, poked at by the barrage of events and sensation that had brought her to this point. Poked out of sleep by the old dream, it drew her to the surface.

In the dense half-wakeful state, suddenly, arbitrarily, it happened. The face in the dream came into focus. She knew who the woman was, and the street and the flapping white shapes and the gesturing arms. It was Mrs. Rodriguez, it was Second Street. Her gesticulations were sign language—Mrs. Rodriguez was deaf. Victor had known Mrs. Rodriguez for years, he kept an eye on her, she had fed Violet countless times and taught her sign language. Violet's favorite stories and Mrs. Rodriguez's long folk tales were enchanting in a new way, performed in this silent visual script.

But why? Why the months of this dream, its mystery and sense of violence? Each time the dream occurred, its images were followed by the memories of the day Victor died. In sleep or out, her mind had jumped from the billowing white shapes to Victor in his shroud. Even now, with the source of the dream solved, its connection with Victor remained a question. It was the last link, the final uncommitted detail. Because of this the dream still held some power and intrigue.

It pushed her out of bed and into clothes. She needed some air.

She wandered in this dazed blanket, the darkness welcome, the crisscross of images not. She walked unseeing until she finally looked up and found herself on the corner of B and Second, as if drawn by a magnet. When she stopped and looked up she was directly in front of the apartment building of Mrs. Rodriguez, the center of the exhausting dream. There was light coming out of the front first-floor apartment windows. Though it was the middle of the night, Violet pressed the buzzer that lit up the flashing red light in the living room. Knowing Mrs. Rodriguez would not answer the door at that hour, Violet stepped off the stairs and stood in front of the windows, in plain view. A hand moved the curtain slightly. The door buzzed, and Violet ran and let herself in.

Mrs. Rodriguez came to the front door and peered through the hole, then opened it, smiling. Tears came to both of them at once, they embraced, Mrs. Rodriguez led Violet over to the couch and they both sat down. Violet spoke rather than signed, it had been so long she had lost some of it and Mrs. Rodriguez read her lips in a concentrated study. Violet told her what the date was, and said she couldn't sleep and was walking the neighborhood, that she missed Victor.

They started out awkwardly, as Mrs. Rodriguez signed and Violet spoke, her lone voice sounding abnormally loud in the otherwise silent space. Finally, after tea and an update on their lives, and her first rough attempts at signing again, Violet felt so peaceful she almost forgot why she was there.

With great difficulty and many pauses Violet signed her dream, not stressing the level of anxiety it caused, or its repetition.

"For one thing," Mrs. Rodriguez replied in sign, "you must remember we haven't seen each other since the day of the funeral. Perhaps it's part of that memory that you dream about. It's also true I was the first one you saw the day it happened."

"Yes, you're right. I saw you first . . . then the police . . . then what seemed to be the entire neighborhood clamoring in front of the house." Violet was struggling with the gestures; she signed very slowly.

"But I do remember something specific . . . You were trying to tell me something, and were obviously very upset . . . I got dragged off by the police at that point. In the dream you were insistent . . . Do you remember what you said that was so important?"

Mrs. Rodriguez shrugged. Her hands moved rapidly; they were fluttering birds. Violet was always struck by the grace of this form of communication.

"I was only repeating what I told the police, who didn't seem to care, about the man leaving the building right before Victor was found. I was afraid the police did not understand me, though they kept saying they did, and I wanted to make sure you knew, in case he could help, and would repeat it to the police. No one asked me about it later, so I figured it meant nothing."

"Yes, I'm sure you're right," answered Violet, unwilling to admit that she had been so upset that day that she too had not paid proper attention to the specifics of what Mrs. Rodriguez had told her.

"I was on my way to the market for some ice. What a day it was, maybe the hottest all summer. It was an ugly day." Violet gently grasped Mrs. Rodriguez's hands and asked her to slow down. Mrs. Rodriguez nodded, smiling.

"I was walking behind Victor's building when all of a sudden a man came out of the basement door. He ran right into me. He nearly knocked me over. My purse fell to the ground and he picked it up and handed it to me. I laughed, because he was wearing a baseball uniform. Men in baseball uniforms remind me of little boys. When he handed me the purse I noticed his hands. They were so smooth, not like a man who played sports, and I noticed his ring, and a small scar like a smile, right on his finger below the ring. You know how I am, I notice everything. I asked him about the insignia on his ring"—she traced a pattern in the air—"and I teased him about his uniform. He said he had stopped by to convince Victor to play in a softball game that Victor said he had no time for. He tipped his cap and left. He was a very nice man. Not a bad memory for an old woman, what do you think?

"It seemed important to tell you and the police because he came out of the back door, and might have seen something. Does that help? Do you remember now?"

Violet's heart caved in. Not nicely, not inch by inch, but in a rush, a flood, a streaking comet—stove in, collapsed. This is how it felt: her blood ran downward, pouring out of her shoes on the carpet; it flowed from her hands and temples. The room stood cockeyed. Everything she thought she knew, counted on, or held dear was smashed and thrown askew. Flung toward the corners of the earth, speeding away from her. She was suddenly rootless, empty, and therefore, utterly, totally calm. This downfall took place in an instant, a split second. Mrs. Rodriguez failed to notice.

Violet took a deep breath. The calm was icy, positively Antarctic. She was the Dead Sea. She managed to speak.

"Yes I do, you're so right, isn't it funny that it was that simple." She took Mrs. Rodriguez's hands into her own, gave them an affectionate squeeze, then released them.

"I know it's crazy that I came, but I know you understand. I'll be in better touch, I promise." Mrs. Rodriguez beamed.

"Take good care of yourself, Violet. And please know I loved Victor like a son and have not forgotten him, not for a minute." They nodded to each other and rose. She led Violet to the door, kissed her, and locked the door after Violet's retreating figure.

Violet was cold, ice cold, filled with a pristine calm. The air was wet with dark. The moon was a pale wafer, hovering. The street shone, unfolding away from her in a ribbony black line. She was so cold, so calm, she could taste it in her mouth like snow. She moved forward on feet of ice, skating down the ribbony black line, racing toward the fateful; her destination was heaven and hell in a split decision. She opened the door and entered, the definition of smooth, all her joints greased with a righteous truth. She was gliding; she was dancing up to the zenith.

She spoke.

"Hi, darling, what are you doing awake?"

Paul stood up and turned to face her, a glass in his hand.

"I guess it's not a good night to sleep for either of us."

Bach was playing softly on the stereo. "I guess too much has happened to let go, no matter how altered. Where have you been?"

In answer Violet went to the closet and hung up her coat, reaching up to the top shelf for a moment, then turned to him. Wordlessly she walked toward him in the comfortable dimness. Wordlessly she pulled the small automatic from behind her back and leveled it at him, aimed, clasping it with both hands.

"So, you were out of town the day Victor died, isn't that what you said?"

Paul was alarmed, his eyes flew wide open in surprise.

"Why, Paul?" her words were extrusions of lead. "Why would you want to spend your life with the woman whose father you murdered?" Her tone was even, icy. "You were up for the name on the mastheads, the big journalistic hard-on. What else did he promise? What did it have to do with me? I get the power aspect of it, Paul, the seduction. What is a Paul Renault anyway? Some kind of social disease, some odd strain that crawled out of the East River?

"Come on, Paul, say something. Say something moving, say something to keep me from shooting your prick to Baltimore." In shock her composure was starting to slip; she was swaying a little, unraveling a little. Paul started to flutter, gave a small moan of panic; he thrust his arms up, palms out, supplicating.

"Violet, honey, Vi, think for a minute. Everything I did I did for us. That first day I saw you at Victor's kitchen table I wanted you, I wanted to bring you with me. It was for us. When we talked you were so vivid, I thought you understood. It was for us." Paul was edging toward sheer hysteria rivaled by survival. Violet was unmoved. Violet was glacial.

"Us? What 'us' is that—the us that murdered Victor, the us that wanted to rule the press via Yardley? I don't understand, Paul. I need to understand."

Paul steadied himself, lowering his arms, and spoke in a tone she had never heard before. His eyes were blunt. His voice stopped shaking, he was near sarcasm.

"Poor Violet. Poor shrinking Violet. You and your axiomatic hairshirts." He sounded fed up, relieved, almost grateful to have the chance to explain.

"You have no idea what goes on out there, what it really takes. You're just a childlike little pie-in-the-sky fool. I wanted to bring you with me. I wanted to educate you. I wanted to give you everything, but you live in a dream state. You think people are basically good, you think love makes a difference. Lately I've been afraid that I could never explain myself to you. When I try I have to listen to another one of your diatribes . . . But John understood. With John I could get some things done. John is a realist, and his power is enormous—"

"Maybe you should have fucked John. Maybe you should have married him. I guess you did."

Violet's eyes glowed with pain, their message unmistakable. Paul caught the message, his sentence—the jury was in. He shivered; he was floundering, looking for a way out. Violet blinked, the click of a shutter at a headline event.

"Did you kill Victor?" she said simply.

"Yes," he said, resigned. "It was a test of faith. John demanded it. He knew how I felt about you, he was being plagued by Victor."

"Why—" It was a cry, the shortest distance between two points.

"Because he found out about Kate and Cobb Hill and a lot of other things he was going to nail John on and it would have ruined everything. John was what I had been looking for, he was magnificent, we were going to—"

"And Max?"

"No, of course not. But listen, with John, I could have made a difference, to contribute on a large scale, to—"

"And Christine," she said quietly, her voice an industrial diamond, her tone more frightening than the gun.

"Yes, yes, I did that. I had to stop you somehow, you were getting too close. I was going to kill Anita, but I couldn't, you see? I loved you too much." Violet jumped internally at the use of the word "love" in this context. Her trembling was a shimmer, grief sloughed off her in waves, in wide accordion pleats, a slip falling from under a dress. Her arms ached. She was close to fainting from the intensity of emotion. Paul tried to wedge his way in.

"Violet, think, it's all in place now. John is probably gone, it's all ours, it's all mine, we can create—"

She cut him off with a look, the look encompassed what they had shared, it encompassed what she had let fall away to expose herself to him. They both saw the images, against the background of "Bach for Cello," of their drops into intimacy; the room was crowded with those moments. The Bach in question was swirling around them. Sirens were heard outside, yet no sound was louder than their panicked breathing.

Paul was rustling through his jacket, "Violet, you're out of your mind. It's just as wrong as what I have done. Give me the gun, we'll talk—"

He pulled out a small automatic and pointed it at her. They looked at each other, strangers on a train.

The sounds of the Bach swelled, an unwilling adjective, as Violet felt the enormity of the betrayal push her finger against the trigger, with Paul saying, "You're just the same as all the rest, and you're in my way—"

The explosions sounded so loud in the middle of his voice, all the sounds of the twentieth century rang out from her gun and flew to the target. The loud sounds shoved their way into his chest, in intimate proximity to his heart; blood spurted out in little red-dash semaphores as he collapsed in seeming slow motion, in an abbreviated scream. Violet's own motions were a parallel to his; she spun into darkness while watching on the way down, pitching onto the Oriental rug, onto that landscape without light.

25

Violet's first sensation was cottony; her head was wrapped in swaddling clothes. She heard murmurs. Her chest hurt. She felt cold, as though her body was filled with snow; she was lying on a table of furry ice.

She squeezed an eye open and was filled with wonder. There was a tableau of faces around her.

Romaine was closest. Donald she recognized next. Anita was perched on the end of the bed. David stood behind Anita, arms filled with flowers.

Violet tried hard to comprehend. Near David stood Jackie, hair loose of its chignon. Next to Jackie was Kate. Standing at the foot of the bed was Zar, arms folded. Back against a wall was Cindy, who waved shyly when Violet saw her.

Violet tried hard again, her mouth filled with chalk.

"Did I miss something?" she said softly. "Is it Thanksgiving or did somebody die?"

There were smiles all around.

A presence at Violet's right shoulder moved into view.

It was Dr. Brush in her greens. "The bullet just missed your heart," she said solemnly.

"Sounds like business as usual," was Violet's weak reply.

"Don't talk," Dr. Brush said sternly. "No talking, and these characters have to go. This is totally against regulations and I'll probably be thrown out of here. I'll check in on you later." She briefly pressed her palm against Violet's forehead and left the room.

Don was the first to move closer. With a finger to his lips he said, "You were right all along, you monkey. We'll talk about it later."

Violet dragged a hand up to place on Don's arm. "Yardley?" she whispered.

"He made it. It's only the beginning for him."

"Paul?"

Donald shook his head. As he did, the large circuit of fate and circumstance, from Borneo to Violet in her hospital bed, stopped whirring around. Yet surprisingly the pain had not lessened. Tears started; she wanted Paul back, the Paul who had not killed Victor, the Paul who wasn't afraid of her challenges. Donald looked at her; their eyes bled into each other's. "Later, amigo," he managed, and left.

Violet's tears made her vision even more blurred. As Donald left, Dr. Brush reappeared. "I mean it, go. She's okay, come back tomorrow," she said to the group.

They did leave, in front of her folded arms.

Anita was first, bending down and gently kissing each of

Violet's cheeks. "We'll recuperate together, don't you think?" she said, and walked rather quickly out the door.

Anita's reference to her absent partner reinforced the shock of the alien Paul. The weight of disappointment was suddenly crushing Violet's chest, pressing her heart down into a black ingot. A thick swirl of pain reduced her vision with the sweep of a pointillist's dark dots.

Cindy moved into her field of vision. At first the pain intensified in a spasm, but it lessened at the sight of Cindy's face, unlined and rosy as a child's, eyes searching. For a split second Violet was rushed back in time to a place before their uncertainties, before their stagger. Cindy sat on the bed carefully, picked up one of Violet's hands and kissed her palm, then held her hand tightly.

"I've come to realize you were right about things," she said softly. "We are all we've got." She brushed her fingers lightly over Violet's forehead. "I know the timing is bizarre, but when you get out, how about a date?"

Violet smiled sadly, and nodded a fraction. Cindy disappeared.

David placed his flowers on the table. His thumb traced a careful line on her arm. "The studio is a god-awful mess," he dared, and walked out.

Kate sat close. "Lunch in the park?"

Violet started to laugh but stopped, painfully. Kate kissed her brow and retreated.

Jackie placed several newspapers on Violet's stomach, and knelt next to the bed. They were eye to eye. "I'm out again. I'll tell you all about it later. Thank you." She was whispering. "It's your fault." She smiled impishly, and disappeared.

Romaine got as close as she could. "If you ever drag me through something like this again you'll never get to borrow a stitch of my wardrobe. Am I making an impact?"

Violet nodded, smiling. "That's the worst threat I've heard so far," she said softly. "I'm properly warned at least. No excuses next time." Romaine kissed her lips gently and walked off. Violet wanted to follow. There was so much to say.

Zar was left, still standing at the end of the bed. Dr.

Brush was impatient. "Her lung is a mess, we're not out of the woods yet—please."

Zar reached down next to Violet and picked up a cassette machine. She carefully placed it on Violet's bedside table.

"I've cued the tape for the good part. Obviously you're going to miss the performance." She looked annoyed.

"I'll tell you about the broadcast later, and how Romaine kept me out of jail. You just have to get better soon so I can fill you in. Call it over, Vi, call it done. Maybe we can work on something together, okay?" She brushed her hand over Violet's, pushed the PLAY button on the machine and left, accompanied by Dr. Brush.

Violet lay in their absence feeling acutely lonely, alienated; her senses were jammed with disaffection.

She heard a low thrum next to her; it sounded like a foghorn pushing out through mist. She felt for the papers in front of her. Picking one up, a stray piece of paper came with it. She strained to read: "I am with you. Call if hospital food too awful." It was a telegram from Bernard. She drew it under her shoulder to sleep with.

She pressed her head into the cool pillow and searched for a sensation of peace with Victor, but it was too soon. Had he witnessed her efforts? Did he know?

The sounds from the tape started to fill the room, a plaid of greys.

She shifted a newspaper in front of her eyes to read. The headline said: LIBBERS LAMENT LADIES LOT ON LIVE TV TAKEOVER. She let this drop on the bed, and picked up the next one: DOUBLE TROUBLE DAME SHOOTS TWO DUDES. She let them slip to the floor, wondering how long she had been unconscious and who had been blabbing. She marveled at the surrealism of being the subject of a headline instead of its collector.

She gazed at the white expanse of ceiling, her own version of headlines forming there, crowding out the others.

>GIRL SAVES WOMAN FROM DROWNING
>DAUGHTER SAYS LAST GOOD-BYE TO DEAD DAD
>A VIOLET CAN BLOOM ANYWHERE

The music filled the room in a rush, a crescendo with wind in the middle. It was the sound of titanium white, it was the sound of pure hope.

Barbara Machin
South of the Border

Based on the BBC TV series created by
Susan Wilkins

'*South of the Border* . . . a rare and wonderful phenomenon . . . which brilliantly intertwines social issues with fast action and dialogue' *New Statesman*

The BBC TV Series *South of the Border* was acclaimed for challenging the predictability of popular television crime. Rated by *Time Out* as one of the top drama series of the year, it won the critics' hearts and attracted enormous viewing audiences.

Here – making their first appearance in book form – Pearl and Finn star in a fast moving adventure born of trade union–management strife. Pearl, black, gritty and glamorous, and Finn, a laconic Geordie recently paroled for stealing, unmask the criminals when union boss John Foxton suspects corruption within his organisation, and worse, embezzlement of vital strike funds.

An action-packed mystery featuring TV's most likeable and unlikely detective duo.

Fiction/The Women's Press Crime £4.50
ISBN: 0 7043 4227 8

Hannah Wakefield
A February Mourning

'**Enormously attractive is the voice of the narrator — friendly, ordinary, honest, doubtful, with an unself-righteous integrity, this voice is intimate and even sexy**' Nicci Gerrard

Solicitor-sleuth Dee Street, heroine of *The Price You Pay*, is back and up to her neck in legal trouble. Her client Alison is in Holloway, accused of the murder of her best friend Annie. And to her horror Dee inherits a suspect in the first IRA supergrass case to come to trial in London.

But is there a mysterious link between the two cases? So Dee starts to suspect, as the trails lead from London to a missile base, and the streets of occupied Belfast. Meanwhile Dee has troubles of her own: she's pregnant and single, and her lover is leaving the country . . .

Praise for *The Price You Pay*, Hannah Wakefield's first novel, published by The Women's Press:
'Excellent and original' Jessica Mann
'An un-put-downable espionage novel, rivals Le Carré for twists of plot and morality' *Bookpeople*
'Witty, thrilling and compulsive' *Tribune*

Fiction/The Women's Press Crime £4.95
ISBN: 0 7043 4207 3

Barbara Paul
Your Eyelids Are Growing Heavy

'Bright, bloodless, comedy-thriller' *The Guardian*
'Really ingenious' *The Listener*

Memory loss is a frightening business... Megan Phillips was scared out of her wits when she woke up on the fairway of an unfamiliar golf course without the faintest idea of how she came to be there. Megan didn't drink, and lost weekends just weren't in her repertoire. Now she had to confront a thirty-eight-hour blank in her life.

Her neighbour Gus couldn't help her construct the missing day-and-a-half. Even Henrietta Snooks, her psychiatrist, ran up against a block in her unconscious which seemed inpenetrable.

Then Megan started to get the phonecalls, conversations she forgot as soon as she hung up, and it soon became clear her blackout was no isolated event. Someone had abducted her, someone had hypnotised her to respond to a secret command. Megan knew she had to find her mysterious hypnotist somehow, and regain control of her life – if she had to kill to do it.

A chilling mystery by the acclaimed author of *The Fourth Wall*, also published by The Women's Press.

Fiction/The Women's Press Crime £4.50
ISBN: 0 7043 4215 4

Barbara Wilson
Murder in the Collective

'A paragon whodunnit' *The Times*

Two print collectives, one left-wing and one radical lesbian, plan to merge. But hidden tensions explode when one of the collective members is found – murdered.

Pam Nilsen is determined to uncover the truth, however disturbing. No one is free of suspicion. The Filipino resistance movement, the CIA, a drunken feminist on a binge, a fugitive in the attic, arms running, blackmail and a pair of unusual contact lenses are all involved before the mystery can be solved.

Sisters of the Road by Barbara Wilson is also available in The Women's Press Crime Series.

Fiction/The Women's Press Crime £4.50
ISBN: 0 7043 3943 9
Hardcover: £7.50
ISBN: 0 7043 2854 2